night

break

nightSHADE

1

carey decevito

acknowledgments

An author cannot be where they are without the movers and shakers that help make them who they are today.

Eric—your talented eye behind that camera lens of yours has gifted me with so many covers over the last year and a half. Six to be exact! You managed to take David Wills, and transform him into the Dalton I always pictured for this book.

David—thank you for your perfect portrayal of Dalton. I can't believe you and Eric have braved the "ghetto" of Las Vegas for this shot. I'll forever be in your debt.

Clarise—here we are on series number two! Your amazing ability to take Eric's work and transform it into a jaw-dropping cover will always astound me.

Joanne—it hasn't even been a year since we first crossed paths but girl, I've never been more grateful in meeting the industry's least well-known, yet most well-connected person. You've been an amazing colleague, proofreader, beta...hell, a Jackie-of-all-trades really, and an even more amazing friend.

Karen—we were brought together by Joanne, but you've also proven to be an amazing addition to my book team as my editor, and I love you just as much as those Oxford commas you like using my friend!

Nick, Isabella & Addison—I could write all the books in the world, but none of what I do would mean a thing without you three at my back. My family means the world, and you make life brighter simply by being mine. I love you.

Betas—a huge thank you to Joanne, Becky, Melissa, Kristine, Jessica, Pam, Christie, Shannon and Keri. You ladies rock!

My dearest readers—I wouldn't be where I'm at today without

each and every one of you. I'm so grateful for your continuing support and encouragement, and I so do hope that you enjoy Dalton's journey.

prologue

DALTON

ONE YEAR AGO…

IF I HAD to deliver that fucker's obituary, this is how it would read:

Rick Donnelly—Wannabe war hero, traitor, terrorist. May he burn in hell.

In truth, he was the scum who managed to kidnap my friend Theo Lowell's nephew, Jasper, then made off with the man's woman, all for the sake of petty revenge and furthering his stance in organized crime.

Now, he was nothing but a piece of shit, sprawled forward, split in half, and wedged between Warehouse Ten and the front end of Theo's brother's pickup truck—dead.

Collapsing to my back, Theo held onto his woman, Morgan, at my side. Allowing a long, drawn-out breath to escape, it helped ease the tension in my body as I began to deal with the pain in my hand and leg. The damn bastard might be dead, but he did some damage before Morgan drove a truck straight through him. My shooting hand now possessed a hole through it, and since I was reaching for the weapon in my ankle holster at the time, the fucking bullet managed to hit my already bad knee.

It was over—thank God for crazy-assed women, great friends... and random strangers.

Jasper was safe.

Morgan was secured.

And my buddy Theo could settle into the life he thought he'd all but lost only hours before.

Sounding on the verge of tears, he uttered, "Huss?" through our comms.

With an adrenaline drop to rival that of someone in the aftermath of military combat, I couldn't blame his emotional state. The same gamut of emotions was reeling through me too, and I hadn't had to track down two loved ones; nor had I had the displeasure of being held hostage, having to free myself, then do the same for the woman I loved. All this with some unknown cyber vigilante, who'd popped out of nowhere, to help us out. One we'd been forced to have blind faith in.

I'm your girl, Mr. T.

Yeah, Hussy had been our girl tonight—definitely.

"Yeah?" she said through that voice distorter of hers.

"Thank you." Theo's voice lodged in his throat, leaving the man incapable to add to his words.

It took a few seconds to get a response, but when it came, albeit in that robotically masculine voice again, it was just as overwrought with the same jumble of emotion Theo and I seemed to be experiencing. "You're welcome, Mr. T," she whispered.

Hussy's earlier concerned outburst to my being shot jumped to the forefront of my mind, spurring me into action. I didn't know why I felt compelled to reassure her, but I found myself unable to stop myself from doing it. Hussy wasn't one of my team at Nightshade Security, yet tonight, she had come through for all of us. Despite never having met, a bond had been forged between the team, Hussy, and me. Plus, I've always been one to listen to my gut, and it's proven me right every time, so it was why I said what I did.

"Huss?" I managed.

Her distorted voice caught, "Yeah?"

"I'll be okay," I swallowed the ball of emotion that made my voice come out sounding like gravel, "but I'm going to need your name, honey."

What I got next was an unaltered, breathless sounding, "Kip," that made my lungs seize, my body tighten, and a part of my anatomy take notice in a very visceral way.

I had no idea who this woman was, and she'd only spoken a single word—the nickname she'd given me based on my last name—Kippers. But that's all I needed. I can't explain the electrical charge that rolled through me, or the sense that something greater was at play here. I simply needed more of that voice. Needed more of *her*. "I want to know—"

A subtle thump on the other end of the line was followed by a long sigh.

I never thought a sigh could hold so much untold emotion, but hers did.

Exhaustion.

Wistfulness.

Hesitation.

Fear.

Defeat.

"Don't," she whispered, and I could have sworn I'd heard her add a soft "please" to that. "Let's just leave it at this." I didn't want to. A gnawing feeling in my gut told me I needed her still; that I wanted her. "I only did what needed to be done. It's what I do."

Something told me pushing her right then would be ineffective, so I gave in, much to my displeasure. But I did it in a way that left the proverbial door open and the ball in her court. "Okay, Huss. If you ever need anything—"

She seemed to contemplate my words for all-too-short of a moment. "I won't." The tone of finality in her answer had disappointment weighing me down until she continued, "But tell you what, I'll be in touch if something ever comes up."

Frustration fled and hope took its place. This was as good as I was going to get. "Okay."

Silence dominated the next ten seconds before Hussy broke it. "I'm going to sign off now."

"Huss?" I was desperate and I didn't care who knew. I wanted to reach through the communication device shoved in my ear canal and yank her to where I lay, so I could see the face that belonged to the voice. I wanted to figure out why she was how she was, what made her tick, what set her off. Hell, I'd have been happy to wait out the medics and the slew of first responders with her voice in my ear, reassuring me, just like Theo was doing with Morgan.

Before I could do or say anything else, the line went dead, all comms were down, and sirens could be heard in the distance.

I could feel Theo's gaze aimed at the side of my face. He probably wanted to know what the fuck was going on with me.

Ignoring the man, I thumped my head onto the dock in sheer frustration and closed my eyes. "Bye, Huss," I whispered.

one

Devolin

PRESENT DAY...

COME ON. *Come on. Come on!*

"Come. *On!*" I bounced in place as I watched the progress bar run its course, then punched the air in victory once it hit one hundred percent. "Gotcha!"

Disconnecting the thumb drive from my laptop, and slamming the top down on it, I scooted out of bed and proceeded to stuff the lot into my satchel.

There was no other option than to go straight to *him*.

This was life or death, and everything hinged on what I did next. I'd long since made a promise to myself that I'd never risk making contact with the team I'd bonded with after one night of mayhem. But promise or not, this information I'd just dug up wasn't something I could relay to him over the phone or some encrypted file share.

It needed to be seen.

Analyzed.

Discussed.

And that meant I needed to see Dalton Kippers. In the flesh. Talk to him. Show him what I'd found and what he was in for.

Then I needed to get far away from him, and move on already, because this crazy obsession I had developed over the man was getting out of hand. My best friend, Skylar, had told me as much on multiple occasions. And when Skylar deemed it fit to force her wisdom upon me, I needed to listen. It's been a little over a year since I helped Dalton and his team rescue Jasper Lowell and Morgan Smyth for Christ's sake—plenty of time to get over my crazy attachment.

On a snort, I shrugged off where my thoughts were heading and zipped up my bag.

"What are you doing?"

The breath in my lungs seized. "Sky!" Hand clutched at my chest, I turned to face the woman, and waited for my erratic heartbeat to calm. "You scared the living shit out of me."

Skylar leaned against the doorjamb, dressed in wrinkled hot pink scrubs from a hard day's work, smirking. "Well, at least we know one of us is capable of getting that ticker of yours up above a slow trot now, don't we?" She breezed into the room, nodded toward my satchel, a glimmer of curiosity entering her gaze. "What's going on?"

I bit my bottom lip, cognizant that guilt showed on my face for what I was about to ask of my dearest friend. Then I blurted, "Sky, I need your help."

"Do I need to worry that the cops will be coming in here to cart your ass off to jail?" she asked.

"I need to get out of here for a few hours."

"Dev, you know I can't—"

"It's life or death, Sky."

Skylar's eyes widened. "Dev, what in the hell have you gotten yourself into now?"

I headed toward the cabinet that passed itself off as a closet and grabbed the pair of jeans and t-shirt I'd been wearing when I had been admitted. My irritation at the lack of immediate support showed with every jerky movement I made to get ready. "Can you or can't you help me out?" I turned to look at her from over my shoulder.

Crossing her arms over her chest, Skylar took a seat in the chair closest to my hospital bed. "You look flushed. How're you feeling; and tell me the truth."

Oh no, not that no-nonsense tone of hers. If I told my friend, who incidentally was a nurse, that I was feeling *off* for lack of a better description, there'd be no way Skylar would let me walk out of here, say nothing of her covering for my absence with Doris, the nurse that was currently on duty. The woman was so old, she should have retired a decade ago, but seemed to find it amusing to torture her patients. It's why Skylar and I had dubbed her Nurse Battle-Axe. Because of this, and the fact I needed to get out of there, I went with, "I'm fine," and hoped that my bad acting, let alone lying skills wouldn't give me away.

Unfortunately, the lack of conviction my words held, and the pause I had to take to brace myself against the wall to wait out the subtle wave of dizziness that hit me, didn't help my cause.

"Uh-huh…"

"I'm not kidding, Sky. I need to do this." I whipped my pajama top off and flung it at the bed, slipping my shirt on. "This case…it's *big*."

"Dev—"

"No!" I persisted, yanking down my pajama bottoms, then headed to the bed for needed support. Leaning on it, I slid my legs into my jeans, wiggling them up over my ample hips. "*He*'s in danger."

Her eyes rounded when realization hit her. "He, as in *he*?" I nodded. "I thought we'd discussed this, Dev." She sighed.

"No, *you* discussed it. I merely heard you out. You told me to move on and I will. I just…" My frustration came out in a huff. "I have to see this through. It's my fault he took this case in the first place, so by default, it's my responsibility to make sure he knows what he's heading into. The people he'll be dealing with…" Another sigh accompanied my shake of the head. "They're not good." And I wasn't about to get into how I knew that with her. Not then, anyway.

"Okay," Skylar paused mid-thought. "Say I let you leave. How the hell am I supposed to keep Doris out of here?"

"She knows you come in here after your shifts. She never bothers to check in on me when you're here, you know that."

"So you want me to...?" She let her words hang so I could fill the gap.

"I know it's not right for me to ask this of you, but can you stay here, as in this room, until I get back? I promise it won't be more than a couple hours tops." Biting my lip in that nervous tick of mine, I continued, "And I'll need your keycard."

"Devolin!" she scolded.

Both of us looked toward the room's door and listened for a short moment to see if Skylar's outburst had generated any attention.

"I'll take the back way out and come in the same way. The emergency stairwell is just outside that door."

"I can get fired for that," she whisper-yelled, shooting the door another glance. Still, the woman pulled her access pass and handed it over.

I snapped it up from her hand then shrugged as I slid it into my jeans pocket. "Just say you lost it if anyone asks."

"Yeah, yeah. You're lucky I love you, woman," she grumbled.

Knowing I had her where I wanted her, I grinned. "So you'll help me out?"

On a curt nod, Skylar got to her feet. "Yeah." Her eyes did a full head to toe appraisal before she shared my smile. "But we need to do something about your hair and makeup first."

I blew out a relieved sigh, hoping my eyes conveyed my appreciation. I really would have left against hospital advice—sure, I'd return after my duty was done, dealing with the ramifications from my healthcare providers—because a life, if not lives, hung in the balance and it was all my fault.

Fucking Max, I thought not for the first or tenth time today.

Sneaking out of my room, and down the stairwell, proved to be easy enough. Nurse Battle-Axe was out on the floor and away from the nurses' station. Heading down two floors, I exited the staircase, and made my way toward the bank of elevators that would take me the rest of the way down to the main lobby. When I got there, I jumped in the first cab I spotted, rattling off my home address.

Upon my arrival, my adrenaline running at an all-time high, I hurried to my vehicle. Finding it parked in its usual spot of my mother's garage, I thanked the powers up above when I noticed the bay next to it was empty, appreciating the fact I wouldn't have to deal with dear old Mom right now.

Hitting the fob, I opened the door, dropped my bag on the passenger seat, then settled into the driver's side.

"Hello, baby," I cooed to my newest acquisition, the leather upholstered finish and new car smell had yet to fade, even after nearly a year of ownership.

Hitting the button that would open my bay's door from the controller on my visor, I put the key in the ignition and turned it. Sending my destination from my phone to the car's GPS, I took a few short seconds to enjoy the purr of the Charger's engine, then I shifted my ride into reverse.

Nightshade Security Investigations—Dalton's company—was closed, so I made my way to the former corporal's home to find that it too lacked the one man I was trying to locate. I took the time to admire the two rockers on his front wraparound porch and the American flag hanging in a place of pride on one of the support pillars framing the steps.

I hope I'm not too late.

I wasn't sure what I'd do if Dalton had already skipped town. Just as quickly as that thought popped into my head, another followed.

Theo would know where he is.

Reprogramming my GPS for Theo and Morgan's place, I reared out of the drive and floored the gas pedal. Fifteen minutes later, my lead foot caused me to nearly miss the entry to the driveway as I reached my third, and hopefully, final destination.

It wasn't until my finger released the doorbell that I realized how truly horrible I was feeling. To make matters worse, my nerves had also kicked in, and I had a fleeting thought that perhaps I should have given myself a quick cursory glance in the mirror before exiting the car. There were no do-overs on first meetings, and I was about to meet more than just Theo and possibly Morgan today, seeing as it looked like they had a visitor, judging by the third vehicle parked at the front of the house.

As luck would have it, someone was home.

I would have cried out my relief at the sight of the pregnant woman before me, but a whispered, "Morgan," was the only thing I could muster as soon as the door opened.

The woman's eyebrows furrowed in apparent confusion. "Do I know you?"

I shook my head, indicating the negative, because that's all I could do. I was too busy fighting a sudden dizzying bout of nausea. Next thing I knew, my vision blurred, then dimmed, and my knees gave out.

At the feel of a cool damp rag sponged against the hollow of my throat, over my forehead, my cheeks, and then back again, some of my faculties returned. The sensation was like heaven on my over-heated flesh. I sighed one second, and a whispered, "Mr. T," escaped me in the next.

"W-what, did she say?" I recognized Dalton's voice immediately—even a year or so later, I still haven't forgotten his deep baritone. Unable to get my eyes to cooperate and open, a thump came from right beside me, accompanied by the heat of another body warming the side of my torso.

"Danger...Kip," I forced the mumble, and then everything started to fade again.

Before I was able to embrace the darkness that swooped in, I felt the palm of Dalton's callused hand gently cup my cheek as he whispered, "Huss?"

two

Dalton

WITH A LOT of convincing to get the medics to allow me to be there, here I was, sitting in the back of an ambulance with who I suspected was Hussy, the cyber ghost I'd set Brycen to tracking in his spare time over the last year.

Her name: Devolin Payton Taylor. At least that's what the ID in her bag said when I managed to sneak a look at it before handing it to the paramedics as they loaded her up. I wouldn't be surprised if she'd faked her own identity, seeing as she seemed hellbent on remaining anonymous.

Leaning forward onto my knees, I peered at the woman splayed out onto the gurney before me—out cold.

Morgan told me that Hussy looked panicked when she'd first opened the door. Then she'd collapsed and Theo had called 911. Morgan rushed to get me a cold cloth, and I'd been left with an unconscious woman, her head resting in my lap as I tried to decipher what her few short words had meant—and why she'd chosen now to show herself.

Devolin whimpered in her sleep, causing me to reach out and grab the hand closest to me—her very tiny, dainty, exceptionally soft hand.

My eyes trailed up from her digits, her arm, her shoulder, the

11

delicate neck that held a thrumming but steady pulse, to her face. Her license said she had green eyes, but I wondered if they'd shimmer like emeralds, taper closer to the hazel side of things, or would be bright like aquamarines. Beyond that, her lips were full, dark pink—almost rosy—reminding me of bubble gum. A fleeting curiosity of if she'd taste as such washed over me, but I shrugged it off. It was her hair that had me begging to set it free and run my fingers through it. It was a deep auburn, with streaks of darker reddish hues mixed in. Her skin was pale, but I knew, with the small line of freckles over the bridge of her cute nose, her complexion wasn't that much darker when she wasn't ill like she seemed to be now.

What the fuck is the matter with you? I scolded myself internally for waxing poetic about an unconscious woman, one I'd had a past with, yet had never met before. Bowing my head, I tried to devise a plan of action on what I would do next now that I had bullied my way into being by her side.

DEVOLIN

I woke up in what had to have been the back of an ambulance, my hand clutched in a firm and warm grasp.

Allowing my head to tilt sideways, I found myself looking at Dalton, who sat beside me. His head was bent forward, shoulders hunched. He was leaning onto his knees, one of them bouncing out of what I surmised must have been anxiety. I could only imagine what went through his, Theo's, and Morgan's heads when I had shown up out of nowhere, and before I could explain anything, I pulled a Sleeping Beauty maneuver on their asses. That thought had me rolling my eyes, cringing internally.

Dalton had yet to notice I'd woken up, so I took the opportunity for a more thorough perusal of the unguarded man before me while I had it.

Dalton's dark brown, almost black hair was due for a cut, as it fell slightly over his eyes. I wondered how it would feel between my fingers if I were to brush it away. He had a chiseled jaw with a slight square shape, full lips, strong and masculine features that guaranteed him to look mean one minute, yet soft when the time called for it. His nose had a slight bend, most likely from it being broken at one point or another—maybe from combat—as with the small scar on the side of his right cheek, by his hairline. I could only assume since I'd only been able to access small portions of his service records. He looked infinitely better in person than in any of the photos I'd dug up, too. Trust me, I'd searched those babies out despite him not being on social media, if only to indulge my insane obsession over a man I've never met and had spoken with once.

Damn!

Dalton must have sensed I was conscious for his head shot up and his steel grey eyes connected with mine. "You're awake." The silk of his voice ran over me, goosebumps exploding on my skin, making me withdraw my hand from his so I wouldn't give myself, or my reaction to him, away.

Double damn! Wait, was that my voice? Embarrassment filled me as a grin broke over his face, solidifying the fact that I had spoken aloud. That look though... Had I felt anywhere close to one hundred percent, the look on his face would have melted my panties. I'm sure of it.

As it was, my mouth had gone dry, my tongue feeling as if it had tripled in size. "Uh."

"If you're going to look, I'd rather you be doing it while I can watch." His grin transformed into a smile.

My mouth opened for a rebuttal to his bold statement, then closed because words evaded me.

Light danced in the man's eyes. "The gig is up, Huss." His words were filled with confidence. "Or should I say Devolin Payton Taylor?"

"How'd?" He patted my hand then twined his fingers through mine, setting off another chain of goosebumps, and I knew how he'd figured it out. "You went through my stuff."

He followed his curt nod with, "How are you feeling?"

I tried to pry my hand from his like before, but he didn't give this time. "Where's my bag? I—I need to show you something."

"I asked you a question, Devolin."

I pulled at my hand again. Stuck. "Just let me—"

Instead of the gentle tone he'd led with, this time his words brokered no argument—all alpha-like. "Don't. Brush. Me. Off, Devolin."

"But—" My words ceased halfway out of my mouth when his lips formed a thin line in warning, and his hand squeezed mine as an added cautionary measure.

I tried to lift my head but collapsed back onto the stretcher's pillow when the nausea and dizziness that had been absent since my waking set in again. For the first time today, I started to really worry. This was all too reminiscent. Closing my eyes, I begged the powers that be, *Please don't let it be back. I can't deal with this right now.*

"What is it?"

My eyes snapped open. The paramedics had to have given me drugs or something. It could be the only reason why I couldn't keep my thoughts to myself—right?

Dalton leaned closer, the squeeze on my hand a gentle one. "What's back? What's the matter? Come on, Dev, talk to me."

He couldn't know. I didn't want him to know. I was there simply because I felt responsible to warn him, to keep him and his team at NSI safe. I should have known that exploring my connection with Dalton couldn't lead to... And what was it that I wanted it to lead to? A happily ever after? I snorted at the notion, then averted his questing gaze by turning my head to look up at the ambulance's ceiling. No, there would be none of that romance book nonsense for me. If I was having a relapse of some kind, it would solidify why I had to push him away. It was better to do the leaving instead of being left behind—it was something I'd learned early on in life. Yes, I was best making sure he had what he needed for his case, then disappear from his life like I'd done the first go around. And this time, I'd stay away for good.

With impatience clearly showing, Dalton groaned, "Devolin."

I closed my eyes, soaking in the warmth growing inside me, all due to the sound of his voice. Trying to breathe away my nausea, I silently prayed he'd say my name again. "You smell good. Like soap, mint, and man," I whispered. It was so not what I'd planned on saying.

"Devolin?" He sounded humored.

I chose to ignore him, until I felt his other hand cup my cheek. Then I couldn't.

Before I could react, deflect, possibly shove my foot in my mouth further, "Sir, we're at the hospital," came from one of the medics at the front of the vehicle. "We need you to clear out." The back door to the ambulance opened with the other attendant standing there.

"Wait," I cried out as Dalton began to back out of the rig, "my bag!"

"What is it with you and that bag?" Dalton grumbled and lifted the messenger satchel to show me that it had been with us all along.

"Take it. There are things on the thumb drives you need to see." The medics proceeded to unload my stretcher from the rig as Dalton stood at my side. "It's about the Wentworth case."

His body stiffened, eyes narrowing on me. "How do you know about that?" he clipped.

I wasn't about to apologize for doing what was right, even if he made me feel like a scolded child just then.

Showing my stubbornness, I jutted my chin up and said, "It doesn't matter. You need to do it right away. Before anyone heads to Mexico." I'd be damned if something happened to him or a member of his team when I'd been the one to put them in this mess, all thanks to a personal connection. Yes, damn Max, indeed.

"Fine. I'll get Brycen to meet me here, then you can show us what you've got when the doctor gives you the all-clear."

"No!" Being around him was the last thing I needed. Hell, if working together on that one mission had caused me to lose my head about him, I feared what working with him and his team in person would do. "Just take it, Dalton. Take the drives and the laptops, too. There's more stuff on those than has to do with your case but take it anyway. Brycen will know what to do with it. You won't need me. Just leave me my wallet. Of everything that's in there, it's all I need."

The man got right in my face, anger—or was it exasperation—emanating from him. It caused me to jerk back into the stretcher's cushions. "You're not getting away from me this time, Devolin," he snapped, his nostrils flaring.

"That's not—"

"You two can do this later," the driver stated. "Miss Taylor, we need to get you back to your room and get the doctor to check you out."

"What?"

Ignoring Dalton's outburst, the medics wheeled me toward the hospital entrance, leaving him behind.

three

DALTON

I WAS FUCKING OBSESSED.

Years ago, I swore I'd never get like this over a woman again and now look at me—taking that same old stroll down that same old road. Yet, despite how it turned out for me the first time around, here I was, spending the last year using my own company's resources to track down someone who would be deemed, by anyone with a functioning brain, a ghost.

From the moment the mission to rescue Theo's nephew and Morgan ended, White Hat Hussy had disappeared from the deep web, never to be seen or heard from again. Well...sort of.

It was bad enough her voice has haunted me since *that* night.

The silky, smooth, low, and sultry cadence, with a subtle Northern lilt, was never far from my mind. I heard it while out on missions. It was there again when I fell asleep.

Truth be told, I had no idea why, or how for that matter, this woman had infiltrated my thoughts. Random things reminded me of her. I found myself imagining what she looked like. I wondered how old she was, or if she thought of me as often as I did her.

It had been months since I'd seen sign of life from her. A year since I'd last heard her voice. The guys at Nightshade Securities still gave me hell when I inquired if they'd turned anything up. They thought I'd fallen off my rocker. Maybe I had.

Then again, White Hat Hussy—or Huss as we'd dubbed her over the last year—had made it impossible to forget her.

When my ass landed in the hospital after being shot, she sent me flowers. I'm not talking about one of those *get-well* bouquets, either. Hell, she'd gone overboard, embarrassing me in front of the others. Even Morgan, a florist for Christ's sake, asked me if I intended on becoming a rival of hers, what with every surface available—and some of the floor, too—being covered in vase after vase.

But Huss, our little cyber angel, had gone the extra mile. I hadn't been the only one to suffer her wacky sense of humor or been blessed with her generosity.

With Shane, she'd helped close a bunch of cases that had either gone cold or lacked information to proceed with their current lead. For Morgan and Theo, she'd sent the man a *Mr. T* doll, and a few other more meaningful gifts in celebration of their nuptials and, most recently, Morgan's pregnancy. Hell, Brycen might not have thought of it as funny at the time, but the rest of the guys from that night—me included—thought it was hilarious how she'd infiltrated the computer wiz's system, repeatedly, only to leave dancing trolls for him to find. Shit, even Theo's nephew hadn't been left untouched. Jasper had a custom blanket delivered to him, with each one of us guys' names on it. The note it came with, typed up mind you, commended him on his bravery. She also told him that if things ever got scary again, all he had to do was hide under the blanket and he'd be safe.

Each gift or act had thought put into it. Maybe that's why I was hung up on her, I don't know. Which is why, with every delivery, I pushed the guys to track her down in their spare time.

But each box or envelope lacked the return address they needed. And forget fingerprints. Every service utilized had no way of providing the billing information—items had been either paid by in cash or any information in their computers had been erased because she'd gotten into their systems. The surveillance systems were of no help either. The woman had thought of everything to make sure she remained incognito.

Yet now I'd found her.

Technically, she found you.

And by the looks of things, she wasn't doing very well. So naturally, when a nurse approached me, volunteering to show me to the waiting room, I followed her.

It wasn't until my ass landed in a seat of the Chronic Care Ward, that worry hit me. About the same time it did, so did my stubbornness.

If Devolin thought she could get rid of me, she was mistaken. I'd sit there and wait for as long as it took until I could get to her. I didn't want answers on the Wentworth case from what Brycen could find on her devices. I wanted those answers straight from the source—Devolin herself.

four

ABOUT TWO-POINT-FIVE SECONDS after the nurse left me in the waiting room, I pulled out my phone and dialed up Brycen. I might have wanted Devolin to give me the information, but depending on the severity of her illness, it might not be soon enough, and time was of the essence with this particular case.

Within half an hour, the man was sitting next to me, pounding away at Devolin's hardware. Shortly thereafter, another nurse—one named Doris, according to her nametag, who looked like a witch with an axe to grind—came by to convey a verbal message that Devolin was fine and she wanted me out of there.

Nope. It wasn't going to happen. I told the lady as much too and sent her on her way with a handwritten note to boot.

With Brycen exploring Devolin's computers, we weren't going to be moving anytime soon.

Turning to my computer specialist, I asked Brycen, "What can you tell me so far?"

The man looked up, his eyes wide with a look of wonderment. "Is this chick for real?" The confusion on my face must have shown because he didn't hesitate to elaborate with a shit-load of enthusiasm, so much so, his hands became part of the conversation. "I wish I could borrow her brain for a day. She's a fucking genius, D!" For him to say that about someone he'd loathed for the better part of a year because she'd bested him repeatedly was something else. "This tracking software she's created puts mine to shame." He shuffled closer, tilting one of the laptops so I could check things out. "This is what I've been missing. This is what we need for NSI, D. You should see the codes she's written. Fucking hell! If you won't offer her a job, I will."

I *had* planned to do that a year ago, but before I could, Devolin shut me down, citing that parting ways after Morgan's rescue was best for everyone. As I've mentioned before, I hadn't stopped at that, but she was like smoke—there one second, gone the next. Invisible. Today had been the biggest break I'd gotten where she was concerned.

Before I could share this with Brycen, I spotted my half-sister heading my way. "Sky?" Getting to my feet, I took a few steps toward her, then waited for her to come the rest of the way.

She greeted me with a hug. "What are you doing here?"

I squeezed her back, "Waiting on someone."

She pulled back from me, her eyes filled with worry. "Is it one of the guys?" Then she peered over my shoulder, eyes going wide, reflecting recognition. Her face filled with shock. "That's Devolin's bag!" Clearly agitated, her arm shot out and her finger pointed in Brycen's direction. "Those are her computers! What's he doing with her computers, D?"

What in the ever-fucking fuck? She knows Devolin?

My stance widened, my arms crossed over my chest, and my eyes studied the woman in front of me. Skylar bit her lip nervously, her eyes darting between me and my partner, who was diligently tapping away on one laptop, then switching to the other, muttering nonsensical things to himself, all the while oblivious to this latest development.

"Skylar, how do you know her?"

"She told me she was fine," she explained, and tried to move past me to get to Brycen, but I shot out an arm to stop her. She sighed and looked up into my eyes. "Dalton, is she in trouble?"

Despite her evident concern, I didn't answer. Instead, I

repeated my earlier question. "No bullshit, Sky. How do you know her?"

Fire flashed through her irises and my sister's trademark stubbornness kicked in.

Getting onto the tips of her toes, her index poked me in the chest. "She's a friend." Another poke. "A good friend. The best I've had in the last two years as a matter of fact." She kept punctuating each point with that finger of hers. "Tell me what's going on, D, because whatever you think she's done—"

"Sky—"

"No! Listen to me, D." She wasn't backing down. Like a dog with a bone that one. "She wouldn't do—"

I was officially past the point of exasperation. "Would you shut the fuck up and listen to what I have to say?"

"You can't take this away from her, D," she whispered. "It's all she's got. She's been sick for—"

"Sick?"

"Yeah, sick, and not the cold or flu kind. You do realize you're in the Chronic Care Ward, right?" She paused, shaking her head before letting it drop to her chest. "I just…" A sigh. "I just thought that this last time would be it," she whispered, but I heard her loud and clear. "She doesn't deserve this to be happening to her. She doesn't need more shit in her life." Her eyes flew up to mine and I was faced with a protective Skylar. "You need to leave her alone. Whatever it is that you caught her doing, she's doing it for good, you get me? Leave. Her. Be. Dalton." She finished this with her chest rising and falling rapidly, eyes shining with unshed tears.

Grabbing onto her shoulders, I pulled her into a hug, offering her comfort. "Had you given me a word in edgewise," I started softly into her hair, "I'd have told you that Brycen, the guys, and I have been looking for Devolin for quite some time." Skylar's body went solid as a rock. Nodding against her head, I continued, "She helped me out a while back." I chuckled. "She's given us quite the runaround, too." Pulling away, I set her back, a subtle smile on my face. "Aside from the fact that I wanted to track her down to thank her for getting involved, I—"

Skylar's eyes widened. "This is about Theo and Morgan, isn't it?"

What the fuck?

"I heard her that night, D." Her voice shook. "I was working the nightshift and had planned to stop by on my break like I usually do, but I heard her. The panic in her voice. The resolve in it...her defeat. I had no idea what she was doing, but I knew it had something to do with her computers."

"Skylar?" She turned to face the same nurse who'd given me Devolin's message earlier. "Your girl's looking for you."

Skylar nodded to the woman, "Thanks, Doris," then turned to me once more. "I..."

"Go," I told her. "Make sure she's alright. We can talk about this later."

She nodded. "Can I ask you something?"

Smirking, I nodded. "Doesn't mean I'll answer."

"D..." She rolled her eyes.

"Fine."

"She's the one with the flowers and gifts, isn't she?" Her lips quirked up at my subtle nod. "I'm going to tell you this, but I swear I'll hunt you down in your sleep and kill you if you tell her this came from me..."

That was the moment when I knew I had an ally in Skylar.

five

I STARED down at the note Doris had handed me.

I'm staying.
—D

Funny how those two words incited a gamut of conflicting emotions. At first, dread filled me, quickly being replaced by excitement, only for that to shift to nervousness, then to doubt, followed by excitement yet again, then to depression as thoughts of my most likely failing health interrupted the merry-go-round that was Dalton Kippers.

Now, I was making myself busy, staring at the far wall of my hospital room, trying to figure out how I could evade the man in question.

That's when Skylar came barreling through the door, a murderous look upon her face. "When were you going to tell me that you knew D?"

My body went rigid, my shoulders bunching up by my ears as I whispered, "What?" D was Dalton? What the fuck were the odds?

"Those are your bag and your laptops out there, are they not?"

"Well—"

"He's the one you've been hung up on all these months, isn't he?"

Mouth hanging open, I nodded, then tried my luck. "Sky—"

The woman threw her hands in the air. "I can't believe this!" She began to pace the room. "What the hell are you doing, Dev?" Skylar aimed a perplexed gaze my way. "I told you that you'd get in trouble with your little—"

"Let me—"

Skylar's feet halted, pivoting abruptly to face me. "You know you'll be lucky to escape jail this time, right? D isn't someone to mess with. He's by the book. Black and white...ain't any shades of gray with that man. Fuck, Dev, what did you do?"

"You don't understand." I bit my lip, trying to figure out what to say. Skylar gave me a look that demanded an explanation whether I was ready to give one or not. "It's not like I planned to get involved on purpose. I had no idea he was your brother; you two don't even share the same last name."

"It's a sore point with Dad. Mom gave me her last name when I was born. I'm thinking about having it changed though." She snorted. "I don't want any ties to her after the shit she's pulled, my genetics are enough."

I nodded. "When I looked into him, I didn't need to know about his family affiliations. Plus, you call him D! How was I supposed to know that was short for Dalton?" Pausing to take a breath, I continued, "I had to make sure I was helping out a group of good guys. The night we crossed paths, electronically-speaking, I was creeping online and saw the video footage. I couldn't sit there and do nothing!" I hated confrontation when it came to me having to justify the ethics I abided by regarding my work. The term hacker wasn't one taken in a positive light, that's for sure, but people needed to know there was a difference in the stereotypical hacker and one known as a white hat. Skylar was aware of the differences thanks to previous conversations, but my friend was too blinded by her emotions to even thinking straight.

"You should have let Brycen handle things," Skylar bit out.

"He *didn't* have a handle on things," I growled in defence.

"That's the point I'm trying to make. He underestimated the target and got tagged. There wasn't any time, Sky. Morgan would have died. I didn't know about Jasper until after the men pulled him out of that old garage, and I had just joined the party by then." Party, yeah. We'd had a rockin' good time that night. Not!

As quick as Skylar was to rage, the woman's temper was diffused just as fast, if the look of empathy strewn across her face was anything to go by.

"Then explain to me, why it is my brother's computer guru has his hands on your precious computers right now? Tell me you haven't found trouble. Devolin, I warned you—"

"I'm not the one in trouble," I whispered.

Skylar's eyes rounded. "You mean— When you left earlier..."

I nodded. "There's a case he landed recently."

"Have you been working together all this time and you haven't told me?" The woman's brows furrowed. "No, that can't be right."

Right then, I thought it best to answer the question my friend had yet to ask. "We haven't been in touch since Morgan's kidnapping. I gave him the slip, and I've been giving Brycen and the rest of the guys working for your brother the same treatment since then."

Skylar's eyes widened. "That's just over a year ago now!"

I nodded. "I know."

On a sigh, Skylar let herself drop into the chair at my bedside. "Then how'd you know about this new case of his?" she asked.

I knew guilt centered in my expression. "I referred that particular client to Dalton, that's how I know. The authorities haven't been able to make heads or tails of anything, so I sent him to your brother. For the last year, I've been..." I had to find a way to explain to her, in a manner that didn't make me seem as creepy as it did in my head. "I, uh...the night when Morgan was taken..." I looked down at my hands, my fingers clutching at each other, knuckles turning white. "We...that is, *I* felt a connection...to them. After everything went down, I just couldn't let them go." It had become somewhat of an obsession, really, and it hadn't just been with Dalton. I'd felt protective of the entire NSI team after that night.

"Oh, honey." Skylar's hand covered mine. "You've been

watching over them, haven't you?" I avoided her gaze but nodded, relieved that she had figured it out without my having to explain further. "Thank you."

My head snapped up. "What?" I whispered.

Skylar's eyes glittered with unshed tears. "You had my brother's back. The shooting, the flowers...the other gifts—" Her eyes rounded as she emitted a gasp. "You need to forget what I've been telling you."

"You've been telling me to do a lot of things since we've known each other, Sky."

"Don't move on, Dev," she whispered.

"What?" I choked out.

"Woman, he's just as obsessed with you as you've been with him. Don't. Move. On," she repeated.

"What?" I parroted my earlier words.

Oh no! This wasn't good. Not good at all. The last thing I needed was a man—one who set my motor running more than any other man—and that was before even having met him face-to-face. I didn't know any other way to deal with my friend's request other than to panic, and she immediately picked up on it.

"Just hear me out..." Skylar began.

So what if he likes my quirkiness? It doesn't make him Mr. Right, does it?

"How do you know?" Skylar broke me from my musings.

"Huh?"

"How do you know he's not your Mr. Right, Dev? He's a good guy. He—"

I cut her off. "It's not him. It's me. It's because I don't do well with people. I've been stuck here for months, and when I'm not here, I'm at my mother's. My mother's, Sky! I'm a socially awkward dork. I'm anxious all the time, and I don't trust easily. I don't trust—"

Skylar made a grab for my hands, stopping that incessant finger twisting of mine and whispered, "You don't think your health is going to get any better, do you?" I shook my head, no. "And today has freaked you out?"

"Yeah," I sniffled, my voice having gone thick. "You know my history, Sky. You know that just when things start looking up, they usually fall to pieces. Aside from Mom and you, I'm better off alone —everyone else always leaves. I can't relate to anything in Dalton's world or yours, for that matter. I don't know what it is to be normal anymore."

"Something happened that night, didn't it?"

"What do you mean?"

"Don't play coy with me, Dev." Skylar crossed her arms over her chest, her chin jutting out in defiance. "You two formed some kind of bond working that case."

I shrugged. "I already told you we did. We *all* did. It doesn't—"

"Yeah, but there's something more there with D than with the others." Her gaze softened when she saw me pull my lips in between my teeth so I couldn't confirm or deny her allegations. "I heard you that night, Dev."

"What?" whooshed out of me.

"I'm thinking you must have been wearing a headset, because I could only hear your part of the exchange. Well, the parts after I heard you shrieking someone's name," she explained. "You sounded so sad. Like you didn't know your place in the world." She was right on her mark. "It's as if being alone is easier even though I know it's been hell on you."

"Yeah, but the price everyone else pays when I can't be part of their everyday lives is worth being alone, Sky," I managed through the lump in my throat. "It hurts less all around in the end."

"But—"

I shook my head. "No, Sky. It's bad enough I can't seem to get him off my mind. You were right. If I can't bring myself to open up, then I might as well just leave well enough alone. So that's why I need you to make sure that he goes away and stops looking for me."

My friend shook her head, eyes locking on mine as she leaned closer. "You don't know him, Dev. He won't stop. Now that he knows who you are, he's not just going to let things go. You've just dangled prey in front of the beast. Do you honestly think he's going to pull up stakes now?"

"He has to," I whispered.

"No, Dev, that's where you're wrong. D doesn't have to do shit. He does what he does because he wants to. Finding out who you are was only part of the puzzle." Skylar got up and backed toward the room's door. "Listen, you need your rest, so I'll buy you some time. I'll send him away but know that he'll come looking for you. And when he does get to you, you better be ready to answer to him, especially if you keep giving him the runaround. Since you're so good at disappearing, I suspect he might just threaten to break out the cuffs."

"Cuffs?" I gulped.

"I know," she leaned against the doorjamb, sporting a saucy grin, "kinky, right?"

"Please don't tell him anything about what I've been through."

"I haven't. I won't. That's something best coming from you, but know that he's already put two and two together. He will be asking you about you being sick, and why you left the hospital when you are a patient. I suggest that you're honest about it all. If not, I can bet, now that he knows your identity, he'll set Brycen to the task of figuring out who you are. I'm going home for a little R&R, and I'll be back later."

With that, Skylar disappeared, leaving me with assorted images that worked themselves into one hell of a sexy scenario. It's too bad I refused to do anything about it.

six

IF IT WEREN'T for Skylar's promise to help me out with Devolin, I would have never left the hospital that very first day.

The next morning, I was right back in that waiting room—sans Brycen—who was still working on deciphering Devolin's information. I'd also tasked him with searching for some background on our little white hat hacker.

Suffice to say, after our official meeting, I figured a gentler approach might be more successful at getting Devolin to spare me some time. It seemed to me, what the woman needed most, was a friend.

When she denied me her time and presence that next day, I called up Morgan and had five dozen pink roses delivered to Devolin's room. It had cost me a small fortune, but how else was I supposed to convey my thanks for everything she'd done a year ago?

I was again denied entry the following day.

This warranted another five dozen roses. I also got a call from my half-sister, stating if I was aiming for impact, I'd hit my mark. Skylar also told me if I wanted to really sweeten Devolin up, stargazer lilies were her favorite.

So that's what I tried next.

When I walked into the waiting room on that third day, I had a rather large, not to mention, extremely fragrant vase full of stargazer lilies in my hands.

"I see the big guns have come out." Skylar smirked from her chair behind the nurses' station. "Did you get the rest?"

I nodded.

She clapped her hands, shot to her feet, then extended her arms toward me. "Good. Now, give me those and let me do my thing."

My third floral delivery must have been a charm—or maybe it was because Skylar got in on things even more and wouldn't let her friend get away with pushing me out any longer.

My phone was in hand.

The number was dialed.

All I had to do was hit *call*.

I didn't. Instead, I found myself so deep in my head, I never noticed Skylar standing right in front of me.

"She said she'll see you."

That got my attention. When my head snapped up, the woman was grinning like a loon.

I cancelled out from my call log, pushed myself up to my feet, and shoved my phone in my back pocket. "She will?"

She nodded. "But I suggest you let her go at her own pace." I gulped down the sudden bout of nerves that overwhelmed me, taking in what my sister's words. "Don't push her, D."

"What made her change her mind?" I asked.

Skylar laughed softly. "You mean, beside you proving me right by being a pushy bastard?" She licked her lips before explaining, "I think it was something I said. Then again, she got some great news earlier this morning, so it could have something to do with that, too." Skylar's smile brightened her whole face, making me itch to ask her what the good news was about. Call me crazy, but I was hoping Devolin would be the one to impart that knowledge when I spoke with her. Therefore, I didn't ask.

Taking a few steps toward my sister, I grabbed her by the

shoulders, and pulled her toward me in a loose hug. "Thank you, Sky," I said into her hair before kissing it, then set her back.

"Go get her, tiger. She's in room 506." With a wink, she turned to leave. "I'll be back later to check on things."

Right as I was going to head toward Devolin's room, my phone chimed with an incoming text from NSI.

BRYCEN:

Call me. ASAP.

So, that's what I did.

"Yo!"

"You talk to our girl yet?" Brycen asked.

"Just heading that way, now."

"You got in?"

"Yes, dumbass, now cut to the chase."

"Alright, alright!" He sounded as if he was smiling. "I was doing what you asked me to do."

"Get with it," I growled.

"Our girl is good, D."

Tell me something I don't know.

"But it's surprising how much one can find out about a person, once you know their legal name," the man said.

"Alright..." I left my word hanging, hoping that Brycen would lead into his explanation.

He didn't disappoint.

"She works for Gordon Hewitt, man," he growled.

Fuck.

Damn.

Shit.

Sonofabitch!

"You've got to be shitting me!" I said a little too loudly. A few people in the waiting room gave me the stink eye.

Gordon Hewitt was a man NSI's been investigating for quite some time. A real estate mogul, born with a silver spoon in his mouth, unlike his father, Gordon Sr., he was a crook. But the slippery fucker knew how to get by undetected, and I knew this first-hand. He had a bevy of lackeys, and they were loyal fuckers, willing to do his dirty work. He was far enough removed from the stink of his men that you knew he was the puppet master, but you couldn't point the finger at the douchebag without making yourself look like the fool.

"So what are you saying?" I asked Brycen.

"I've looked into the work she's doing for him," the man paused, "I can't say if she's in deep with the guy, but she is on the payroll, and everything looks legit. She didn't leave much on her system except for existing projects, and to be honest, that shit was encrypted to the nth degree."

"Brycen—"

"So far as I can tell she's clean." A relieved breath escaped me. "But I'll caution you to tread lightly with this one until we figure out how she got involved with the guy."

Well, that was a short-lived spell. "Got it," I ground out.

"And, D?"

"Yeah?"

"The shit I just found about the work she does for him, I'm getting the sense that she's not entirely on board with it all."

Well, that was something. So I asked, "How so?"

The man chuckled. "Let's just say, if any of this information were to get into the wrong hands, a whole lot of shit could come raining down on a whole lotta heads."

"Bryce—"

"I'm talking politicians, CEOs... Hell, she's even got a file a mile long on Hewitt himself." I didn't quite share Brycen's humor, but that last bit, I took it as good news. It meant that she knew how to protect herself against any possible backlash. Including one from her own boss.

"Anything we can use?"

"Some of it ties in with bits we've been able to uncover," the man responded.

"You're just going to leave me hanging?"

"Yeah." He chuckled once more. "I want a deeper look into things before I give you the goods on that jackass."

"Sounds good."

"Give her a kiss from me, will ya?"

"Babyface—" Before I could finish warning the man, I was met with dead air.

seven

I CAN'T BELIEVE *you gave in.*

But I had.

It was impossible not to fall for Dalton's charm, when I'd never been the recipient of such efforts before. I had been contemplating giving in, and when those lilies arrived, I knew holding the man back would be futile, my resolve entirely decimated.

Dalton's said efforts also made me wonder about how the man would be if he had a woman in his life, especially if he took such great pains to woo a mere stranger. Of course, this set a slew of various scenarios to play about in my head; ones that caused me to dream—day and night.

He'll be here any minute!

Deep breathing, a few cursory glances in the bathroom mirror, or all the shifting I did, making sure my clothes looked just right, even if they were pajamas, did nothing to assuage my nerves.

I was as ready as I'd ever be.

When Dalton walked through the door to my hospital room though, I knew right then there was never truly such a thing as being ready for a man like him.

One just had to brace.

So I did just that, and then I also proceeded to soak in the sheer masculinity of him. That usual strand of dark hair still hung over his eyes. His silvery-blue gaze was open, friendly, yet assessing at the same time. His broad shoulders and chest were hugged by his signature black t-shirt. I wondered, not for the first time, how he ever got those things on...or off, for that matter.

My eyes trailed lower, pleased he'd forgone his black cargo pants and was sporting a distressed looking pair of jeans. The denim, soft and overworn, hung low at his hips, hugging those massively powerful thighs and what I figured, but had never witnessed, would be a spectacularly firm derriere. His hands were bare, but I noticed his left wrist had leatherwork wrapped around it: a bracelet of sorts. It went well with the dog tags hanging from his neck and the combat boots on his feet.

However, it wasn't the appearance of the man per se that drew me to him. It had been his unwavering loyalty to his friend, Theo, and the surefooted way he led his team. Sure, all the other guys had that same confidence in spades, but something about Dalton's strength, his sense of humor on that dark night, his intellect, not to mention, the quick thinking and seamless adapting to the situation, that had pulled me in. He was a perfect picture of leadership and control in a life where I never had any.

A throat cleared, "Devolin?"

Just one word. With that deep baritone of his, it was all it took for my already erratic heartbeat to hammer harder, for my sweaty palms to grow damper, and for my hormones to shift into hyperdrive.

Oh shit, I'm in trouble!

The man shut the door behind him, his long stride bringing him to the bedside chair in five steps. Dropping his large frame into the seat, he set his elbows on his knees, and leaned forward, his eyes keeping mine captive. "Thanks for agreeing to see me."

"Thank you for the flowers," I said softly, feeling the heat of my blush suffusing my cheeks. Seriously, if ten dozen roses and a bouquet of lilies made my room look like a miniature garden, I couldn't help but wonder what the result of my granting him with that same gesture what felt like an eternity ago, albeit in a much more insane quantity, had looked like.

His lips tipped up, his gaze going warm and intense. "You're welcome. I owed you payback," he winked.

I couldn't look away. "I'm getting out," I blurted.

His brows rose. "Huh?"

"The doctor came in this morning." I licked my dry lips. "He said if everything holds up, I'll be home in a week. Two at the most."

"That's great news, Devolin." He reached out to take my hand in his, and I let him. He seemed to be a very tactile person. I'd noticed it at Theo and Morgan's, during my very limited amount of consciousness, then again in the ambulance, and now. "Can...can I ask what—"

I cringed. "You're telling me you don't know? I would have thought you'd have had Brycen look me up by now."

Dalton had the decency to look affronted. "I can't say he didn't try," he confessed. "Most of your records are sealed. Then again, when I found out what he was researching had nothing to do with the Wentworth case, I got pissed and reamed his ass."

This necessitated a giggle on my part. "I'm sure he would have figured out a way to get to those records somehow." Dalton's expression turned thoughtful at this. "But since you've most likely seen or heard about the files I've built on you and your team, and in the interest of being fair, I'll tell you a bit of what I've gone through."

eight

GODDAMN! *I need a shot of Jack*, I thought on my drive home from the hospital.

And a cold shower.

Followed closely by another round of Jack, and maybe a beer chaser.

Yes, it had been that kind of day.

The first shot of Jack would be a digestive to the information that had poured out of Devolin, going a long way to explain why she was the person she was. Fuck, but with all she'd told me, I found it damn near impossible to ignore the innate urge to protect her. She'd been through so much.

The cold shower would be for the fact the woman was a wet dream come true for me. Sweet, innocent, funny as all hell, and somehow, despite being slightly socially awkward according to her, she had so much sass and sarcasm in her, it made her all the more endearing. Regardless of those girlie flannel pajamas of hers, my cock still flew at full-mast throughout most of the afternoon. Despite their full coverage, those cutesy things did nothing to hide her curves. It had been a decadent kind of pain, even if inappropriate. I was there as a friend—not to pick up—and perhaps, if luck was on my side, an eventual boss.

As for the second shot of Jack and its beer chaser, those would serve to help me figure out how I was going to deal with the slew of unanswered calls and texts I'd received throughout the day from *her*.

This *her* being my ex-fiancée: Suzanna. The bitch I thought I'd finally been rid of for the last six months even though we'd been over for nearly five years now.

On that thought, I pulled into my drive, only to come up short when I spotted Skylar's car in the extra parking space.

What the fuck?

I parked in front of the garage, turned the key, then pulled it out of the ignition. It was just my luck Skylar would need me for something.

Just like your stepmother needed your dad for everything. No. That wasn't it. Skylar never asked for anything. Not before. Not now. And I didn't expect that to change in the future. If anything, I'd always appointed myself as her protector when she least wanted it. Skylar had always been the queen-of-sticky-situations, but she'd also been an expert at getting out of said situations on her own. So it shocked me to see she'd come to see me, let alone, had helped herself in with the key I'd given her five years ago, when I retired from the army and bought this house.

Maybe she's here about Devolin.

Now that made sense.

With that assumption, I stormed the front steps and let myself in, shouting out, "Sky?" The scent of fried steak and sautéed mushrooms assaulted me from the threshold.

"In the kitchen!" I heard, followed by the crash-bang of pots and pans and the sizzling of searing meat.

I entered the kitchen and let out a groan of pleasure, "Goddamn that smells good," then I dropped my phone on the counter and made a beeline for the liquor hutch, pulling out my trusty bottle of Jack Daniels, along with two tumblers.

Pouring myself two fingers, I lifted the glass to my lips and downed it before doing it again, filling the second glass along with it, knowing Skylar had an appreciation for the stuff. The perk of having your sister in your house, unannounced no less, was that the need for a cold shower was curtailed.

I turned to find Skylar sporting that assessing gaze our father always gave me. I swear, she had more of Hank Kippers in her than I ever did.

As I slid the extra tumbler toward my vegetable-chopping sister, her gaze came up to mine as she took a moment to study me. "Rough one?" she stated more than inquired.

"You could say that," I sighed, running a hand through my hair and giving her a pointed look. "I, uh..."

Her eyes held a knowing glint. "She laid it all out for you, didn't she?"

I nodded, swallowed hard, "Yeah."

Skylar set her knife on the counter, picked up the cutting board, swiping the green onions, radishes, tomatoes, and celery onto the mixed greens in the bowl next to her, before taking a sip of the drink I'd poured her. Then she turned to the stove, flipped the switch on the necessary burners, took the steaks off, then, after shoving the pan in the oven, she faced me again, leaning onto the island counter.

"Heavy, isn't it?"

No words sufficed to express the weight Devolin had held on her shoulders with very limited support, so I nodded as she studied me further. "Seems too easy a description, to be honest, sis," I said as I ran a hand through my hair.

"Hmm," she nodded. "The steaks have another ten minutes to finish, why don't you go wash up?" Having encroached on my property, she read me like a book, knowing all too well that I needed a moment to myself.

Leaving my phone on the counter, I headed for my bedroom to freshen up.

"She's calling you!" Skylar shrieked, my phone in her upheld hand as I came back from the bathroom ten minutes later. "What the hell does that bitch want?"

"Let it go, Sky," I warned.

"You want to know how many times *this*," she waved my phone in the air, "went off while you were cleaning up?" She didn't wait for my response. "Five fucking times, D! *Five!*"

"What would you have me do, Sky? She's calling NSI's number; it's not like I can change it."

She set the phone down on the counter, then reached to start loading our plates with food. "You've talked to her?" She paused in her task to peer at me.

"I've tried that, and I thought it worked, but I guess it didn't stick." I went to the fridge, pulling two beers out, and popping their tops off. "I'll get Shane to put one of the guys on the force on it," I assured her, as I set our drinks on the table.

"I'd slap a restraining order on that woman so fast her head would spin," she grumbled.

I didn't have the heart to tell her I'd already done that and it had gotten me nowhere.

"So," I wiped at my mouth with the napkin, my plate now empty. "We've talked about my work, yours, how Dad's doing, but you're leaving something out and I'm itching to know."

Skylar shoved her last bite of steak in her mouth, an obvious effort to stall the conversation. It was something she did all the time when we were growing up, particularly when she knew she was in trouble and our father would question her.

My gaze narrowed. "What's this visit about, sis?"

She swallowed her food, her jaw clenching before she proceeded. "Devolin's going home," she whispered.

"I know. In about a week it looks like."

Skylar's grin was so contagious I felt my lips tug upward. "Tell me you're hiring her, D. You can't have spent nearly an entire day with her and not—"

"Uh, Sky?" I rubbed at the back of my neck. "We didn't exactly discuss work."

My sister's brows furrowed. "You didn't? But I thought—"

"Nope." We hadn't, and despite the urgency with which she'd

hunted me down, I wasn't all that upset with the lack of information right then.

When I said I'd learned all about what made Devolin the person she was, I meant it. My mettle was tested when I enlisted with the Rangers. Hers had been tested at the tender age of eight. Relentlessly.

nine

Devolin

HERE I WAS, laying in my hospital bed recollecting how my day had turned out.

I figured, once Dalton was granted a visit, he would have been all about business.

He hadn't been.

Instead, we'd made light chitchat. I never figured the man to be much of a talker, simply because of what Skylar had told me about him, but it was evident that my best friend didn't see her brother in the same light I did.

All the fuss I'd made over my pending visitor had been for naught. Within minutes, Dalton had me so at ease, it felt like second nature to tell him all about myself.

I began my story when I'd lost consciousness at summer camp right before my ninth birthday. I'd been unusually tired and nauseous. My skin was pale, I had ached all over, and bruises started popping up with the slightest bumps into things. I wasn't hungry, and despite this, my belly had grown hard as a rock to the point it bulged out, resembling that of a malnourished child in some Third World country. Everyone thought I was coming down with a cold or some sort of flu bug.

But it wasn't that at all.

I lived in Canada, one of Toronto's suburbs, at the time, so my mother had picked me up and brought me to the Toronto General Hospital.

When I spoke about the multiple sessions of poking and prodding, the incessant questions about my symptoms, the innumerable screening tests, Dalton's nose had scrunched up to the point I had laughed. Yeah, no one enjoyed the hospital—Dalton was no exception.

"It sounds worse than what it was." I patted his hand in reassurance. "Trust me, worse things came along after that."

"It's so much for a young kid to deal with," his voice, although empathetic, was soft—tortured.

Admittedly, the whole experience had freaked me out. And perhaps, having had my nose in my father's old biology and pathophysiology textbooks may have not been that bright of an idea at the time. I was smart. Freakishly smart, that is. With that kind of gift, the thirst for knowledge had beckoned me and my parents had indulged my harmless endeavor.

"From the General," I licked my lips. That's when Dalton had also poured me a glass of water, handing it over for me to take a sip. "They sent me to Toronto Hospital for Sick Children. I felt like I was stuck in an episode of *Star Trek* or something."

There'd been MRIs, CT scans, more X-rays since my lungs had been rattling badly by then. Hell, they'd even done an ultrasound, but my least favorite of all diagnostic tests had been the lumbar puncture.

"I can't imagine how hard it must have been on your parents," Dalton said.

Snorting at that, I turned to set my glass of water on the bedside table.

My mother had dealt with it well enough; she'd given in to her OCD impulses and kept everything in sight clean and sterile. My father, on the other hand, his reaction I didn't understand. I'd simply chalked it up to when life throws you a curveball, some rolled with the punches, and others—well, to put it simply—they just ran.

"At this point, I'd been hospitalized for three days. My mother never left my side. Dad, being the only man I adored—who inspired me to be the best at everything I did—had a job to do. He couldn't stay and I got it. He was a doctor. He helped kids like me get better every day. Since he worked in the same hospital I was in, I knew I had it good because Daddy would stop in whenever he had time between patients."

Dalton took this in, and seemed to know without my saying it that this was a major turning point in my life's story. "Something happened, didn't it?"

My head fell to my chest and I whispered, "They diagnosed me with leukemia."

Dalton's hand covered my twisted fingers, his other coming up to tilt my chin until our gazes met. "I'm so sorry, sweetheart," he whispered. "So fucking sorry."

All I could do at his heartfelt words was shrug in a what-can-you-do manner. What was done was done, so I continued with my tale.

"Dad's visits grew more and more infrequent, until they stopped altogether."

"Fucking coward," Dalton growled.

I agreed with him wholeheartedly.

It had broken me. It had decimated my mother. It had also filled me with the resolve I needed to beat that cancer bitch with everything I had. Back then, I'd thought that if I'd beat the leukemia, I'd get my father back. It took five years, multiple relapses, not to mention loads of pills, chemotherapy, and radiation, but the day came where I was told I had won the battle.

Except that wasn't all.

And Daddy-Dearest never came back.

"After that, Mom took us and moved us to Jacksonville before the ink had dried on my parents' divorce papers." I giggled softly at how we ended up here in the first place.

Dalton smiled, then asked, "What is it?"

Shaking my head, I explained, "When I asked her why she chose North Carolina, she told me she'd fallen in love with the idea of it because of one of her favorite authors."

Dalton's eyebrows rose as he laughed. "You're shitting me, right?"

I shook my head and met his disbelieving gaze. "Mom is Mom. She's flaky at times, but if you're one of hers, she'll lay her life down for you without hesitation. So my life was uprooted, thanks to Nicholas Sparks, when I was fourteen. Even though we have no family around here, I loved it immediately. I still do."

It had been heaven for Mom and me.

For a short two years at least.

It turned out that numerous sessions of chemo and radiation caught up with me—times two.

"They always say bad things come in threes, and I was destined to live it, I guess." I shrugged. "I was out with a bunch of friends, enjoying the last of the summer vacation before school started up again. We were at the beach. Ian, my boyfriend at the time, and I had snuck off from the rest of the gang that surrounded the bonfire we'd built for some one-on-one time.

"The headache hit me like a ton of bricks. Then the nausea and the dizziness followed."

Dalton's eyes widened in realization. "You thought the leukemia was back, didn't you?"

His question had been rhetorical, but I nodded just the same. "The moment my mother saw me, she rushed me here to Onslow Memorial Hospital." Since they knew of my history with leukemia, they ran the necessary tests and came back with nothing until they ran additional ones. "I was diagnosed with lupus and a rare type of anemia," I grumbled.

The man groaned. "Seriously?"

"They put me on iron therapy to correct the anemia they found, but when that didn't work, they tested my marrow and found I had very few stem cells," I explained. "As if lupus wasn't enough, I also was diagnosed with aplastic anemia. My doctors had informed me that both the lupus and anemia were most likely caused by the various treatments I'd received for my cancer."

Dalton's head fell forward to his chest on a heavy sigh. His hands flew into his hair, pushing it out of his face. "Fuck, Dev," came out, sounding pained before his tortured gaze met mine again.

"So that's me," I ended on a whisper.

"*Fuck!*" Then his hands reached for mine. He got to his feet, his ass found the side of my bed, and he pulled me into his arms for a hug.

I sighed at the memory of feeling Dalton's arms around me. Unused to physical attention, especially from a male, I never expected for my body to melt at this intimate contact as quickly as it did.

His heat.

His kindness.

His safety.

As exhaustion set in, I held on to the feel of him wrapped around me, falling asleep with a smile on my face for more than just the simple reason that I'd be able to leave the hospital really soon.

ten

DALTON

IS THIS A SETUP?

I marched straight from the conference room, into my office, slamming the door.

I couldn't believe what Bryce had just filled me in on. If Wentworth wanted me on this wild goose chase for him, the jackass should have been honest with me from the get-go. For the first time, I cursed the anonymous referral that had sent the politician my way.

And I couldn't be any more thankful for Devolin's warnings.

With the latest information gathered by the woman, then assessed by both Brycen and myself, I picked up the desk phone and punched in the number to Minister Wentworth's personal line.

"Mr. Kippers," was my greeting upon the third ring. For a man whose son was incarcerated in Mexico, pending trial for being involved in the Canadian cabinet minister's fiancée's disappearance, possible manslaughter what with the extensive amount of blood at the scene, he was a little too chipper for my liking. "Do you have something for me?"

"The Juan Cartel is involved?" That's right. Fuck polite. Fuck the pleasantries.

"How'd—?"

"When were you going to divulge the fact you've had personal and business dealings with criminals, not only known in Mexico but throughout the continental U.S.?" I was seething. "This changes everything, Minister—"

"Kippers—"

"I'm done sitting on this shit and playing this your way." I was so finished with these pompous assholes. If the money wasn't so damn good, I'd be more selective of my cases, but I wasn't quite at that level yet. I needed more manpower before that could happen. "From now on, we're doing this my way. That means I'm going to be dealing with the RCMP, Global Affairs Canada, and the Canadian Consulate directly. Any new information you receive, you forward to me or my colleague, Brycen Matthews, immediately. Answers are given when they come and not a second before, Wentworth. Be warned, the bill you thought you were going to be footing just got a fuck of a lot heftier. Do I make myself clear?"

"Now wait just a goddamn minute!" the man bellowed.

"No! You omitted information that put me and my team at risk. We're prepared to risk everything, our lives included, but playing me by being selective of the information I get, or don't, doesn't work well in this business." I paused long enough to make sure the man got me with my next point. "You've got twenty-four fucking hours to get back to me on the suitability of this new agreement before I bill you for hours worked and we part ways." I slammed the phone into its cradle.

Seconds.

It was all it took before my line rang and I picked up the receiver.

"Find her." Then the line went dead.

"I'm glad we could agree on something," I grumbled to my office walls.

Reclining in my chair, my arms up, fingers interlaced behind my head, I released a long tension-filled sigh, as I turned my chair toward the large corkboard bolted to the wall behind my desk.

I'd spent the better part of the day leaving messages and speaking with the proper channels to each Canadian agency, including the City of Ottawa Police. I also pulled my marker with my contact with the Mexican authorities, Miguel Sanchez, who happened to be a drinking buddy of the lead investigator in charge of the abduction and Wentworth's son's subsequent arrest.

Suffice to say, that massive board was getting loaded with information, from the dishearteningly graphic images of the hotel crime scene to the various names associated with the victim, Nadia Alvarez-soon-to-be-Wentworth. Minister Max Wentworth and his son, Scott's known associates were listed there as well, and that list was rapidly growing.

I took a minute to focus on both Wentworth men's associates, drawing one parallel aside from the fact they shared blood: Enrique Ortiz.

After a quick search of the INTERPOL Criminal Information System, Ortiz was now an open book to me. Well, what various law enforcement had been able to gather over the years that is. With the rap sheet on that fucker, I knew I'd have my work cut out for me.

Ortiz was one of the Juan Cartel's chapter leaders. He was also on multiple international watch lists for crimes such as drug and human trafficking. The guy spent more time on U.S. soil than Mexican, tending mostly to the Southwest region of the States, but some Southeast parts were also in the mix now, which incidentally put him in my backyard. There'd been multiple attempts to indict him, all of which had failed. Let's just say the man had a knack at making people disappear. Being a massive man, at roughly two-hundred and ninety pounds of solid muscle and six foot six, people learned to fear him early on in his career, mainly because of his days as an enforcer.

I studied the most recent shot of the guy who I'd added to the board. Clean-cut, tailored suit, Italy's best if I had to guess. He was good-looking, confident in his stance. From that shot alone, notwithstanding the others I'd perused, he seemed to hold a certain approachability, a charisma that most likely got him a whole hell of a lot more than women.

My email chimed, pulling me away from my target of study.

Scott Wentworth's rap sheet.

An unsealed one, delineating each and every single infraction in the kid's life.

At a quick glance, nothing seemed out of the ordinary: petty misdemeanors, theft, drug and weapons possession, small-time dealing, solicitation...all since the age of fourteen.

The minister's son sure had been busy. If I were to hypothesize the reasons for the trouble the kid got into, I'd have to say everything he'd done had been a push for attention from his father.

He was now twenty-one, and if Nadia Alvarez, his father's soon-to-be-wife was found dead, Scott could be facing up to twenty years, with no possibility of parole, for murder in the second degree. At the very least, I was confident the man would see at least four years for being an accessory to kidnapping. And since these alleged crimes were committed in Mexico, he would have to go through their system, and suffer the less than desirable accommodations and treatment. If he wasn't already, I'd be willing to bet he'd wager double his sentence for the comfort of a Canadian cell right now.

As I scanned the rest of the email on Scott Wentworth, my cell began a vibrating dance to the *Criminal Minds* show tune. When Devolin had given me her number, I'd programmed it in to that jingle, seeing as she was a fan of the show, but mostly because she likened herself to Penelope Garcia, the program's resident hacking guru.

This warranted a smile from me.

Probably the first of the day, and it was overdue considering it was past quitting time, and I was hungry.

"Have you eaten yet?" I asked in place of a greeting.

"Hello to you, too." She giggled. "They just delivered my tray."

"Don't eat it," I ordered. "How do you feel about burgers and fries?"

"Love 'em."

"Then hold on, I'll be there in half an hour."

"Kip?" Devolin said, a smile in her voice.

Wedging my phone between my ear and shoulder, I pressed the series of keys to lock down my system. "Yeah?"

There was a long pause before she answered. It was as if she couldn't decide what she wanted to say. "I'll be here," she whispered.

eleven

Dalton

"I HAVE A CONFESSION TO MAKE," Devolin said with a mouthful of fries.

Within minutes of my arrival, we were set up and chowing down on the dinner I'd picked up for us.

I paused with my burger halfway up to my mouth and met her gaze, "You do?" then bit into the beefy goodness, courtesy of Fairfax, a local pub owned by an acquaintance of mine.

She nodded, swallowed her food, then grinned. "Not that the food isn't great, but I had an ulterior motive in calling you."

Maybe I hadn't been the only one who had grown fond of our visits. To be honest, they were the best part of my days. This, combined with her words, made me grin. "Is that so?"

"Mm-hmm..." She licked at the drop of mustard that had landed onto her finger.

The act, although innocent in nature, set about a chain reaction that had me shifting slightly in my seat to ease the tightening in my pants. To say I was flustered with how this woman affected me would be an understatement, but then again, I'd been obsessed with her for the better part of a year, and that was all before laying eyes on her.

"I was hoping we could talk about what I found," she looked down to her food, "that is, if you can."

Well that knocked me out of my musings about her. Staring at her, I hesitated. "Dev…"

"It's okay," she paused. "I understand—"

Setting my burger down, I was quick to reach over her lap and cover her empty hand. "That's not why I'm here, Devolin."

Her eyes rounded. "It's not?"

I shook my head, smiling. "I like you." She swallowed hard. "I'm here as a…friend." This got me a relieved expression, when I would have hoped to have seen one holding a bit of disappointment. "I'd be lying if I said I wasn't interested in discussing how you came about those files we found on your laptops, but it's not why I pushed for our visits."

She remained silent, coyly averting her eyes from my intense gaze.

Fucking sweet.

Adorable.

Hot.

And completely clueless about her appeal.

"Look at me," I demanded, making her eyes snap to mine. She studied my face. "At this point, with all that you've shared, with what I've told you about me, I'd like to think of us as friends. Are we not?" She gave me a subtle nod that had me relaxing. "Good. And since Bryce isn't completely done with pulling the information from your devices, and we're far from piecing all that shit together, I'd rather not talk about the case just yet."

"But—"

"Not yet," I warned. This seemed to frustrate her, if the sour expression on her face was anything to go by. "Don't worry, I will come to you when it's time."

Instead of acknowledging my words, she huffed, then shoved a couple of fries in her mouth, remaining mum for the next few minutes. Then, in a very petulant tone, she asked, "Then when am I getting my laptops back?"

Had it come from any other woman but her, it would have

grated on my nerves, but from Devolin, it was cute. So cute she had me laughing, which seemed to incense her further.

"I'm being serious, Dalton. I need to work."

The humor was knocked out of me, her words serving as a reminder she worked for that criminal, Hewitt.

"About that," I cleared my throat. "You work for Gordon Hewitt?"

"Oh, no! Not you too!" She shook her head from side to side, her demeanor going from irritated to outright furious. "I got it from your sister and my mom, who think Gordon's creepy, and I didn't take it from them, but I'm certainly not going to take it from you!" She proceeded to drop her food in the Styrofoam container and closed it, pushing it at me. "I think we're done here. Take your food and go, Dalton." She wiped at her face with the napkin, then threw it onto her bedside table. To further prove her stubbornness, she jutted her chin out, nose up in the air, and concentrated on the wall in front of her.

"Dev—"

"Gordon's been nothing but good to me," she defended. "He stuck with me when I had to reduce my hours. He let me work from my damn hospital bed! He's been nothing but nice. He is a little eccentric, but..."

I set my food down as she rambled on. Much like my sister, I could tell that if I didn't find a way to stop her, she'd go on and on and on. Standing, I bent forward, then pinched and held her chin with a stern, "Devolin!" Her mouth snapped shut, her head turned toward me, eyes freezing on mine.

"I've got to work, Kip," she whispered.

With a softened gaze, my head moved toward hers. I knew her eyes were green, but since when did they glimmer like emeralds with tiny flecks of gold like that?

"Sweetheart..." I licked my lips, feeling the warmth of her breath fanning over my mouth. Fuck, I needed a taste of her. Just a small one. Ensnared, I inched closer until my lips barely brushed hers.

Devolin emitted a tortured sound, turning her head away from me. "Dalton, no."

That subtle contact had affected her as much as it had me. Even though she'd tilted her head, she wasn't pulling away. As much as I wanted to push the boundaries, I knew I had to give her what she wanted right then. Something told me this connection of ours was too important to rush things.

Therefore, I didn't give into my baser instincts to lean back in and devour that sinful mouth of hers.

Instead, I leaned my forehead onto hers. "I'm sorry," I whispered.

She nodded her assent, then reached for my hand which had somehow found itself wrapped around the side of her neck, and pulled it away. Giving it a squeeze, she released my hand, then set hers on my forearms, easing me backward, where my ass found itself back in its seat.

"You..." Her fingers touched her lips. "You need to go."

"Sweet—"

"Please," she begged softly.

I managed to croak an, "I'll go," before I got up, left the uneaten half of my dinner where it was—on the floor—and took one look back at the woman who was doing a number on my head, before dragging my ass out of there, trying to figure out how something that felt so right could have turned out so wrong.

twelve

Devolin

THIS IS IT!

I'd waited a lifetime for this. Well, okay, maybe more like a year.

Ten more steps, Dev!

Staring up at the building looming before me, I paused to let it all soak in. Truth was, this newfound reality of mine was a little daunting to say the least. A year ago, I'd have laughed if anyone had told me that this day would come. Things had looked too grim for me to even entertain the thought of where I would be a week, a month, let alone a year later.

Then a miracle happened...

"What is it, baby?" My mother's hand squeezed my shoulder. "Are you feeling okay? Should we go back—?"

"Mom!" A nervous laugh escaped me. "I'm fine. This is just a lot to take in, is all."

Drawing a deep breath, a relieved look overtook her worried expression. "You're sure?"

I turned toward my mother, squeezing her hand then met her gaze. "This is just a new step for me. A big one." The older woman's expression softened. "Besides, you knew you were going to have to cut the apron strings at some point, Mama." Holding out my keychain, I jingled the keys to prove my point, but more or less to lighten the mood.

"You look flushed, maybe I should call Janet and tell her—"

"Mom, I'm fine!" I growled, then marched up the building's steps and punched in the code to the main door, heading straight for the elevator. I was so tired of being treated like an invalid. It was why I'd insisted on my own place if I were ever to be discharged from the hospital. When I got word from the doctor that I was being released, I'd had my mother check out a few places for me before settling on this one.

The older woman was hot on my heels. "Don't take that tone with me, young lady!"

Snickering as she entered the elevator, I said, "*Young lady,* Mom?" My finger hit the button that would take us to the twelfth floor. "I'm twenty-nine." Kissing her cheek, I offered her a smile of reassurance, just as the doors opened, delivering us to our destination. Finding apartment 1203, I turned to my mother again, sure that my excitement was written clearly across my face. "Now, can I please take a look around and see what you've done to this place?"

I took the time to peruse what Mom had done with my new apartment. The woman had gone completely OCD on my new digs, but it had been that way since I was eight. Everything had to be clean. Sterile. But there was a mountain of reasons as to the why, and because my mother had been my rock throughout my life, I'd forgive her anything.

With my apartment unpacked for me, I headed toward the one room that beckoned my attention. It was the one room that had been left untouched at my request—mostly.

Adrenaline pumped through my veins, my excited smile becoming larger. When the knob turned, granting me access to my home office, I couldn't suppress my gasp.

"Oh, Mom!" I whispered as I surveyed the room.

Floor-to-ceiling windows had their curtains pushed to the side; a massive U-shaped desk was up against them, the bottom of the U up against the wall where I envisioned positioning my three large monitors. A TV was mounted to the wall above that. Space for my two laptops, which were still with Brycen, was set up by the windows, where I'd be able to take in the view of the city skyline at night. Against the wall, by the room's entrance, was a five-drawer filing cabinet that matched my desk. A massive vase of fresh sunflowers sat atop it, with what remained of Dalton's unspent lilies and roses. The reminder of the man himself made my pulse quicken. Beside the flowers sat a photograph of my mother and me, taken the week before, in the hospital gardens. It was the day I'd received the good news the stem cell treatment for my anemia was finally working and I'd most likely be able to go home soon.

The rest of my office space contained my favorite couch and throw pillows, which matched the abstract paintings that covered the other two walls that would have been otherwise bare.

As soon as I sensed my mother's presence, I turned toward her, utterly speechless.

"Do you like it?"

My voice shook as I said, "This is too much, Mom."

She cleared her throat, an indication she was feeling as emotional as I was. "It's never too much, baby girl. You deserve to know how proud I am of the difference you make in the world."

I groaned, cupping my forehead, feeling overwhelmed. "Mom, I'm just some computer geek."

"You're more than that, and you know it." She sighed. "I may not understand this draw you have to this technology thing, but you have a gift, baby. You're smart, you're creative—"

"I'm a sickly recluse that thrives on puzzles," I mumbled.

"Devolin Payton Taylor!"

"What?" I shrugged. "It's true."

"You're beautiful, baby girl, and someone's going to see that someday." I didn't bother to say anything, knowing all too well I'd be inciting a never-ending dispute with the woman. God forbid she found out anything about Dalton and his visits. The flowers had caused more than enough of a ruckus. "Just promise me something."

Cue the internal groan. "And what's that?"

"Promise me, now that you're on your own, you won't stay

cooped up in this new office of yours. Promise me, you'll find some semblance of normalcy. Go out, make some new friends—"

"I have friends!" That defensive tone did nothing to convince even myself, to say nothing of convincing my mother.

"I'm talking about *real* people, with real faces, in a social setting where you're in the same room. Not those cartoon characters on your screen."

I didn't blame her for saying something like that. Still, it burned because ultimately, she was right.

"They're called avatars, Mom."

My mother's determined gaze caught mine and held it. "Promise me, Devolin."

Giving her a nod, I added, "I'll try."

She snorted. "I suppose I'll take that. Meanwhile, I'll leave you to it." She proceeded to the hallway, toward the apartment's door, with me following behind her. "I didn't want to mess with all those wires of yours and screw up your system, and since you didn't want anyone tinkering with your stuff, I let it be."

"Mom." I grabbed the older woman's hand. "I love it. And you."

"I know you'll ignore me if I tell you to take it easy and that your cyber world can wait until tomorrow, but please don't work too much tonight. Get some rest. And call me tomorrow to let me know that you're okay."

Ever the worrisome mother.

"I will, Mom. Go have yourself the weekend with the girls you've been planning." *For more than a year* was left unsaid as I hugged her, because we both know how long she'd had to put off living her life again. "Love you."

"Love you, baby girl. You'll call if—"

"Promise, Mama."

Just like that, I was alone. In my own apartment, no less!

thirteen

Dalton

FOUR DAYS.

In those days, I called, I texted, yet Devolin never returned any of my messages. This show of stubbornness of hers pissed me off.

If she wanted her fucking laptops back, she'd have at least given me a sign of life, dammit!

After four days, I took matters into my own hands.

Sitting on the front stoop of the building Skylar had given me the address to, I spied a car pull up to park at the curb, then two women exited as soon as the engine was turned off. Their playful banter and giggling halted the moment Devolin's gaze landed on me.

Hurrying to my feet, I took the ten or so steps that would take me to her.

"Dalton..." She turned to peer at the older woman, who had joined her at her side. That's when I noticed the resemblance. This had to be her mother.

"Devolin, who's this?" the older woman asked, her eyes directed at me in blatant appraisal.

"Mama, it's—"

I had her right where I wanted her. Flustered.

"My name is Dalton Kippers, ma'am." I stepped up and stuck out my hand. "I'm a friend of your daughter's."

"Joleen or Jo Taylor." She gave me a dazzling smile. "So what brings you here, Mr. Kippers?"

"Dalton, please." She nodded. "You see, Devolin helped me out a while back, and I have yet to have the opportunity to thank her, let alone repay the favor. And it seems I won't be doing that any time soon, since I'm here on business, and it looks like I need her expertise once again." I gave her my best sheepish look.

The woman looked over her shoulder at her daughter. "Is that so?" All Devolin seemed to be able to do was nod, her gaze meeting mine and defiantly holding it.

"I have something of yours." I hefted up her satchel. "It would be nice to talk about your findings, if you have time?"

"Now?" Her voice squeaked.

Her reaction had me grinning. "No better time, don't you think, Devolin?"

"O-okay."

"Baby girl, we'll do dinner tomorrow instead." Joleen kissed Devolin's cheek.

"But—"

"Just give me a call later," the older woman continued.

"Are you sure? You could—"

"I'm pretty sure that three's a crowd." She smirked, then threw me a wink.

"Mom!" The duo had me chuckling. "It's not like that."

"A mother can dream, can't she?" she said, as she proceeded toward the driver's side. "Mr. Kippers, go easy on her. She shouldn't overexert herself. Doctor's orders and all."

"Mama!" Devolin scolded.

"I figure since the topic at hand comes rather easily to your daughter, our conversation shouldn't be too strenuous." I flashed Devolin's mother a smile. "As it is, I'm hoping I can steal her from the one who's currently utilizing her skills."

The woman's eyes flashed toward her daughter, her approval at my statement palpable. "I hope that works out for you. Her friend, Skylar, and I believe she could do better."

"I do, too. I guess I'll just have to convince her of that." It was my turn to wink at the woman. "It was lovely meeting you, Jo."

On a nod, Devolin's mother smiled, rounded her car, got in, and drove off.

63

"I can't believe you!" Devolin exploded, as soon as her mother's taillights had disappeared around the corner. "Have you lost your mind?"

"Nope." I smirked down at her, then set a hand on her lower back and swooped the other in front of us. "Shall we?"

On a disgruntled sigh, she led the way.

fourteen

THE NERVE OF HIM! What a manipulative sexy-assed man he was!

I shook the latter out of my mind, concentrating on the manipulative aspect of his character.

Where the hell does he get off on strong-arming me?

He'd bullied me into speaking with him. Alone! It was just the kind of situation I was trying to avoid.

After that whatever-barely-there-kiss we shared earlier in the week, I knew it was imperative that I keep my distance. But seeing as it was my place, it's not like I could run off on him now could I?

Not once did I imagine that helping Dalton and his team a year ago would result in meeting him in the flesh, say nothing of having him physically sitting in front of me on that too small loveseat—all hot—making me want things I shouldn't want. It was the only place we could talk aside from sitting in the kitchen.

The kitchen!

That was a brilliant idea.

"Um… Can I get you something to drink? Or eat?" *Rope to tie me down with, since I'm liable to run away from here any second?* I thought as I headed toward the room in question, trying to find a way to get him out of my place as quickly and painlessly as possible. Let it be noted that if I were normal, I'd be so on board for that last extracurricular.

The man burst out laughing. His deep baritone stopped me in my tracks, my shoulders bunching toward my ears.

"Personally, I prefer cuffs." Shocked at the casualness in his tone, I spun around on my heel, finding him right on up in my personal space. I lost my balance. "Whoa." He grabbed my arms to stabilize me but didn't let go when my footing was regained. It seemed his reaction matched the shock I knew was showing on my face. Someone once told me I shouldn't play poker because of my tells, and right then I knew why. Dalton still had a hold of me and wasn't showing any sign of backing away. In fact, his eyes were fused to mine, darkened in unquestionable hunger. Damn the man was potent. "But I can see myself amending that statement," he whispered.

My lips formed the letter without the word, "Oh," escaping. As much as his words shocked me, they also piqued my curiosity to the point of thrilling me. "How so?" My God, what was the matter with me? Why was I pushing this somewhere I swore I wasn't going to go?

Without blinking, he gave me his answer. "I'd simply prefer to be the one doing the holding instead of having an aid." My traitorous body leaned toward him, as quick as his words were out. Dalton broke eye contact first, effectively ending this supercharged magnetic moment of ours, and stepped back a few paces, his face closing down as if I'd imagined the effect I had on him. "You mind talking in the kitchen?"

Yes, the kitchen. Where it was safe. Well...*safer*. With a table that could provide a barrier between us.

I cleared my throat. "That's probably a good thing if we need my computers."

"I need you with me." Dalton's words were honest, almost desperate, after we'd finished discussing the information I'd gathered. He'd even shared what he and the team had obtained on their end, as well as their various hypothesises.

"Brycen's got everything I have here to help you out. You guys seem to be doing just fine, so far. He can do as good of a job as I can," I told him.

"You can't tell me that you actually enjoy working for Gordon Hewitt, can you?"

My chin dropped to my chest as I made to grab a handful of hair at the back of my head, bunching it in my hands and I growled a, "Not this again."

"He's scum, Devolin."

I looked at Dalton, knowing there'd always been something shady about my boss. Other than the fact that I suspected the information I provided the man with was used—more often than not—to strong-arm certain investors, let alone clients, it was nothing significant enough—*yet*.

"I know you have a file on him. I'm getting the sense that you're not too crazy about some of the jobs he's assigned you. I'm telling you that your instincts are right. You're right in following your gut and looking into the man, Dev. The guy's a criminal."

"What?" I shrieked.

"I worked a case for a client a few years ago. A friend of mine, who's a cop, was working that same case, but from his own angle. Please say you'll at least think about coming to work for me." Dalton's hand made to grab mine, but I pulled back, our fingers brushing. This made him withdraw, dry-scrubbing his face, and giving away the stress he was under as his chin dipped toward his chest in a show of defeat.

I felt for him.

I really did.

"Dalton..." I sighed. "Look—"

"I'll double whatever he's paying you. We've got a great benefits package. If you ever need to work from home—" I winced at that. "I don't care what it takes. You were amazing when it came to finding Morgan. This case is worse. Trickier, and you know it, or you wouldn't have tracked me down to make sure I wasn't flying blind all the way to Mexico. You'd still be in the wind, and I'd still be running around in circles trying to make sense of why you didn't want to be found." His chuckle was low, sending shivers down my spine. "I can triple it, if you'd like," he persisted. "No, fuck that...I'll quadruple it."

My heart skipped a beat as it often seemed to do whenever I was around this man.

"You don't have to do that." I had the feeling I needed to buck up. Maybe it was Skylar's voice in the back of my mind, telling me I was better than my job with Gordon. Maybe I needed to fish or cut bait—for a lack of better terms—when it came to my insane infatuation with the man sitting before me. The moment my hand touched his forearm, I knew what I was going to do before I did it. There was no denying what was going on here. "I'll do it."

His head snapped up so fast, I feared it would pop off his shoulders. "What?"

"For no other reason than you've been honest with me." My gaze held his. "But if you need another, it's because I'm personally vested in this." What a fucking understatement! "I told you that Brycen is good enough to handle the logistics from here on out, and I have every confidence that he can, since I know he's most definitely copied my software by now." I gave him a prideful grin. "And even without that, I've been inside his system so many times over the last year, I know he's equipped to get you through the Wentworth case."

"I can't help but sense there's a but in there somewhere."

He was right.

I nodded. "I can't sit here and say I'll keep out of things. It's not in my nature," I explained. "I have to see this through to the end."

"What's in it for you, aside from the salary?"

"Isn't that enough?" I knew he'd say no, so I elaborated. "I get to close a door for once in my life, instead of having someone close it for me."

"What's that mean?"

"It means that I knew it wasn't the end when I shut down the comms on you guys a year ago." I bowed my head toward the tabletop. That was the hardest confession I'd ever had to disclose yet. "Maybe it would have been had I not been obsessed with keeping tabs, but..." I picked at my nails.

"So you felt that...connection?"

I nodded. "You made me wish I was there. That I was part of the team. You made me want to run away and hide, too. I work alone for a reason."

His brows furrowed. "But why?"

"Because it's easier."

"It's lonely, and something tells me you've had your fair share of lonely."

I shrugged. "It's not all that bad."

"Bullshit."

My head snapped up, eyes narrowing on him. "Excuse me?"

"I said—"

I bolted to my feet, fisting my hands on my hips. "I know what you said. Now explain why you said it."

He pushed back from his chair and came to stand toe-to-toe with me. I had no choice but to look up and up...and up. Christ on a crutch he was tall. "I don't know what happened to you to make you pull away from people, but I can see it in your eyes, Dev." His voice softened, having the same effect on my anger. "You want to be a part of something, but you're scared."

I couldn't look at him. So I tilted my head down and to the side. This man—one I'd only recently met—saw right through me. If I wasn't careful, he would see it all: my flaws, my weaknesses, my scars.

And he'll run like all the others.

With my face averted from him, I tried to tamp down the tears of frustration and sadness that threatened. "I don't know you."

Fingers at my chin tilted my face up. Seconds feeling more like hours, he studied me. "You know me." He stated that with far too much conviction for my liking. "You know everything about me, down to my record of service, even though that was classified information." His gaze narrowed on mine with his words, but I couldn't help the shy smirk as I caught the corner of his lips twitching up. "You know everything about my team. Hell, you probably know everything about everyone you've ever met in your adult life, even though you don't have their files on those super computers of yours." It seemed Brycen had done a fine job gathering information from my systems.

"Some, yes. Most, never. And before you ask, I got to know Skylar the old-fashioned way. I can do that when I want."

His hands cupped both sides of my face and he leaned in close. Close enough to feel his breath fanning over my face. My brain was getting foggy from his nearness. "The problem, as I see it, is that you're trying to close doors when you should be opening one in particular; the one that'll let us...that'll let *me* know you."

I tried to shake my head, deny the truth of his words, but his grasp prevented me from doing so. "You don't want to get mixed up with the likes of me," I said.

"Let me be the judge of that," he whispered, pressing his forehead to mine, his eyes closing for a moment. "Let me in, Dev."

"Easier said than done, Dalt—"

He hushed me with a gentle press of his lips before I could get his entire name out. A press that ended far too quickly for my liking, but he never moved too far away, leaving his eyes closed, his forehead still touching mine. Then he sighed. "I've been waiting to say this for a long-assed time because of your skill and extreme stubbornness."

"What is it?" Fuck, could I sound any more breathless?

"I know we haven't brought up that night from a year ago in our conversations, so thank you." He opened his eyes, and I was ensnared with what I saw there. "Thank you for stumbling onto Morgan's video. Thank you for stepping up to the plate and getting involved. Thank you for being our eyes and ears where we couldn't have them. Just...thanks." Then he pressed his mouth against mine once more, running his tongue over the seam of my lips. I opened for him on a moan of capitulation. My hands braced themselves on his shoulders, what with how weak-kneed he made me with the thoroughness of his kiss. It's as if he was inhaling me. I liked it. Liked it a lot. Maybe a little too much.

"Do you think Brycen will be okay with me joining you guys on this case?" I blurted out as soon as we separated for much-needed air.

Dalton leaned back, humored disbelief strewn across his face. "I kiss you like that and you're thinking of Matthews?"

"I'm sorry." I pecked his playful pout without thinking. I

couldn't help myself. "It's just, I know how it is between hackers. We're a little territorial."

"Well, he'll just have to deal with it." His matter-of-factness filled me with warmth. "You're running point on this one."

Say what? That's when reality hit me. "Shit."

"The guys, all but Bryce, will probably think I've officially lost my mind when I tell them tomorrow, but I'll deal with it. If anyone gives you trouble, let me know." His tone held authority so I played into it.

"Sir, yes, sir!" I saluted.

fifteen

DALTON

THE FOLLOWING MORNING, I headed into the office for our weekly team meeting. As soon as I'd made it to the conference room, I found Brycen, Cade, Tate, and Theo already waiting for me. I had asked Devolin to show up a half-hour after our usual start time, so I'd have enough time to make the big announcement, and feed everyone's curiosity, not to mention, possibly extinguish a few fires.

When I noticed Shane hadn't arrived, I asked, "Where's Peters?" to the room at large.

"Here," the man in question answered as he entered, then dropped into one of the vacant seats. "Sorry I'm late."

"So, D, you want to let us in on why the hell these two are here?" Cade motioned toward Shane and Theo, who did work for me from time to time, but they had day jobs of their own. Then again, so did Cade.

"I asked them here because I have some news that plays into the Wentworth case. With the calls pouring in, business is booming." A few heads nodded. "I'm bringing someone in." Judging by everyone's gaze intent on me, it seemed that my latest piece of information was being taken in easily enough. "As you all know, Canada's Foreign Affairs Minister, Max Wentworth, has contacted

71

us, and it's come to my attention recently that a one-man effort isn't going to cut it, what with the information Brycen and I have discovered this week."

"I was wondering why you hadn't left town yet," Tate, the newest on the team said.

"The Wentworth clusterfuck is only part of why I haven't left. My gut tells me I need more boots on the ground. People I can trust to be on task for this one. This goes without saying, if I didn't trust you, you wouldn't be here." Heads nodded, and I continued. "If everything stays on schedule, I'll be heading to Ottawa on Tuesday to talk with the cabinet minister. I'll need all of you to come along when Mexico comes into play. I'm telling you right now guys, this reeks of cartel."

"So back to the new guy. What's this person's specialty?" Tate asked.

"Computers."

That got Brycen's attention.

"Did I just hear you right?" he asked, his eyes widening.

"Matthews, you've been busting a nut to get out from behind the desk these last couple of months. You have the field training, and I could use someone who's good with computers in the field, in case we run into something that can't be tackled remotely from headquarters."

"So who's—" The man's eyes glimmered with excitement. "You're not serious! You're bringing *her* in?"

I nodded.

Cade leaned forward, looking between the two of us, an annoyed expression crossing his features. "Who? Why didn't we know about this shit until now?"

"Hello?" came from out in the hall.

"In here," I called out. Within seconds, my eyes set themselves on a suit-clad woman I barely recognized. I should have told her that kind of attire wasn't needed unless she was to be in a client meeting. Then again, I wasn't disappointed with what I saw. She carried the office-assistant-slash-hot-librarian look better than any other woman I knew. Complete with small eyeglasses, tucked in her lapel pocket.

"What the fuck?" Tate broke me out of my musings.

I cleared my throat, proceeding with introductions. "Men, I'd like you to meet our newest team member, Devolin Taylor, also known around here as Hussy, Huss, or White Hat Hussy."

The room had gone so silent that I swear I could have heard crickets.

Cade was the first to break silence with a whispered, "Holy shit, you found her!"

Brycen was second, and far from subtle. "Marry me. We'll make a bunch of beautiful, little dancing computer genius trolls together." At this, Devolin burst out laughing. The laughter was cut short when the man found his feet and walked over to her, grabbing her hands in his.

Devolin immediately fought to reclaim her personal space by yanking her hands from my teammate. It got my attention enough that I moved to get between them. "Do you mind?" I pushed Brycen back gently. "Sit down."

"Okay, okay." He leaned to the side to peer over my shoulder and watched Devolin reclaim her composure. "I'm sorry, hon."

She nodded despite her obvious discomfort and embarrassment.

Theo, with a guarded air to him, got up next and approached her. A foot now separated him from the woman as they studied each other. "Huss?" His voice was husky.

"Theo," whooshed out of her.

He extended his arms before asking, "Can I?" Before he even finished, Devolin stepped into his arms for a bear hug. "Goddamn, sweetheart, but you gave us the scare of a lifetime that day you showed up on my doorstep. I know I said it last year when everything went down but thank you for what you did that night."

She nodded into his chest. "You're welcome, and I'm sorry I freaked you all out." It came muffled due to the big lug's tight hold on her. "I'm okay."

"I can see that." He chuckled. "But do us all a favor and quit wasting poor D's resources. They've had a tough go chasing a ghost around this last year."

"I make no promises, but I'm here for now." Devolin pulled away and gave him a sheepish smile.

"Right." I clapped my hands together once. "Now that we have the introductions out of the way, let's talk about how we're going to do this job."

sixteen

MY KNUCKLES MET the hard wood of Dalton's office door.

"Come in."

Peeking from around the door, whatever seemed to be bothering the man disappeared as his gaze warmed when it landed on me.

"I got the paperwork filled out." I waved the pile of forms Dalton had given me to complete. From payroll and benefits, it was all there as promised along with a formal letter of offer.

He got to his feet and rounded his desk while holding out his hand, which I promptly filled with my delivery.

Dropping them onto the top of his desk without a glance, his gaze turned assessing on me. It made me fidget, wondering what he saw as he looked at me.

I felt like an idiot. Here I was, dressed to the nines for some large corporate getup. In my defense, the skirted suit was my regular attire when I worked out of Gordon's office. But here, all my new coworkers were a step up from grease-stained jeans and holier-than-thou t-shirts.

"Did you get yourself settled okay?"

His words seemed to carry a double meaning of sorts. "Yeah, why?"

He approached me slowly, stopping at arm's length. I held my ground, even though my manically beating heart made me want to retreat. "It was a little hard to miss that you were a little..." He looked as if he was trying to choose his words carefully.

Okay, so I was right. He wasn't just being a caring boss, making sure his newest employee was ready to get to the grind come first thing in the morning.

"Skittish?" I supplied. He nodded. "It's part of the curse."

His brows drew together. "Curse?" I nodded. "But you're fine with me. And Theo—"

"Theo asked for permission, but it wasn't as uncomfortable as it's been for me before. And with you..." I let my words hang.

Dalton took another step forward, bringing him close enough to touch. "What about me?" he whispered.

You make me feel safe.

I didn't tell him this. Instead, I led with, "I think it's got something to do with what we—Theo, you, and me—went through last year. It's brought us closer together than with the other guys on the team." There! That's plausible enough, right? To make my point clearer, I added, "Aside from doctors and nurses, I haven't been around many people other than Sky, a few others, and my mother over the years." Dalton reached up and cupped my cheek. "It got worse in my teens, when I couldn't really maintain friendships. I mean, who wants to hang out with the sick girl, right?"

Now why in the hell did I go and say that? It left the door wide open for Dalton and his ever-inquisitive mind, especially when he knew my health history.

The hand on my cheek flexed, Dalton's thumb rubbing a light pattern over my skin, making it difficult for me to focus as the need to nuzzle his palm grew greater. "We're going to have to talk about this need of yours to pull away. Brycen may not have shown it, but the guy was seriously freaked out."

"I'd rather not." I gave into the warmth of his hand and nestled my cheek into it, my gaze on his chest because it was easier for me to hide that way.

"Honey..."

My eyes snapped to his. "Hmm?"

"I have plans for dinner, and since I'm heading to Canada tomorrow, I was really hoping to see you." He shuffled his feet closer. There was nowhere else for me to go. Suddenly, the air I was breathing grew thicker with the scent of his cologne, the warmth of his body. Had I been able to move my feet, I still wouldn't have attempted to go anywhere. "Please say yes?"

Wait a minute. Did he just say he had dinner plans? Talk about a proverbial bucket of cold water to douse the rising flame in my libido.

"I can't." I quickly righted myself and took a step back, putting some much-needed distance between us. "We shouldn't. Kip, I'm working for you. And you're clearly seeing someone."

Dalton's shoulders began to shake right before a boisterous laugh left him. I couldn't help but watch his reaction, even though there really wasn't anything to laugh at.

"I—I should go." I backed toward the door.

Before I could get too far, Dalton wrapped a hand around my upper arm and moved us until my back pressed against the cold wooden surface of my only exit. The tick in his jaw was the only thing that showed his annoyance. His eyes, although firm in intensity, still held a slight hint of softness. "I'm not the cheating kind, Dev."

I swallowed the lump in my throat. "I didn't say you were."

He pressed his front to mine, the sensation making my body tingle. That was new to me. And delightful. And just a little scary, if I allowed myself to feel the full extent of my emotions. "You alluded to it, sweetheart." He released my arm, only to lean closer by resting his elbow onto the wood above my head. His free hand came up to draw soothing patterns on the side of my neck, making me shiver. "Am I scaring you?" he whispered against my cheek, nuzzling it. The man was as potent as he was scary, but the fear was of the unknown for me, not the man himself per se.

"Uh-uh." I gulped as his questing digits traced my bottom lip, one that felt so dry that I set to wet it, unintentionally licking his trailing finger.

Dalton's eyes dilated, and the unmistakable look of lust in

those orbs fed the fluttering sensation that had taken residence in my stomach.

"Good." He pecked my cheek, then proceeded to nuzzle my jaw before pulling far enough away to make eye contact. "I've changed my mind."

I blinked, confusion setting in. "What?"

"You're coming home with me. Right now."

"What?"

"You heard me." He smirked. "Skylar is dropping by for a family dinner."

My eyes widened. "Oh no!"

"Oh yes," he chimed. "And before she shows up, we have a few things to discuss."

My apprehension to his statement rose a notch or a hundred. "We do?"

"You're going to tell me all about this whole skittishness of yours. While we're at it, we're going to discuss how to get you past it. If we have time, we'll talk about other things." The last, he growled as he watched my reaction. He knew when the fear hit me. "Sweetheart, you've got to know by now, there's nothing you can say that'll scare me off."

That went a long way to appease my mind. Not! "O-okay."

He gifted me with a smile, appreciation reflected in his silvery-blue eyes. "And when Skylar leaves..." He pushed his groin harder into my stomach. The feel of his rock-hard cock rubbing against me couldn't be missed. It also caused me to gasp, my eyes widening as I felt the warmth of a very thorough blush spread to more than just my face. "We'll see where the night takes us."

It wouldn't be taking us very far, of that I was certain. Regardless, I couldn't bring myself to deny him anything. It was easier to agree than to fight him right then. So I nodded my assent. The rest I'd deal with when the time came.

seventeen

DALTON

THINGS TOOK a major turn for the awkward as soon as we arrived at my place.

Devolin pulled up and parked behind my truck as I stood leaning against the tailgate, waiting for her. That's when I saw her conflicted look warring with one of panic on her face. All of this as she remained unmoving behind the wheel.

I approached her vehicle without her noticing me, then opened her car door for her.

When she still didn't budge, or acknowledged my presence, I crouched down and softly prompted her. "Devolin? Honey, what's the matter?"

"I-I don't think I can do this."

"This? This what?"

"I can deal with telling you all about me. The bad. The ugly." She licked her lips. "But—"

I couldn't help myself. Something told me I needed to re-establish our connection, and the easiest way to do that was by touching her. Grabbing her hand, I squeezed it. "Look at me." She gave. "We don't have to do anything that'll make you feel uncomfortable."

"But that's just it." Her sigh came heavy with frustration. "I'm uncomfortable all of the time. I don't know how to deal with this. I don't know how to deal with you. Me. Us."

Isolated. Alone. Not used to contact outside of her small circle. I had to remind myself of these facts, even as I tried to figure what it all meant in the grand scheme of things for us.

"Will you still come in?" I asked. In the state she was in, I wasn't above begging, even if it was just to make sure she was in the right frame of mind before letting her leave. "If it makes you feel better, you pick one end of the room and I'll stick to the opposite side of it. I won't push you to give me any more than you're ready for."

Her nod came hesitantly, albeit determined.

As soon as she'd made it to the couch, Devolin let herself drop to the edge of the cushion, her fingers automatically clasping each other, turning white with what I'd discovered to be a nervous tick of hers.

Instead of going to her, I asked, "Something to drink? There's water, unless you want something stronger, in which case it would be a Bud Light or JD."

Her answer of "Both," shocked me into simply nodding and heading to the kitchen cabinet, then the fridge, and my hutch to fetch our refreshments, all the while worried about my guest's extreme discomfort.

When I entered the living room, Devolin looked a bit more at ease, even though her skin remained pale and her movements were a little abrupt, with the way she grabbed the beer I handed her. As soon as I set the two tumblers and the bottle of Jack down on the coffee table, I straightened with the intention of doing as I'd told her I would earlier and head for the other end of the room. She put a stop to that by grabbing onto my wrist.

"Sit," she whispered, "I'm fine."

"Are you sure?"

"I can't tell you all about me with you being at the other end of the room." Her nose scrunched up. "It would be weird."

With that, my ass found the next cushion over and settled in for everything Devolin was willing to share. If I knew now what I'd know afterward, she'd say that the alcohol was more for me than for her. She'd barely touched her beer.

I was dying.

I had to be.

My body was running at a fever pitch; my mind was scrambled. And all I had to blame it on was a one hundred and ten pound, auburn-haired, bright-eyed angel straddling my lap, her shaking hands, questing over my shirt-covered chest.

A fucking virgin!

I was in hell.

I was in heaven.

How the fuck could I figure out where I was when I couldn't make out up from down with Devolin's little gasps and the awestruck look strewn upon her face.

All because I'd won her trust.

All because she'd asked something so little of me, in such an innocent fashion, that I would have given her anything.

I was so busy trying to keep my hands off Devolin that the touch of her tongue, where my shirt collar started, had my body jumping as if she'd hit me with a live wire.

At my groan, Devolin jumped back to the point I had no choice but to brace my arms around her to prevent her from toppling off my lap.

Embarrassment rolled off her in droves. "Did I do something wrong?"

"Are you kidding me?" I croaked, moving my hands so I could feel the skin of her bare arms, rubbing them soothingly. "Sweetheart, I can't even begin to tell you what you're doing to me." With that, I arched my pelvis into her, causing her skin to flush with the most adorable blush and her emerald eyes to widen.

Her mouth opened, then closed. "Well..." Her eyes were trained to the side of my neck.

"Come here," I whispered, pulling her toward me, as a hand went up to sift into her hair, coming away with the clip that had secured the twist that had been in it all day. Her arms rounded my shoulders and held onto the back of the couch as she came will-ingly, collapsing against my chest, her head laying in the crook of my neck, her breath fanning over my Adam's apple. I gave her a squeeze. She fit so fucking perfectly in my arms, I'd be happy if she stayed there for the rest of my life. "I don't want to let you go."

Devolin's body tensed, but as soon as it had, she relaxed against me. "Then don't," she whispered. After a moment of silence, she added, "Will you...will you let me know if I do some-thing you don't like?"

This had me chuckling, which proved not be the best of reactions.

As Devolin fought to get off me, I pulled her in, locking my arms behind her back once again. "Stay."

"I'm not a dog, Dalton!"

I pecked her scrunched up nose, watching as her annoyance melted away before my eyes and she settled. "I want to kiss you."

"I'm not sure I want your kisses if you're going to laugh at me," she snipped.

Okay, so she was still annoyed.

"Baby..." That got her attention. "I can guaran-damn-tee that there's nothing you could do that I won't like."

Her forehead dropped to my shoulder. "But what if there is?"

I turned my head to kiss her temple, whispering, "There isn't." Unlocking my hands so I could reach into her hair and fist it, I pulled her head back gently, eliciting a gasp from her. As soon as her shocked gaze met mine, her irises turned a dark green, her pupils dilated. She was turned on. This was my chance.

And I took it.

Crashing my mouth down to hers, I took what she was willing to give me. For a split-second there, I was worried about my forwardness. When that pleasured mewl of hers came out, I took the opportunity to get a more thorough taste of her. Fuck she was sweet, all bubble-mint with a hint of something darker. Chocolate. The pure decadence that was Devolin had me wondering if the rest of her would taste as sinful if I drizzled the creamy treat all over her.

Devolin wriggled over my lap, one hand holding my head to her, the other sifting its fingers through my hair, her nails scoring my scalp. I wanted those nails embedded in my ass as I fucked her. I wanted them buried in my shoulders and back while I made love to her, showed her the varying degrees of pleasure that could exist when two people get as close as possible.

My mouth trailed from her lips, down to her chin, her neck, her collarbone, where I stopped to nibble.

Devolin was completely gone. In her place was some sort of siren. She arched back, holding onto the sides of my neck as I mumbled, "Christ you're hot," right above the swell of her breasts, bared where her blouse buttons parted. This necessitated her grinding down on my swollen cock, which felt like it was being strangled in my jeans. "Fuck," I groaned, then buried my face in her neck. She smelled of perfume, shampoo, sweat, and a little bit of what made Devolin her own unique blend of aphrodisiac, specifically tailored with me in mind. "We need to slow this down," I mumbled against the skin of her jaw, nipping it before pulling back.

Devolin's eyes were on fire at this point. She dropped her forehead to mine, her breath fanning against my face.

I couldn't help myself, I lifted my chin to peck her lips lightly.

"Oh, God! Oh, damn! Oh, shit! Shit! Shit!" came from the entrance before the front door slammed shut.

My head fell to rest on the back of the couch on a sighed, "Fuck," while Devolin's body began to shake. Within seconds, she burst out laughing.

"That..." she huffed through her giggles, "that was..." another bout of hilarity, "payback." She dissolved in another fit of laughter before finally finding her wits. "That was for the times she's—"

"Oh, no, no, no, no, no!" I cut her off. "I don't need to know who and what my sister's business with guys is. I don't even want the vaguest of idea. Get me?" My eyes narrowed on hers to prove how much I didn't want her to finish that sentence of hers.

The smile she gave me lit up her entire face and I was mesmerized. "I got you, Kip," she whispered onto my lips before giving the lower one a nip, then licking away the sting.

"Are you sure you've never done this?" I groaned, as she shimmied back and started to get off me. "You're killing me here."

Her short laugh did nothing to conceal her humor. "Want me to kiss it and make it better?" As soon as her words were out, her eyes went wide, she blanched, then blushed, and I couldn't help the grin that spread on my face.

If I were to take things beyond simple pecks here and there and make out sessions, I'd have to find out how much Devolin had experienced in her limited freedom over the years.

Getting to my feet, I shifted myself in my jeans in hopes to restore some circulation in my cock, then wrapped a hand around the back of Devolin's neck, pulling her into my chest.

"I—I..."

"Sweetheart, when the time is right, and when you're ready, I'll give you free reign to do just that, but not before we discuss things first," I said, then kissed her stupid before releasing her, and headed for the front door. Skylar was waiting after all.

eighteen

AS SOON AS Skylar came back in, I gave her a hug in greeting then excused myself to the washroom.

What the hell had I just gone and done?

Staring at myself in the mirror, I couldn't help but notice the rosy tint to my cheeks, the glimmer in my eyes, my swollen lips, or the sex-kitten tussle going on with my hair. My inventory caused me to smile like a loon.

That had been one hell of a clinch I'd found myself in. One, if I didn't allow my worries to take over, I'd admit I wanted to partake in again and again.

I liked the way Dalton was hard one moment, then soft with me the next. I adored how conscientious he was about my experience—or lack thereof. I especially loved just how attuned he was with my feelings, willing to push when he read that I was ready, and pulling back when it was the right thing to do.

Safe.

For what felt like the hundredth time today, I embraced the warmth inside me I hadn't experienced a lot of in my twenty-nine years.

Contemplating if I should fix my hair, then realizing I didn't have my clip with me, I decided that maybe it was high time I embraced that dormant inner vixen of mine and made my way back to Dalton and Skylar.

"She's not like the rest of them, D!" Skylar whisper-shouted.

"You think I don't know that?" Dalton growled.

Here I thought I'd be able to get back to the two half-siblings when I heard their not-so-quiet discussion. As much as I wanted to, I couldn't move away from the conversation nor move into their line of sight for them to realize their chat was no longer a private one.

"Please be careful."

"Sky, this isn't some sick conquest thing," Dalton said, making my building panic ebb a little. "Devolin means something to me."

Silence.

"Don't mess it up, D." Butterfly flutters started up in my stomach. "You might be my brother, but you hurt her, you've got me to answer to, bucko." Fuck, I had the greatest best friend. "I'm going to go check on her. Lord knows she's probably mortified and looking for a way to escape."

Shit! Fuck!

I looked around to try and figure out what I should do. If I stayed put, I'd be found out. If I headed back where I'd come from, odds were Skylar would catch me before I had the chance to turn around and make my way back to them.

Forward. I had to move forward.

I smirked internally at that thought. It seemed to be the motto to my life as of late: moving forward.

"Oh, hey! You okay?" Skylar asked as I rounded the corner into the kitchen.

Meeting my friend's gaze briefly, I was more concerned about what I'd read in Dalton's when I looked at him. When I did turn to him, the man held himself steadfast and with an air of confidence. The moment his gaze met mine, after he'd given me a discreet perusal, taking notice of my hair, his eyes dilated, and his lips arched up in a cocky grin before he threw a wink my way.

Returning his smile with a shy one of my own, I shifted my

attention back to Skylar and answered her earlier question. "I'm fine."

"I'm so sorry—"

"Sky...really. It's okay."

She made quick study of my face, and once satisfied, nodded and turned to her brother. "So what's for dinner?"

nineteen

DALTON

I MUST BE TURNING into a girl. Fuck, I should just hand my man card to the closest fucker around with how jealous I've been feeling over the last hour.

A call came in from Shane and I had to take it, so I left my sister and my...well, my Devolin.

My Devolin?

My mind froze as it stuck to those two words, my body feeling a calm I hadn't felt in far too long.

Yes. *My* Devolin.

Fuck it sounded good.

See?

Man card.

Gone.

What was odd about that was the fact that I didn't give two shits about that single factoid. So I left the women on my back deck for a visit, while I took my cell to my office to see what Detective Peters had to say.

By the time I made it back to the women, Skylar and Devolin were up on their feet, their arms wrapped around each other giggling. I

88

hadn't realized until then, how long it had been since I'd heard my sister truly laugh. Of course she laughed, but there always seemed to lack genuine happiness, or more like there was an underlying melancholy to her bouts of humor, over the last little while. To hear her laugh like she meant it filled me with warmth.

Grinning at the sight before me, I asked. "What's going on?"

The women turned toward me, their smiles intact, both sets of eyes twinkling.

"Ask your woman," Skylar said cryptically.

"Sky, I'm not—" The moment Devolin's eyes met mine, she found herself unable to finish her sentence.

She's getting it.

Truth be told, whether we wanted it to happen or not, despite the time in our lives where it took root, no matter all external circumstances, she was mine. To even contemplate another man laying his hands on her, to be kissing on her, made me see red. Even if a relationship was the furthest thing from my mind; the way she'd been giving me bits of herself since we met, putting her trust in me, something she rarely did with anyone, meant the world to me. Let's not forget how electric we were together earlier. As ridiculous as it sounded to me, I had no doubt Devolin Taylor was going to end up in my arms again. And in my bed. She was already firmly rooted in my head, and I couldn't ignore the fact that she was slowly creeping into my heart, too.

"D?" This came from Skylar, knocking me out of my thoughts and back to the present. "Did you hear anything I said?"

"Huh?"

Skylar's mischievous smile came out to play. I swear she could read me better than anyone else I knew. "Never mind," she said, turning to Devolin, who was biting her bottom lip as if trying to prevent herself from laughing. "I'm glad you're moving on, girl. I'll see you on Wednesday night."

"Yeah, but I'm not cooking," she smirked.

Skylar turned to me once more, then approached. "I'm out of here." Wrapping her arms around my torso, I gave her a squeeze back. "Any chance you'll be back by Sunday?"

"Sky..." I groaned. I knew what that meant.

"You haven't seen him in a month, D," she said about our father.

"So long as she's not there, then yeah, I'll be there," I tell her about her mother.

"Okay." Her eyes reflected her relief. "I'll let him know."

"Love you, squirt." I kissed the top of her head.

"Love you, too." She gave me one last squeeze before backing away with her usual warning. "Be safe."

I grinned at her words. "It's just a routine meeting."

She studied me for a while longer than felt comfortable. I didn't give away any of the apprehension I felt about the resulting trip that would come out of visiting our country's northern neighbor.

Once Skylar was happy with what she saw, she gave Devolin a quick finger wave, saying, "Wednesday, doll," as she made her way off the patio, to the side of my house, toward the front yard.

I didn't waste time. As soon as Skylar was gone, my feet set me toward Devolin, whose gaze resembled that of a deer caught in headlights.

The moment my arms wrapped around her, her taut body relaxed, and her hands came to rest on my chest.

"I should go," she whispered. "You have an early flight tomorrow."

"Stay."

"But—"

"I want you to stay." I pressed my lips to hers. "Just for a bit longer." I pulled back to find tat her eyes had changed to that dark forest green again. Smirking, I flicked the tip of her nose. "And not for that, sweetheart. I'd be happy if we just talked."

"Talked?" she squeaked.

My nod was curt. "Talked," I repeated, as I pulled her toward the patio door, leading the way toward the living room couch.

Instead of taking a seat beside me like I thought she would, she surprised me by hitching her skirt up to straddle my thighs, a self-assured smirk on her face.

My eyes narrowed suspiciously. "What are you doing?"

"Do we really have to talk?" She leaned forward, nipping my jaw.

I groaned. "Dev."

"I'd rather keep going from where we left off earlier." Her fingers reached into my hair, pulling at the strands, thus keeping my head hostage.

"Sweetheart," I tried again.

She nuzzled just below my ear before whispering, "Don't you?" as she settled her crotch nice and tight against mine.

"Baby," I hissed out, "we really," she nipped at my lips and I let her, "need," her tongue snuck out, "to," I pecked her mouth, because I couldn't help myself, "talk," I finished on another peck.

Releasing the hold she had on my hair, she pulled back to cup the sides of my neck, avoiding my gaze.

By this point, my hands were fisted at my sides. This was reason one why we needed to talk. By now, had she been any other woman, I would have been all over her. But because of her tendency to freeze up, even though she had been fine earlier, I really needed to find out where my boundaries lay.

"Dev—"

"What are we doing here, Dalton?"

"We're trying to feel things out for an us, sweetheart." I slowly wrapped my arms around Devolin's torso, letting my hand settle on the small of her back, my fingers itching to reach into the back of her skirt and grab a handful of her ass. "I—"

Her irritated expression softened, and her eyes met mine as she surmised, "You're scared you're going to push me too far."

"Yeah." I swallowed. "I'm not exactly what they call a gentleman," I confessed. "I know what I want, how I want it, and I'm not above taking it." My eyes searched hers. "Baby, I don't know what I'll do that'll set you off," I explained further. "I guess, what I'm saying is that I need to know where your head is at with this. It's new to you, sweet—"

She shut me up with a tender press of her mouth to mine that ended too soon. "I can't say I'm not scared too, Kip." She nuzzled my nose. Normally, I hated being called by that shortened version of my last name; Devolin using it, however, I found that I loved it. "But what I can say is that for tonight, I want your arms around me." Punctuating the latter with a quick peck, she continued, "Your lips on me." Another peck. "Maybe a few less articles of clothing." Another. "And some heavy petting?" she whispered the last over my lips before pulling back, her eyes hopeful. "It's been so long since I've had some petting, Kip."

"Christ, woman, you're a wet dream come to life," escaped in one long breath before I leaned forward, snagging her mouth with mine.

twenty

OH. *My. God.*

Dalton's hands were on my ass! Over my underwear, but they were on my ass nonetheless, clutching the cheeks I always thought were too round and jiggly. Grinding our pelvises together, a delicious shiver ran through my body the moment he nipped where my neck met my shoulder.

"Mmm," I moaned.

It was the only thing I could muster. Words were no longer part of my vocabulary. I was reduced to moans, groans, and other unintelligible nonsense, much like a caveman, and I didn't give two shits about it. It felt too good to care. Dalton felt good. Amazing!

That's when I decided to give him some of the same in return.

Grinding down on him, I rubbed my chest against his like a cat in heat. My hands wandered down his pecs, journeying their way to his waist, and I proceeded to hitch up his t-shirt.

"Off," I grunted with my effort, the shirt having snagged behind his back.

The man's laugh rumbled in his chest as I leaned back to give him enough room while he leaned forward. He reached behind his neck and ripped the shirt from his body, chucking it to land somewhere behind the couch.

Not for the first time, I wondered how his hard to my soft would feel against my skin. The urge was so strong that with no hesitation, I reached up to the top button of my blouse and released it from its eyelet, rushing to the next. Dalton's larger hands put my smaller, much daintier ones to a halt.

My head snapped up and found Dalton's smile—not to mention his fiery gaze—on me.

"Let me." He leaned in and kissed my lips gently. His mouth then moved to kiss the expanse of skin that I'd just bared before meeting my eyes.

My nod was hurried, my breath choppy. "O-okay."

With each subsequently released button, Dalton proceeded to kiss and lick the newly exposed flesh of my front, until he couldn't bend further. That didn't mean that his fingers stopped though. He pulled on the hem of my shirt, finished undoing the garment, then proceeded with pushing it off my shoulders, aiding me with the sleeves, all the while nibbling on my shoulders.

Pulling at my bra strap with his teeth, he released it to snap against my skin, the pinch a sweet kind of pain that didn't hurt at all.

As soon as I was divested of my top, Dalton's hands skimmed up the skin of my arms. Goosebumps broke out over my heated flesh. His nose nuzzled just below my ear, his breath coming out in warm gusts feathering down my chest. His palms stopped on either side of my neck, his eyes ensnaring me when he pulled back slightly.

"You're exquisite, baby," he whispered. The reverence in his voice caused me to melt further into him.

If I wasn't careful, I could lose more than myself in this man. I could lose my heart. My soul.

I couldn't let that happen—at least not yet. Not until he knew my deepest secret.

It hadn't been my fault that I hadn't shared that part of myself just yet. We'd gotten a little sidetracked with our earlier exploration.

And now… Well, now wasn't the time for it either.

Talk about a mood killer.

The feel of Dalton's mouth blowing a heated breath over my left nipple, through the white lace of my bra, had me snapping back to reality on a moan.

"Where'd you go just now?" he mumbled against my breast. The nip he gave me there caused me to yelp on a shudder.

"Please," I begged.

He gave me a devilish grin. "You like that?"

"Uh-huh." On a vehement nod, I proved my point further by gripping the back of his head and urging him closer.

But he resisted. "Baby…"

"It's nothing, Kip. Just something I forgot to do, but I'll take care of it later."

His brows furrowed, and his lips thinned with evident frustration. For a minute, I thought he'd read through my lie, but the man's expression changed to one of challenge.

"I must really be doing this all wrong if you have time to think of other things."

"No!" I shook my head from side to side. "Please don't stop, Dalton."

This caused him to smile. "Then stay with me," he whispered, lowering his head down to my breast again, this time, flicking its rigid tip with his tongue before giving me one of his little nips again.

"Fuck!" My eyes closed and my head fell back onto my shoulders.

The man's deep timber of a laugh vibrated from my nipple, straight to my core, causing a spasm. I gasped at the sensation and wriggled to grind harder against his jean-clad length.

"Christ you're a firecracker," he mumbled, switching breasts, his hand working the one he'd just left. Pulling the lace down to expose my chest with his free hand, he went straight to the bared tip and growled. "Fucking delicious."

The moment his mouth sealed itself to that tip, I felt as if the top of my head blew off. Stars exploded in my vision.

I heard a long keening moan from somewhere in the distance

along with Dalton's, "Holy fuck!" Lost to all that was Dalton, I collapsed against his chest.

Had that been me moaning like that? *Shit!* I thought the sound was something exaggerated from the few porn videos I'd seen during late night TV. I didn't think women truly made those noises in real life. Yet I had.

"Dev?" Dalton kissed my temple. "Baby?" His lips met my forehead. "Sweetheart?"

"What the fuck was that?" I mumbled against his neck before pulling back, feeling a little unsteady, not to mention, embarrassed by the inner hussy that had clearly taken over my body.

"Baby, I just made you come for me with my hands and mouth on your tits." He looked like the cat that ate the cream.

I groaned and let my head drop down to Dalton's chest at my analogy. Not because of its tackiness. More because the mere thought of the word *cream* made my sex clench and need flood me once more. Visions of Dalton, and his sinful mouth, exploring my other intimate parts, testing me, forcing more of those keening wails I'd just emitted assaulted me.

"Nope, coming with nipple stimulation alone is definitely not a myth." I felt my face heat, thankful I was able to hide my blush against Dalton's now vibrating body.

"I'm about to debunk the shit out of everything you might think a myth, baby," he said on a chuckle, then kissed the top of my head. "Just you wait and see."

I thought I had quenched my inner hussy's thirst earlier, but the bitch reared up again, the glutton for more of Dalton's attentions that she was.

Giving her what she wanted, I snuck my hand between us and cupped his rather impressive bulge. "By all means, Kip, don't leave me hanging."

twenty-one

DALTON

"WELCOME TO JACKSONVILLE, folks! The current time is nine-oh-five p.m., the temperature is at a balmy…" I drowned out the captain's voice as our flight made its final descent toward the tarmac.

It had been a charged couple of days, filled with meetings with Canadian agencies that had me jumping through hoops due to their red tape processes. One thing I had to hand to our northern neighbors was that they sure knew how to run a tight ship. Where they failed however, was that their government was unable to send anyone into a foreign territory to investigate. They had informants within the Juan Cartel, just simply not in Enrique Ortiz's pocket. I now saw why Wentworth needed an external source to help him out.

With that said, I had another set of worries on my hands, thanks to Brycen and what he'd informed me of this morning, right before takeoff.

To say I was incensed would be an understatement. I wanted this plane of ours to land like yesterday so I could give my woman a piece of my mind.

As soon as the plane had circled the runway, parked at the gate, and the seatbelt sign light turned off, I was up on my feet, making my way toward the exit.

Thirty minutes later, I was at Devolin's apartment building, being let in by what I surmised as one of the place's residents, and on my way up the elevator.

When I got there, however, no amount of loud banging on her door made her answer, which now had me more worried than pissed off.

I whipped out my phone.

> Where are you?

I saw the bubbles indicating that she was writing something, which filled me with relief. It was late enough that I knew she wouldn't be at the office, but where else could she be? She was supposed to be having dinner with Skylar.

Pulling up my sister's contact information, I typed away.

> You still with Dev?

I flicked back to my text to Devolin, only to find nothing and the bubbles had disappeared.

SKY:

> Why?

> Because I'm at her place, no one's here like you said you would be. It's Wednesday, is it not?

A few seconds later...

SKY:

> McAskill's.

Fuck!

What do you mean McAskill's? You two were supposed to be here!

Seconds later, I got a message notification from Devolin herself.

DEVOLIN:

I'm fine. Glad you're back. I'll see you tomorrow.

She was fine? She was glad I was back? She'd see me tomorrow?

What in the ever-loving fuck?

I could tan her sweet, innocent ass right now. Maybe that's what I would do when I found her.

Turning from her door, I headed for the stairs. I had to work off my frustration before I saw the woman, or I'd be liable to do some serious damage.

Locating the two women as soon as I arrived at McAskill's hadn't been a hard task. All I had to do was sniff out the testosterone.

Loud whooping could be heard as some preppy guy, who looked like he was still in college, walked out from the gathering, shoulders hunched.

"Right! Now which one of you's next?" I'd recognize that voice anywhere. The *you* was slurred, but it had come from none other than Tamara, one of Skylar's friends. I groaned. If Tamara was part of the pack, I smelled trouble.

Nudging some of the men to the side, I made my way to the front of the group, sticking my fingers in my mouth and blowing a shrill whistle.

Three female heads turned to face me, making me smirk at their startled expressions. It was the shocked one on Devolin's face, however, that humored me the most.

"I'll play."

"Brother—" Skylar started, but I lifted my hand to silence her as I made my way to Devolin, whose gaze was fused to mine. A twinkle of fear mixed with a spark of defiance shone in them. Some of the male population cleared out and went back to what they'd been doing.

"Get me a beer, will ya, sis?" Without looking her way, I took the cue from my half-sister's hands, my gaze never straying from Devolin's now wide-eyed one.

"Kip," she breathed. If it hadn't been for the subtle glaze in her eyes, I'd have said she was now completely stone cold sober. "I—"

"You're in deep shit already, sweetheart." I pecked her nose because I simply couldn't help myself. "But after I school you in this game, I'm taking you home, and we're having a little chat about what you've been up to these last few days."

Brows furrowing, her eyes narrowed, and her expression turned to one I'd recognize anywhere: sheer pissed off female with a bone to pick.

"Who do you think—"

I grabbed onto the finger she was poking me in the chest with and stared her down. "I wouldn't push me if I were you," I warned. "You've already earned yourself five. You want to earn yourself ten, or even fifteen, that's fine by me. My hand can go all night, babe."

Her mouth snapped shut, her face grew red, then she schooled her features, set her cue on the table's edge and proceeded to mumble, "Neanderthal" as she racked the balls. She might have thought she'd said it low enough not to be heard over the music; she was wrong.

I snorted my annoyance. "I can always take you home now."

"You're not taking me anywhere, mister." She kept on shoving balls in the rack violently without looking at me. "Not tonight." Ball shoved. "Not tomorrow." More balls shoved. "Not any time until you tell me what the fuck crawled up your ass and died!"

twenty-two

I FELT the heat of his fury before his body made contact with the back of mine.

As much as he was pissing me off, part of me wanted to turn, plaster myself to him, and beg him to take me home and explore me the way he had a few short nights ago. Plus those spankings he was alluding to... Mmm.

"Does Hewitt ring a bell, sweetheart?" His breath fanned over my ear and down my neck, making goosebumps rise onto my skin.

I bit my lip. I had purposefully omitted that particular tidbit of information in our many phone calls while he'd been away, knowing all too well he wouldn't be happy with me. Had he approached me like a normal person and asked, instead of storming into the place and telling me we'd be having words later, I probably would have come clean.

Instead of fessing up and explaining, I snapped. "That doesn't concern you."

"Baby, when you're my woman, it does." He nipped my lobe.

My knees felt like they were about to give out. Ignoring the fact my reaction was more about the overbearing dickhead standing too close to me, I chose to blame my reaction on the booze I'd consumed.

"Here you go, D."

Saved by the best friend and her sidekick.

When Tamara had called to invite Skylar out, I hadn't been too sure about coming along. From what Skylar had told me about her, the woman was apparently a magnet for trouble. After meeting the woman in the flesh though, I saw exactly why Skylar was a friend of hers. Although a pathological flirt, Tamara was sweet, caring, and funny as all hell. She was the perfect addition to the evening. It had been a welcomed distraction from what had happened earlier, while Skylar and I had been picking up pizza for our originally planned quiet night in.

Without a word, Dalton backed away from me, effectively knocking me out of my musings and back to reality. Grabbing his beer from Skylar, then meeting my gaze, he proceeded to chug the entire bottle before slamming it down on the table we'd been using for our drinks throughout the night. "I'm going to need a fresh one."

"Got you covered." Tamara turned to Skylar. "I told you he'd do that. You should have ignored him."

Dalton's short laugh lacked humor.

"He deserves what he's about to get," Skylar muttered, and met her brother's gaze, folding her arms across her chest with that we're-gonna-have-a-talk look on her face.

Huffing as I reached for my margarita, I sucked up the dregs of my drink. "Can we get to playing already so he," I pointed at Dalton, "can go home?"

"I'm not going home without you," he growled.

"We'll see." Motioning toward the felt-covered table with a jut of my chin, I said, "Your break."

I cleaned his clock, three out of four times. Skylar and Tamara had laughed themselves practically sick while Dalton and I had played, taunting the man, cheering in my corner. It was hard to ignore, and I felt proud of myself for standing up to my opponent. That Dalton seemed surprised and impressed by my pool skills was an added bonus.

Within seconds of our final game ending, Dalton grabbed my arm at the elbow and started ushering me toward the exit.

"Time to go home."

"D—" Skylar tried to interrupt, distracting him enough so I could wrench my arm out of his grip.

"I'm not going home with you." Venom laced my words.

His gaze was fused to mine, heated and irritated. "Like hell you're not. We've got shit to discuss and—"

As he reached for me again, I jumped back. "And like I said, we'll talk tomorrow. If you don't mind, I'm out with the girls tonight, all thanks to you, and I'd very much like to enjoy my outing without you ruining my buzz." I punctuated this with a feeble push of both hands to Dalton's chest. "Go home, Dalton."

The man didn't budge.

Refusing to let his gaze go, I stood my ground until I simply couldn't anymore. A favorite song of mine chose that moment to start blaring through the pub's speakers, my mood instantly perking up. Turning from the infuriating man in front of me, I grabbed onto Skylar and Tamara's hands, tugging them toward the small clearing in the middle of the bar that served as a dance floor.

"Let's dance!"

He could leave.

He could stay.

I didn't give one good goddamn what he did. I was there to drown my sorrows and forget about the clusterfuck I'd put myself in with Dalton Kippers. That other woman could have him and his overbearing sexy ways.

twenty-three

DALTON

I WAS in no way leaving without her.

Sitting alone in the nearest corner by the dance floor, I watched the three women getting down to the latest mash-up of new versus old tunes that had furthered my woman's endeavor of ignoring me.

Fuck, she could move. And I hadn't been the only one to notice either.

That hip shimmy thing that she was doing was attracting attention from all angles, and by the looks she'd been giving me, Little-Miss-Innocent knew exactly how the local male population was affected.

I'd had enough of her games.

Halfway through their third song, I'd made my decision known.

Sneaking up behind her, I grabbed her by the tops of her arms, turned her to face me, bent forward, and hoisted her over my shoulder. It was a good thing I kept my arms locked around the back of her knees, because her kicking surely would have ended with a shot to the nuts, due to my high-handed behavior.

"Hey! Lemme go!" Devolin shrieked, her fists pounding my lower back.

Meeting both Tamara and Skylar's gazes, my words were clipped. "You can choose to stay, but we're leaving."

"Let. Me. Go, Dalton!" Devolin ordered, still pounding on my back. "Right." Pound. "The fuck." Hit. Hit. "Now!" she growled the last.

My hand found her ass, smacking it five times in quick succession, causing my little spitfire to thrash in my grip, but I held firm. "Woman, don't push me."

"Hmph!" She sighed and then went limp as I turned and made my way toward the door, hearing Skylar and Tamara cackle.

"I'll call you tomorrow," my half-sister called out as Tamara added, "Give 'im hell, sister!"

"So, you're a shark at pool, huh?" I asked within seconds of having Devolin in my truck's passenger seat.

The woman ignored my inquiry, looking out her window.

I sighed, then tried again a few minutes later.

"I missed you," came out just a hair above a whisper.

Nothing.

So I turned to gauge her reaction to my latest proclamation, and found her hunched toward the passenger door, her head leaning on the window, sound asleep.

I was thankful to find an empty spot in front of Devolin's apartment building.

"Sweetheart?" I shook her thigh.

"Hmm?" was all I got from her.

It was impossible to stay mad at this woman. Shaking my head, unable to conceal the small quirk of my lips at her cuteness, I made my decision.

Jumping out of the truck after locating her keys in her purse, I made quick work of releasing Devolin's seatbelt and lifting her into my arms.

"Let's me goes, Dalt," she whispered drowsily against my

collarbone, the effects of the alcohol she'd consumed more evident. "I can walk."

I chuckled. "You can't even lift your head off my shoulder to tell me that, woman. I'm not going to let you walk."

"Stubborn, jackass...heartbreaker."

The last had my breath freezing in my lungs.

What the fuck is she talking about?

As soon as I had her apartment door opened, I closed it behind us, locking the deadbolt, and headed past the living room, kitchen, and then into the hallway to locate her bedroom.

On my left, right off the kitchen, I found a linen closet, the bathroom being next to it. To my right, a soft glow beckoned me. I smiled at the sight I took in. Computers, laptops, a mounted TV, beautiful stylish furniture, and floor-to-ceiling windows. The rest of the décor was pure Devolin. This was her office. Her sanctuary. Not for the first time, it reinforced my desire to get to know the woman in my arms on a deeper level. I wanted to know the ins and outs. What made her tick. Why she was the way that she was. And I swore that I'd make that happen. Even if it meant having to reveal those deepest and darkest parts of myself to get her to stay.

Turning from her office, there was one final door at the end of the hall. Opening it, I was bombarded by the scent that was Devolin. Unlike the rest of her place, you could tell her bedroom was her domain. Where everything else had its place and was tidy to the point of compulsiveness, her bedroom looked as if a hurricane had broken through.

This had a laugh rumbling in my chest as I tried to remain quiet.

Devolin's arms came around my neck as she tried to burrow in deeper into my chest, her nose nuzzling my jaw on a sigh.

With her action, the worry and anger that had been building since Brycen had called me, to let me know she'd been out to meet with Hewitt, eased a bit. The fact that it hadn't been once, but twice during my absence was temporarily forgotten. In this moment, a bit of clarity came. There may be a lot of things I had yet to discover about Devolin, but if there was one thing I knew about the innocent woman with sassy tendencies currently in my arms, it was that she had a kind soul.

Dodging the piles of clothes and shoes on the floor, I made our way to her unmade bed, glad the sheets were already pushed toward the foot of it.

Setting her down, I proceeded to remove her shoes, then I took in her sleeping form as it curled in on itself until she lay on her right side in the fetal position.

Removing my own shoes and socks, I pulled my shirt over my head, stripping down to my boxers before folding the lot and setting it on the edge of her dresser.

Easing myself down behind her, I pulled the sheets and her duvet over us, and I settled onto my back, my left hand tucked behind my head while I stared at the ceiling. Within seconds, Devolin turned, then shimmied her body into my right side. My arm rounded the back of her torso to hold her close as her head came to settle onto my shoulder, her face nestled into my neck.

Next thing I knew, I was sound asleep. I just didn't know how much of that sleep I would need until the sun rose the next day.

twenty-four

DEVOLIN

I KNEW IT WAS MORNING, but I couldn't make myself move what with how nice and warm I felt.

"Why can't I sleep like this every night?" I mumbled to myself.

"When I get back from Mexico, we can do that as often as you'd like," came rumbled from below my head.

Gasping, I proceeded to take in my surroundings without moving an inch.

Heat surrounded my cheek. A cheek pressed to a hard, smooth chest.

My soft belly leaned into the side of an eight-pack of abdominal muscles I was now currently running my hand over. The hand that was attached to the arm that only seconds before, had been wrapped around said abs.

My leg was bent at the knee and draped over what felt like a large, muscular tree trunk of a leg. That leg was now bending upward, bringing my knee dangerously close to...

Escape now!

Bolting to a sitting upright position, it didn't take me long to realize I was wearing nothing but white cotton underwear.

Grabbing one of the sheets, I covered my chest by tucking it under my arms. Brushing my unruly hair away from my face, I turned and stared daggers downward to a still sprawled out, laughing Dalton at my side.

"You did this!" I accused.

"You did, actually," he supplied. "I was a complete gentleman and put you to bed with your clothes on. The only thing I removed were your shoes."

A vague memory from the night before hit me. I'd woken sometime during the night, sweating. Stumbling in the dark, I had shucked my clothes, then collapsed back into bed, reaching for my pillows.

Except, Dalton ended up being said pillow.

My cheeks flushed with a blush I knew was impossible to conceal. "What are you doing here?"

"What, no good morning?" The man had the gall to cajole.

"Morning," I griped. After all, my mother had taught me to mind my manners no matter the situation.

Within seconds, Dalton did an ab-curl, wrapped his beefy arms around me, and I found myself once again tucked against his body.

This had a dual effect on me.

First, I felt as if I could fall asleep on the man for another ten hours, thanks to the headache pounding inside my skull.

Second, my mouth watered at the recollection of how the man had tasted when we'd played before his trip to Canada.

The latter made me shiver.

"What was that about?" he asked against the hair at the top of my head.

"Nothing." I couldn't let him know my thoughts. I was still pissed at him and his high-handed behavior, thinking he could control me, demanding I bend to his will.

"Sweetheart." His arm skimmed the skin of my back along my spine, eliciting another shiver. "We need to—"

"Not right now," I told him.

"Yes, now." His soft tone had altogether disappeared.

"This is my house!" I pushed myself up and out of his grip. Dalton let me go. "You don't tell me what to do!"

Or not.

One second, I thought I'd be able to convince the man to postpone our discussion to later—like maybe once I'd gotten dressed, grabbed a cup of coffee, and taken a couple of aspirin for my hangover—and the next, I was firmly held down, on the flat of my back, with a stern looking Dalton, torso wedged between my thighs, our hands up above my head, and his face in mine. I couldn't miss his rather large erection pressing into my crotch, since it also caused me to see stars as he rubbed himself against my heat.

"Did you hear me?" he asked.

"Huh?"

"Fuck." He let his head drop so his forehead met my shoulder, sighing. Then he surprised me with another one of his delicious hip shifts, which pressed him impossibly closer than we already were. "We're not talking."

"No shit, Sherlock," came out of my mouth.

His chest started to shake over mine, making my nipples stand at attention as his taut flesh rubbed against them, causing my ire to take a back seat as my thoughts once again got scrambled.

Dalton moved our joined hands to wrap my fingers around the slats in the headboard. "Hang on."

Mirth glowed in his eyes as he pulled back to take in my reaction to his command.

Then he claimed my mouth for his own. With the way he set forth to ravage me, if he asked, I'd give him my body, too. What scared me the most, was that I had the distinct feeling I'd give him anything at all if he requested it.

The problem with that, was that I wasn't quite sure he'd return the courtesy. Not after last night.

twenty-five

DALTON

PLEASE.

I fucking loved hearing that plea coming from her mouth.

Pulling my face away from worshipping her tits, I peered up to see Devolin watching me. I moved a hand down toward the edge of her underwear, pausing between her navel and the white cotton's elastic.

Biting down on her bottom lip, a vehement nod urged me to continue as our eyes remained fused to the other's.

My mouth ran dry. "Are you sure?" I rasped.

"Please," she whispered this time.

Her body shook, her breath catching as I snuck my fingers past the band of her underwear. Her unrestrained reaction to my ministrations had my cock so hard I could hammer nails with it.

I broke eye contact and leaned in, pressing my nose to the junction of her parted thighs, nuzzling her heat, and catching the scent of her essence. I delighted in the fact she'd soaked through the garment before I'd had the chance to get her completely bare for my taking.

Lifting her hips as permission, I got up to my knees, using both hands, and gingerly pulled her panties down her legs. I kissed my way down from her sternum, to her pelvic bone, before settling back down onto my stomach, my face mere inches from her treasure.

Taking a good look at the feast that awaited me, I looked up to find Devolin's face averted to the side, sporting a blush, her eyes clenched closed as she gripped the headboard still.

The woman took direction very well.

"Baby, look at me," I said.

Her eyes popped open, and she wearily turned her head to look down. Her pupils dilated at what she saw, and her body seemed to relax.

"You're fucking beautiful." Her licking her lips had me doing the same to mine. "Tell me to taste you, Dev, or this stops right here, right now." There was no fucking way in hell I was pushing for something if she wasn't ready for it.

"Uh...I thought..."

I ran the top of my index finger through her glistening lips, admiring the slickness as my eyes bore into hers.

"Sweetheart—"

"I want you to kiss me...down there," she finally got out.

I dipped my head, parting the lips of her sex, and took a slow leisurely tongue swipe from the rosette of her ass to her clit.

Devolin's back bowed up off the bed, shoving her pussy into my face. "Oh my God! Do that again!"

I did.

"So good," she moaned.

This caused me to chuckle into her folds, making her gasp. That, for me, was my cue to find out what else she liked.

Fuck, the woman was a greedy little hellcat!

Forgetting about keeping her hands above her head, she'd laced her fingers through my hair, pulling my face further into her pussy. Her knees had come up to lock behind my back, her ass had arched up, thrusting her juicy cunt in my face.

Flicking at her clit with my tongue, I thrust two fingers into her heat, curving them upward, locating that sweet spot I knew would set her off.

"Oh shit!" she panted. "Don't, Kip! I—"

I tried to pull my head back so I could look at her, and her grip relented a little.

"You can handle this," I told her.

"I want you inside of me when it happens." She licked her lips, then elaborated. "I've only been able to come once."

This made me smile much like the Cheshire Cat. "Is that a challenge?"

She shook her head. "No. It's just a fact. Every time I've...well, you know...I've only been able to go—"

I chose to ignore her words and dove into her heat again.

Challenge accepted!

"Oh my God! Dalton, no!"

I further ignored her plea and began to prove to her that if done right, multiple orgasms would be all she would see in her future.

With me in charge of them.

twenty-six

DEVOLIN

"OH MY GOD. Is this what heaven feels like?"

"It can be," Dalton said, as he kissed his way back up my body. My very much sated and limp body. All because of his mouth and hands. Again.

As satisfied as I felt, the feel of his skin rubbing against mine, as his body covered it, had my blood heating and my nether regions aching once more.

So I did the only thing I could think of. I let the man lead and went along for the ride. If he could set me off like fireworks on the Fourth by simply eating me out, I wanted—no, I *needed*—to know what his dick filling me would be capable of. After all, everyone knows that the actual deed is supposed to be better than anything else. At least that's what I'd heard and read in my vast collection of erotic romances on my Kindle Fire.

I must have taken too long to respond because before I knew it, Dalton started moving off me.

"No!" I grabbed on to either side of his neck and pulled his face down, pressing my lips firmly against his. Licking the nip I bestowed his lower lip, a new burst of flavor hit my tongue. The unbridled taste of Dalton was still there, but there was an additional one accompanying it.

Is that me?

"It is," Dalton broke me from my musings. I hadn't realized I'd spoken my thoughts aloud. "And." He pecked my lips. "I." He smooched me a bit harder this time. "Like it." He nipped my upper lip before kissing the sting away. "A lot." Then he reared his head to look down at me, his gaze full of lust. "And I hope you like it too, because I can't love on you without being able to kiss you."

My next action conveyed that I was more than fine with his intentions. Pulling his head down to mine once more, I crushed my mouth to his, pressing my tongue against the seam of his lips until he allowed me entrance. Massaging his tongue with mine, I moaned into his mouth, my blood now up from a simmer to a boil.

Moving my lips to his jaw, I kissed up to his earlobe, then whispered, "Get inside me, Kip. I want to feel you."

In the next second, Dalton pushed himself off me and the bed, then walked toward my dresser, grabbing his pants.

Getting up onto my elbows, I stumbled over my words. "W— where are you going?"

The man fished around in his pockets, throwing the jeans onto the floor, and flashed me that devilish grin of his, which made his dimples pop out. I'd make a point to lick them the next time he was smiling like that and within closer range.

He produced a foil square packet for me to see. "Condom."

Coming to a stop beside me and the bed, the man proceeded to shove his boxer briefs down his hips and legs.

My jaw dropped.

The man was physically huge, so I wasn't quite sure why I was surprised he'd be the same below the belt.

"I love the way you look at me," he growled.

My eyes flickered to his before going back down to his groin, then back up again, all the while licking my lips. "You're huge!" I stated the obvious.

He proceeded to tear the packet and slide the condom down his length, stroking himself a few times.

I groaned at the god standing before me in all his naked, delectable glory. My perverted mind had me wondering if he'd ever be amenable to perhaps stroke himself to completion in front of me if I were to request it.

Just as that thought occurred, the mattress dipped at my feet.

"Don't worry, baby. I'll go slow," he said against the skin of my belly, making my stomach muscles flutter.

"Can I watch you...jerk yourself off some time?" As soon as the words left my mouth, I smacked myself in the forehead for allowing my mouth to run away on me. This had Dalton bursting out in laughter, which was cut short when he took in my mortified state.

He gently grabbed my arm and pulled it down between us by the wrist. I still managed to avoid his gaze.

"Sweetheart?" My attention snapped to his as soon as I realized he was leading my hand to his lower stomach, downward until we'd reached his dick. Wrapping my hand around his girth, he covered it with his. I gave an experimental stroke, eliciting a hiss from him, his eyes never straying from mine. "Baby, if that's what you want, then yeah." His hand slid back to my wrist, then grabbed to remove my hand from his length before leaning in closer and kissing my knuckles. "I have no problems fisting my cock for you. I just expect a little entertainment while doing it."

"You mean porn?" I inquired, then nodded. "I can do that."

Lowering his body over mine, he smirked, shaking his head. "No, baby. Why would I want porn when I have you in the room?" I must have looked confused because he elaborated. "If I'm going to jerk myself off, I want it to be so I can watch you do the same to yourself." Before my gasp could escape, the man plunged his tongue inside my mouth and devoured me like I was the world's best treat.

twenty-seven

DALTON

THE FEEL of Devolin's hand gliding over my cock with my guidance had almost been my undoing. I damn near shot off like a geyser. And here I was about to give the woman total control, considering this was her first time. It would be a miracle if I didn't manage to make a fool of myself before I got her off.

"I need you, Kip," Devolin whispered against my lips.

"Take me in. Guide me inside you," I kissed the side of her mouth. "We'll go as fast or as slow as you need."

She slid her nose against the side of mine while nodding.

Her soft shaking hand took hold of me and the air in my lungs froze. My breathing picked up again as soon as she ran the tip of me along the length of her sex, coating it in her juices. My eyes crossed the moment she fit me into her entrance, removing her hand only to skim up my stomach, toward my chest as her legs began to squeeze, putting pressure against my ass to bring me deeper.

I halted my hips' forward progression and took a moment to study the woman laying beneath me. Her eyes met mine as I pulled back, then pushed in again slowly, savoring the tight silken feel of her, the way her inner muscles gave then sucked at my length.

Pulling out, leaving nothing but the tip, I pushed in further than before and continued to do this a few times until I was fully seated inside her. Reality startled me to a full stop, however, when the wince of pain I'd expected never came. Her inner muscles contracting around me had my brows furrowing in suspicion.

Devolin blushed a deep crimson.

"Care to explain?" I growled.

"It isn't what you think."

She tried to soothe me by rubbing her hands over my pecs, but I pulled them away, holding them down between us.

"You're not—"

"I am." Her tone left no room for argument. "I just..." She sighed, "I—"

"Devolin," I growled my impatience.

"I-broke-it-by-accident-while-playing-with-a-vibrator-alright?" came out in one long, exasperated word.

Huh? Had I heard her right? "Come again?"

"I was...you know...playing around with a toy one night." Her gaze was trained to my jaw momentarily before it met mine, a guilt-stricken expression on her face. "It felt so good, and I went too deep, and I—"

Holy fuck!

"Shut up," I snapped.

She ignored me and kept talking.

"I broke my hymen."

"Dev."

"But I'm not going to apologize, because it was the best damn orgasm I've ever had."

"Devolin."

"Next to you of course."

"Sweetheart."

"You're mouth on my boobs was great and all, but your mouth down there?" She sighed, her eyes taking on a dreamlike glimmer.

I smirked. "Babe."

"Pure heaven. I saw stars, Kip." The awe on her face was unmistakable. "I can only imagine what—"

By then, I couldn't help myself. At first, my shoulders were the only things shaking and all too quickly, the rest of my body followed as laughter overcame me.

"What's so fucking funny?"

"You," I said, getting hold of myself and grinning down at her. "Every time we're in the same room, it's one surprise after another. I like it." Images of her playing around with herself floated to the forefront of my mind, causing my cock to flex inside her. Devolin's irritation melted, instantly being replaced by lust.

"Kip?" Her hands feathered into my hair and pulled my face down to hers.

"Yeah?" I whispered.

"Will you fuck me now?" she asked sweetly.

Grinning down at her, I pulled my hips back, then slid right back into her as far as she could take me. "How's that for an answer?"

If I hadn't suspected it earlier, I would have right then. In our post-orgasmic haze, my forehead buried into the pillow next to Devolin's head as we tried to catch our breath, I knew I was falling for her.

Far too soon, reality set in, breaking us from our early morning tryst, as my phone began to ring.

Depositing a kiss to her shoulder, I pushed myself away from Devolin. Her groan of displeasure at our intimate disconnection had me smiling down at her. Turning away from her, I grabbed my pants but not before the cell in its pocket stopped ringing.

Grabbing my phone, thinking to myself that if I were lucky, I'd have Devolin on her back, begging for me to take her again before the sun went down tonight, I activated my screen. A message notification from Brycen was there, front and center.

My mood soured instantly as soon as I heard the voicemail.

Suffice to say, it took six words from the man to dash my hopes of feeling Devolin wrapped around me before the day's end.

"We're off to Mexico, mi amigo."

twenty-eight

DEVOLIN

"YOU'RE HEADING TO MEXICO TODAY?" It didn't make sense. I hadn't even gotten the results of my latest triangulation efforts with the new vectors I'd mashed into my algorithms. If that didn't work, I wasn't quite sure what my next recourse would be.

"When Bryce can't sleep, he works," Dalton said, as if that served as a suitable answer, all the while pouring each of us a travel mug of coffee. It didn't, so I looked over at him while I buttered our breakfast toasts. "He went in early this morning only to find your system going off."

"Motherfucker!" Surprised at this news, I dropped the knife into the margarine container, then spun around to face him.

"Listen—"

My excitement got the better of me. "It worked?" I took the coffee he offered me as he nodded. "It actually, freaking, honest to God worked?"

"Dev—"

"I didn't think I'd have a chance in hell with what you all gave me for the search parameters. And the algorithms I had to modify to—"

Dalton lost his patience. "Fuck your algorithm talk, woman.

120

Quit rambling like a lunatic and finish up because we need to get out of here."

My mouth snapped shut, lips pressing tightly together. Disregarding his snippiness, I folded our toast in napkins, and walked over to the couch. Shouldering my purse, I turned to the short-fused man. "Well, you coming or what?"

The man smirked as he approached. Grabbing me around the waist, he kissed the dickens out of me before leaning his forehead to mine.

"Sorry for snapping."

"It's okay." I tilted my head back and swiped his lips with mine.

"Let's go," he growled against my mouth.

The morning had flown by in a whirlwind of activity.

Men were walking around with what I'd dubbed their game faces on. They all looked so threatening.

It wasn't until I saw Dalton, Theo, and Tate come out of the conference room discussing firepower, shells, night-vision goggles, and a slew of other items I didn't quite know about, that reality started to sink in.

These men were taking off to save Minister Wentworth's fiancée. My supposed soon-to-be-aunt to be more precise. The man himself had only given me three other aunts over the years— each one younger than the one before. But Dalton didn't know this. It wasn't important in the grand scheme of things. What was, however, was that these men stayed safe and came back unharmed.

And I was part of that operation.

I wasn't sure when it was that I'd forgotten I would be assisting these men from HQ. These were men who'd come to mean the world to me, despite my lingering skittishness. They were men who would enter a crime-ridden country, infiltrate a cartel undetected, and rescue a woman who'd been kidnapped because of my fucked-up cousin and politician uncle's shady dealings with that same cartel. I'd read up and done my research on the

Juan Cartel and its many chapter leaders: Enrique Ortiz specifically. Getting caught would surely mean war. They wouldn't be safe down there. Hell, I wasn't sure if they'd ever be safe again if Ortiz ever got his hands on their personal information. Fuck, this whole thing was insane and a massive clusterfuck waiting to happen! I could feel it.

Panic struck me in that instant.

My breathing became choppy. My hands grew cold and sweaty. If I had a mirror, I was sure the color had drained from my face.

Is it hot in here?

"Babe?" Dalton sounded far away.

Why is the room spinning?

"Sweetheart?"

"She's gonna drop, D." This came from Theo.

Within seconds, I felt the warmth of Dalton's arms picking me up, then I gave into the darkness that seemed to have crept up on my periphery from nowhere.

I came to in Dalton's office, cradled against him on his lap.

"You're back," he murmured against my temple. "How are you feeling?"

I didn't want to tell him I was freaking out, although I figured it was pretty evident. I didn't want to say I felt guilt for leading my uncle to Dalton and his team in the first place. If it hadn't been for me, Dalton wouldn't be going off on this potentially deadly mission. I also didn't want to tell him I felt as though we'd missed something. Something crucial. Something that made me doubt my capability for this operation despite his utmost confidence in my skills.

No, I didn't tell him any of that.

He needed to focus.

For himself.

For his team.

Pasting a smile on my face, hoping to all hell I was convincing enough, I looked up at him and said, "I'm okay. Just a little overwhelmed is all."

He didn't seem entirely sold on my reassurances if the expression on his face was anything to go by. "You're sure?"

I nodded, then leaned up and kissed him.

I would be fine.

I had to be.

I would be the pillar of support the team needed—the eyes and ears to their brains and brawn—and I wouldn't fail.

Because failure was not an option.

twenty-nine

DALTON

"I NEED you to do me a favor," I told Theo, as I closed my office door behind us; after making sure Devolin had drunk some juice and had recouped enough from that panic attack of hers. I recognized the signs for what they were the moment they appeared. She wasn't fooling me one bit. Overwhelmed, my ass.

"What's up?" Theo asked.

"I need you to get Morgan to look in on Devolin while we're gone. I've got Skylar, but I think she'd be able to relate more with a woman who knows what it is to have someone she cares for on an intimate level leave on a mission. It might help her out."

Theo nodded. "That's a good idea. It might curb Dev's panic attacks. Does she have those often?"

"You caught that, huh? I don't know. This one was the first I've known about," I said. He nodded again, but I could tell he had something else to say. "What is it?"

"It's just..." he sighed. "She was great back when we were looking for Morgan last year. Trust me, no one will ever be more grateful for her help than I am, but are you sure she can manage this op?" The man was wondering the same thing I'd been asking myself since her episode less than an hour ago. "Things are different when the heart's involved. It's not the same and you know it. It clouds the judgement, fucks with the head."

Don't I know it. As a matter of fact, I had a permanent ache in my leg to remind me how matters of the heart fucked with one's head. All because of my ex-fiancée.

Running my hands through my hair, I interlaced my fingers behind my head, releasing a stress-filled sigh while staring down at my feet. "Call your wife up and give her Devolin's phone numbers and email. We leave in three hours. Make sure whatever loose ends you might have are tied up. I've got a few calls to make, and I need to speak with the guys. See where their heads are at."

"Sure thing." The man headed for the door, while I took my seat at my desk and picked up the phone's receiver. "And, D?" He was facing me when I looked up. "You might want to clear that head of yours, too. This shit's about to get tricky. We don't need no bad juju." He didn't wait for an acknowledgment, he walked out.

He was right. I needed to focus on this mission, our first foreign one as a group. One that could land us in deep water should we not be ready for anything.

After an hour of pulling each man into my office and going over the mission, reiterating contingency after contingency for any scenario that may come up, not to mention, gauging each team member's focus, I called Devolin in.

"I sent Miguel the details on the comms units you wanted," she said, as she entered and shut the door behind her. "He should have them in hand at your connection point."

"Good." I eyed the woman, trying to figure out what it was she was hiding. She hadn't been the same since she came to earlier: avoiding eye contact, body tense, and seemingly jumpy. Even around me. "Sit."

She let herself drop in the free chair across from my desk as I continued to study her with a critical eye. We'd deal with her shit after I'd finished dealing with mine.

"What's—"

"Why'd you meet up with Hewitt?" I asked the question that had been nagging at me since I'd found out about it yesterday.

She shrugged her shoulders. "He wanted to talk."

"Twice?" I snapped. "What could be so important it warranted two separate meetings?"

"It wasn't twice," she defended.

"That's a lie and you know it."

Her face grew red. "It wasn't!" she argued. "He brought me flowers the first time, then we had lunch the next."

"Why?" I demanded.

"He wanted to know why I left him high and dry." Her eyes narrowed on me. "He knows about you. He said—"

"Did he tell you we've investigated him on numerous occasions before?" I bit out. "His file is currently still open, by the way." I paused to gauge her reaction. "Did he tell you more about the dealings that, you yourself have admitted, gave you goosebumps because they seemed fishy?"

"Dalt—"

"Did he tell you about the file Bryce found on his computer, filled with shit about you?" I exploded.

Her jaw dropped. "I—"

"I'm talking emails, phone call recordings, texts, photos, Devolin. Photos of you outside your apartment. In front of my fucking house. What's worse, there are shots of you, sick in your hospital bed, sleeping. I should mention most of those were close-ups." She gasped at this. "It could have been a gun instead of a fucking camera lens and you wouldn't have been the wiser. There're photos as recent as last night at McAskill's."

"I didn't know!" She got up to her feet, panic in her eyes. "I didn't fucking know! Why didn't I know? I have my system at home set up to run a scan of his computer. It's supposed to ping my phone when something new pops up." Then her eyes widened as she connected imaginary dots. "He has another one I didn't know about, doesn't he?"

My nod was curt, then I got up to my feet and ground out, "What. Did. He. Say, Devolin?"

"Dalton..." She began to pace the front of my desk.

"What." I rounded the piece of furniture. "Did." When she was close enough, I grabbed her forearms to stop her. Her head shot up to look at me. "You tell him?" I demanded, giving her a shake.

Her eyes welled with tears. "I didn't say anything!"

"Bullshit!" I declared. "Think, Devolin. Think! It may seem inconsequential, but that man knows how to take the tiniest piece of scrap information and build something that'll take even the best down. Hell, you didn't even know he was having you followed. What did you say to him?"

"I had no idea how he got my address because I hadn't even submitted my change of address form yet," she whispered to herself. "Now it all makes sense."

"That's it, I'm calling Rex in."

"Who's Rex?"

"He's a man who owes me a favor. While I'm gone, he'll be with you the entire time."

"What?" she shrieked. "Why?"

"Have you not heard a single word I've said?" I gave her a perplexed look. "There's no denying the man is obsessed with you." I reached for the file sitting on my desk behind me, then handed it to her. "You think I'm lying about those photos, Devolin? Look for yourself." I gave her time to peruse the file's printed out content. I think I made my point, if the stricken and clearly disgusted expression on her face was anything to go by. Figuring she'd had enough, I took the file from her, and dropped it on the edge of my desk. "I could see separate eyelashes, fanned over your cheeks." My tone faded to one just above a whisper as I lifted a hand to cup her cheek. "While I'm away, I want you at home when you're not at the office. If anyone needs to see you, Rex will be with you for protection until I get back."

"Dalton—"

My thumb rubbed against her jaw to cover her lips and put a halt to her words. "I need you safe, sweetheart. I need my head in the game, and it can't be if I'm worried about you and what that asshole's agenda may be. He's dangerous, Dev, and he's fixated on you."

"When we had lunch," she began, leaning her cheek into my

hand. "I told him I was seeing someone. I didn't tell him who you were, but he knew. He came right out and said your name. He somehow knew I was working for you. When I confirmed it, he started asking me about you, the guys, what kind of stuff we did, if I'd seen some interesting things so far. I didn't give him any information on any of you and what goes on here. I just told him everything was confidential. He then asked for an example. When he realized I wasn't going to give into his cajoling, he asked me out on a real date. I said no. The less I gave him, the more agitated he seemed to get until he just stormed out of the deli, leaving me with the bill. I haven't heard from him since, I swear."

She wouldn't. Not if I could help it.

I pressed my forehead to hers, my hand moving from cupping her face to wrapping around the back of her neck.

"Anything else?" I whispered against her lips, brushing my mouth lightly over hers. She shook her head. "Thank you."

Her hands came up to my chest and pushed me back, her eyes narrowing on mine. "You're welcome, but next time, how about you ditch the caveman attitude from last night, and just now, and ask me what you want to know. Nicely. Didn't anyone ever tell you that you'd catch more flies with honey instead of vinegar?"

I snorted, before grabbing Devolin's arm and pulling her into my body hard enough to get an *oomph* from her.

"I can be sweet," I whispered against her ear, my hands rubbing her upper arms.

She tilted her head back to look up at me, brows arched. "Could have fooled me."

Wrapping my arms around her torso, my hands came to a stop as they cupped her jean-clad ass. "Can I make it up to you when I get back?"

Humor lit her eyes as she shrugged one shoulder. "Maybe."

"Maybe I can take you out on an official date?"

Her eyes warmed, her body melting into mine. "Maybe we can stay in and..." She let her words hang on her suggestive tone.

"Fuck me." I groaned, then dropped my head to nuzzle her nose. "I think I like your idea better, baby."

"Promise me you'll be careful," she whispered. "I'll be watching."

"I promise, I'll do everything I can to get back to you," I vowed.

"I promise to stay with Rex, ignore any communication that comes from Gordon, and do everything I can to make sure this op runs like a well-oiled machine," she said.

Someone's fist pounded on my door. "D, we need to head out."

Tightening my grip on her, I said, "Kiss me, Devolin," wishing we had more time so I could get a read on what was going through my woman's head. Last night's *heartbreaker* comment coming to mind.

"I thought I told you to ask—"

Laughing, I crashed my lips to hers. Pulling her in tight, she held on with all she had. I swallowed her moan, took in the taste, the feel of her, her scent. I memorized her. Imprinted her into my brain as deep as she already was in my heart.

Breathless, and trying to regain our faculties, Devolin whispered, "You should go," before sneaking in one last peck. "Be safe."

"You too, sweetheart." Kissing her forehead, I released her, then headed for the door before turning for one last look at her. "Bye," I rasped.

"Later, Kip." She winked.

thirty

I WATCHED as Dalton and his crew walked out of NSI's front entrance. Once that door latched shut behind them, I turned the deadbolt to the locked position like Theo had instructed me.

I found myself sitting at my desk, my brain running at a hundred miles an hour. Guilt filled me for lying by omission about how Dalton came across this latest case. Worry filled me about the possible dangers that the men's latest jaunt would hold for them. What was worse was the panic that had caused me to lose my shit earlier was threatening to take hold of me again.

"There was never a right time," I whispered to the room as if it was a proper justification for having remained mum about my family connections to this operation.

I knew Dalton wouldn't see it that way, though. Hell, I didn't see it that way. I knew I'd been given the opportunity to come clean just before he left. I could have told him right after I finished pouring my guts out about Gordon. If it were the other way around, I knew I'd be pissed at the man if he withheld important information from me.

With that final thought, I resolved that next time we spoke, which would be when he landed in Houston before connecting with their chartered helicopter, I'd come clean.

Until then, I ran a check of my monitoring systems to assure myself I was ready for when the boys needed me. I estimated another five hours or so before the men would reach their destination. Between now and then, because my gut told me something big was on the horizon, I'd make damn sure I hadn't missed a single thing.

Rex was a bear of a man. A very scary one at that.

When the man came calling at NSI's door, I asked him for his ID, feeling slightly embarrassed when he produced it without hesitation, a look of complete boredom strewn across his face. The approval in his eyes, however, was sign enough that I'd done well.

It turned out Rex wasn't much of a talker either.

I tried to engage him in conversation, but his answers were short, mostly provided with shoulder shrugs and grunts.

In truth, the last three hours in his company had been pure torture.

When my phone rang, I jumped at the chance to make contact with the outside world—a person that wouldn't mimic a fucking robot.

"Hello?"

"Devolin?"

"Who's this?" I asked the woman on the other end of the line.

"It's Morgan. Theo gave me your number earlier when he called to let me know they were on their way out," she explained. "How are you?"

"I'm good," I said, watching as Rex set his motorcycle magazine to the side and got up to do his rounds over the office floor again. That meant another hour had passed since his last check. Yes, I could tell what time it was simply by when the man would move. Clearing my throat, I added, "Much better now, thanks."

"I'm so glad..." Her voice trailed off as if she meant to continue but didn't.

"Is something the matter?" I asked.

"Uh, no. Not exactly," she said. "I...uh...called because I wanted to know if you'd like to join me for dinner."

"Uh—"

"It's just that I know how it feels to have your man take off to parts unknown. Then again, they're not unknown to you now, are they?" She giggled nervously. "I suppose it's probably harder for you to know where they are, and what's going on, and not being able to be there to help them." She sighed. I didn't voice how right the other woman was on that one. I figured I had enough to worry about instead of borrowing additional trouble. "What I'm saying is, after all these years, I've forgotten how it felt when my brother was deployed. Theo taking off—"

I was nodding in agreement throughout Morgan's rambling, then realized the woman wasn't there to see me, so I said, "I get it. It's only been a few hours and I'm sick with worry even though I know they're still up in the air."

Sick with worry didn't cover it. With everything lined up and ready to go, I was simply sitting there, watching my screens, then watching Rex watch me, and twiddling my thumbs. Hell, I'd even given up on playing Candy Crush on my phone. Every hour, when Rex went on his walkarounds, I'd pick up the phone and have Dalton's number half-dialed before I'd set the receiver back in its cradle. Maybe I could pick Morgan's brain on how to come clean to Dalton?

Turning my attention back to the conversation, I said, "I'll tell Rex. I'll be over in half an hour, is that okay?"

"Your ass gets here when it gets here, lady," she said, making me smile. "As for mine, it'll be digging out weeds in the green-house until you get here."

"You need me to bring anything?"

"Nah. We can order something when you get here, so long as you're up for it," she replied.

"Sounds good."

"Now answer me this one thing before I let you go. Who's Rex?"

"My new bodyguard," I said dryly. Before Morgan could ask, I added, "It's a long story. I'll tell you about it when I get there."

• • •

"What do you do, Rex?" Morgan asked, trying to engage the man, who'd yet to utter a single word since our arrival. We'd been there for a couple of hours now and it was after dinner.

"He doesn't talk," I supplied, as I rinsed the dishes we'd used for the pizza.

Morgan's eyes rounded, then studied the behemoth of male muscle standing by the back door, surveying the gardens and the rest of the surroundings.

I swore I saw his lips quirking up at the sides. Good Lord, it was a miracle!

"I talk," he rasped. He sounded like a smoker with a two-pack-a-day habit, but I suspected that the scar etched into his skin across his neck might have something to do with it. Rex's mild-humored expression faded as soon as he noticed my eyeing said scar.

"Then what do you do?" Morgan asked him again, while at the same time, my cell started ringing.

Drying my hands on the dishrag and setting it down, I reached into my back jeans pocket and pulled the device out, noticing the scrambled number that told me Dalton was calling from the satellite phone he'd brought with him. My heart started to race.

"Stay inside," Rex warned.

Nodding, I took a deep breath, slid my finger across the screen, and answered with a breathy, "Hey!"

"Sweetheart." I could hear the smile in his voice. "Everything okay?"

"I feel like I should be asking you that."

"We're good. In Houston. We're just waiting to board the bird."

"Bird?"

"Helicopter," he explained.

Suddenly, Rex burst out laughing in the kitchen. Then Morgan's giggle followed. How the fuck had she managed that? I'd tried everything to engage the man, but he'd remained steadfast and removed the entire time since his arrival.

"What the fuck?" Dalton snapped.

"I'm at Morgan and Theo's," I explained. "She invited me over, and since this might be the only break I have until this operation is over, I figured I'd take her up on her offer."

"I'm glad you did."

"I really like her, Kip," I whispered, my emotions getting the better of me. "And Theo, too. You've got some really great friends, baby."

"Everything okay?"

I nodded yes as I gave him the truth. "No."

It was time.

There was no turning back now.

thirty-one

DALTON

I WASN'T EXPECTING her to tell me that things weren't okay. Knowing Rex was there, because he was in between jobs right now, soothed the panic that would have built had she been entirely on her own.

"Dev, what's wrong?" I asked.

"I...I've got something I need to tell you," she confessed. "I should have told you this long before now."

"What is it?"

"You're not going to like it. I don't want secrets between us. Not like this," she rambled on. "A gift or some other kind of surprise is one thing—"

"Devolin," I snapped. "I need you to focus." Some of the guys were heading toward the helicopter and Preacher was finishing up with fueling the LongRanger. Preacher, our pilot, and I went a long way. Back to Kandahar to be exact, when he did supply drops. He now ran a charter and tour business out of Houston.

"It's about this mission, Dalton," she said.

Somehow, I knew what she was about to tell me. Hell, I'd found out during our twenty-minute drive to Albert J. Ellis, where we caught our first flight. Therefore, I told her as much. "I know."

"Huh?"

135

I sighed. "I know, babe." Then I continued, "I called Wentworth to give him a SITREP—a situation report. He came right out and said that he knew his niece would come through for him."

I heard her gasp. "He did?"

"Imagine my surprise. All this time, man refused to tell me who'd referred him," I explained. "It's not every day that a Canadian diplomat reaches out to some small American security firm, Devolin."

"You're not mad?" she squeaked.

Had I said no, I'd have been lying. At first, I'd been pissed off. Theo and Brycen both made me see reason pretty quickly, though. Shane, too. Hell, everyone who'd had a hand in Morgan's rescue jumped to defend my woman.

"I was," I paused, "but I'm not now."

I heard her relieved exhale over the line. "Please know, I never meant to hold out on you like that for this long," she said. "I just—"

"I get it."

"I asked him not to tell you," she admitted. "I wanted to let you know on my own. Fuck..." I could hear what sounded like her hand smacking against her forehead. "In fact, I had originally planned to tell you that day at Theo's when I went to find you. Afterward, time got away from me. From us. We talked about so much. I got caught up in us. I should have... There's no excuse, Kip. I'm sor—"

Her words warmed me, despite feeling her guilt radiating through the line.

"Sweetheart—"

"He's not a good man, Dalton," she whispered. "But he's family, and Nadia's a nice woman. Young. She's a few years older than me, but she didn't deserve what's happened to her. I regretted sending him to you almost right away."

I felt my brows knit together and curiosity got the better of me. "Then why'd you do it?"

"Because I knew you'd do everything you could to make sure she was safe." Her voice cracked. "My skills with computers aren't a secret in my family. When Uncle Max called to see if I could look into things, I knew I needed someone I could trust to help. I found out a lot of things, that both shocked me and didn't, about Max and Scott. That's why I came to you. That's why I said yes to working with you and the guys. I needed to make sure that I didn't fuck up by sending him your way. I didn't want you to be the one to pay for my stupidity."

"You're not stupid." I was firm about it, too.

"I needed to keep you safe. Even if I couldn't have you, I had to keep you safe." Her voice shook, and I could tell she was crying.

It killed me not to be there to console her. "Babe..." my voice trailed as I tried to find the right words.

"Now that I have you, I don't want to lose you, Kip." Her breath hitched. "I—"

That's when I knew it was time to address my earlier concerns.

"Devolin, listen to me," I said with determination. "You're not going to lose me. I'm not losing anyone on this team, and that includes you. There's a lot going on, and emotions are running high right now. Thank you for telling me. This is why you were acting weird after your panic attack earlier, isn't it?"

"Uh...yeah."

Brycen clapped me on the back as he passed me and got into the bird. I was the only one aside from Preacher, who was running through his pre-flight checklist, left to board.

"Right. Okay." I sighed. "Sweetheart, I have to go."

"It's okay," she sniffled.

"Will you be alright?" I needed to make sure her head was in the game.

"I'm fine. Go, baby," she said, the smile back in her voice. "I don't want the guys waiting because of me."

Smiling too, I said, "I'll call again when we land next. Until then, promise me something."

"Anything," she breathed through the line.

"Get your head back in the game, baby," I told her as the prop motor started up, "because we're going in hot, and I'm not planning on wasting time to get back to you."

"O-okay, Kip."

"Hey, D!" Theo yelled over the noise.

"Gotta go, babe," I said. "Love you." Then I hung up.

thirty-two

"LOVE YOU."

He'd told me he loved me, then hung up. I hadn't had the time to reciprocate. Hell, I didn't even have the time to say goodbye.

He loves me.

Or maybe he didn't. Maybe it was just the emotions running high. Maybe it was just habit.

I had no doubt that the man cared for me. But love? We've had a connection for well over a year.

You only just met. How's it possible that he'd feel that way so soon?

I knew how.

As much as I'd fought the attraction, as much as I rebelled against the idea of finding my own happily ever after, I knew. He was mine, just as I was his.

What did that mean for me—for us—in the long run?

My legs gave way, my ass barely making contact with the edge of the couch cushion beneath me, as the truth stared me in the face.

Fish or cut bait.

Skylar's words from a few weeks back.

It hadn't just been about my job. It had been about Dalton, too.

Smiling, I made a monumental decision. There would be no

more picking and choosing the parts I gave to Dalton. I was going all in. If the man truly loved me, he deserved all of me. Not a quarter. Not half or three-eighths. All. Of. Me. I wasn't quite sure if I could say I was in love with the man as of yet, but I knew I was falling for him and hard.

"What's that smile all about?"

"Morgan!" I shrieked, nearly falling off the couch. "You scared the fuck out of me."

She gave me an apologetic look. "You left so fast, looking like you were heading to your funeral. When I couldn't hear you talking anymore, and you didn't come back, I decided to check on you. Was that Dalton?"

I nodded, unable to keep the smile from spreading on my face.

"What'd he say? Or can you talk about it?"

"They're up over San Antonio most likely," I said, then decided to let Morgan in a bit more. "I left that way because I had something to talk to him about. It wasn't good, and he needed to know about it."

Morgan's gaze narrowed on me, brows arching toward her forehead. "Is that why you were playing that hypothetical game with me earlier?"

"Yeah." My blush suffused my face. "The funny thing is, I expected him to blow up, but he was fine."

"Well that's good."

"Mm-hmm," I mumbled. "He already knew what I had to tell him."

That's when I decided to come clean with Morgan, telling her all about my familial link to the Canadian politician, his abducted beauty queen of a fiancée, and his addict son.

Morgan's enthralled expression was rather comical when I'd finished regaling her with my tale.

I had no idea what possessed me to bare my soul to her, other than the fact that she was genuinely a good person. Much like Skylar and Tamara, she was a ball of energy and hilarious to boot. Not like the other two, however, she had this talk-to-me demeanor that required little to no effort on her part for me to give into.

That meant that I talked myself silly, sharing a bit more about myself, my life, my family, and how I got into hacking.

Morgan shared too, which made me feel that much more secure in the budding friendship we were developing.

"He told you he loves you?" Morgan choked out, eyes wide to the point she looked like she'd swallowed something massive and it got lodged in her throat.

My hand waved at the air as if Dalton's words were inconsequential. "I'm sure it was just a slipup."

"I've only known him for a little over a year, but girl..." She simply let her words hang as she sucked in her bottom lip.

"It's strange, isn't it?" I said, pondering aloud. "I mean, we've known each other for as little as three weeks, then wham!"

Morgan wore the largest grin I'd ever seen. In a matter of seconds, it disappeared before I was met with the other woman's intent gaze. "Dev, no one knows if it's too quick but the two people in the relationship. Hell, I knew I loved Theo within two weeks!"

"You're shitting me, right?"

The woman shook her head. "It's funny how people are brought together." Morgan paused to think over her next words before sharing them. "Theo and I had a lot going on when we first met. My house," she waved her hand all around her, "was in shambles, thanks to a leak in my roof. I called around, but no one was answering until I remembered a friend of mine mentioning Theo's company. Late on a Friday evening, I was shocked when he answered, delighted he was popping by. I think I might have contributed to the accumulating moisture on my floor with the drooling I did when he made it through my front door." She wagged her brows up and down, causing me to burst into giggles.

"He is pretty easy on the eyes, isn't he?"

"Mm-hmm." Morgan winked. "What I'm saying is that we didn't rush to get to how we felt. It just happened. Shit hit the fan all around us: first the flood, then my house being vandalized, Theo's, across the road, was burned down...and then there was the kidnapping. We had no choice but to fight together. We knew we were stronger that way."

"But I—"

Morgan leaned forward and covered my clasped hands. "I know you're going to say that you chose to keep watch over us this past year. I know you're convinced the only reason you're here is because all this is your fault. It's not, Devolin. It never was."

"I wasn't—"

"Your uncle took that trip with his woman and his son. He's the one with the shady dealings. And he's the one who came to you for help. All you did was go with your gut on a recommendation, and you weren't wrong in doing so. Dalton is a solid choice," she said.

"Dalton's just so..."

"Gorgeous? Sweet? Smart? Charming? Did I mention gorgeous?" Morgan supplied on a giggle after the last.

I shook my head, laughing along with her. "I was going to go with high-handed, abrupt, and scary to name a few, but your list is much better." And it was all true. "What you said is why I love the Neanderthal."

"You love him?" Morgan got up, then started shimmying her hips in some sort of Funky Chicken styled happy dance.

Rex poked his head into the room, smirking at the crazy lady, then peered at me where I proceeded to roll my eyes at him right before he ducked out of view once more.

Later that night, Rex shocked the hell out of me as we rode the elevator up to my floor. "Solid man that Dalton," he said.

My head snapped up to look at him. Feeling my gaze on him, he peered down at me and gifted me with a brief smile. A smile!

"In our line of work, a lot of shit can go down. Do him and yourself a favor, doll. Make sure you tell him," he rasped the last, then turned to face forward again.

"Tell him what?"

The man sighed, then gave me that you-know-what look before focusing on the opening elevator doors.

As he exited the elevator, me falling in step beside him, he repeated, "Tell him, Devolin."

I watched Rex from the corner of my eye, seeing through his alert expression. I knew it wasn't my business, but I couldn't help but be curious about what the man had been through to put that haunted look in his eyes. I was pretty sure it had something to do with that scar though.

thirty-three

DALTON

KNOWING DEVOLIN WOULD BE SLEEPING, I pulled up Rex's contact.

"'Lo?"

"It's Dalton. All good?"

"For now," he said.

"Does she know about anything?"

"No. She didn't even realize she had a tail on her throughout the day." He yawned into the phone. "The fucker called a few times, sent texts. I managed to hide the envelope someone slid under her apartment door when we got back from her friend's place, though. Sick fuck."

That meant he'd looked inside the package. I'd already seen the texts, thanks to Brycen, who'd hacked into Devolin's phone and worked his magic. Now, instead of Devolin receiving her old boss's calls and texts, Brycen, Rex, and myself were receiving them.

"He's got cameras in here too, D," he continued. "I've got pictures to prove it. Just so you know, I'm having Stan install a security system in here."

"Get him to install his best," I ordered. "I'll cover it. Now tell me, what was in the envelope?"

"Your ugly ass for one," he growled, "and then some."

A smile crept onto my face despite the burning rage festering in my gut. "Have you done anything about the cameras yet?"

"Fuck yeah, I did. Took me some maneuvering, but I convinced your girl to take a bath to unwind. She was looking wired. I found and dismounted the two in her bedroom while she was in the tub. Did the one in the bathroom's air return before that, just so you know. I searched the rest of her place after she went to bed. Found two high-tech ones with zooms pointed right at her computers in her office, one in her kitchen, two more in the living room," he listed. "She doesn't know about them. I shoved them in a trash bag, smashed everything out on her balcony and dumped it into her kitchen garbage. I'll take care of that when we leave for NSI later."

"Fuck!" I took a calming breath. "You know things are going to escalate now that we've taken away his eye candy, right?"

Rex groaned. "A simple babysitting job this ain't no more, brother."

No, it wasn't.

So, I had to ask, "Are you okay with this? I know—"

"Get your shit done, then get your ass back home to your woman," the man grumped.

"Anything else?"

"Nope."

"Later, then," I said, then hung up. "Yo, Babyface?" I yelled out to Brycen, turning to the men still standing by the LongRanger.

"Yo!"

"ETA on our ride?"

"Ten minutes out."

Right. That meant I had time to call my woman.

"Kip?"

My dick jumped in my black fatigue pants. "You have no idea what that sleepy, sultry voice of yours does to me, baby," I told her.

"Mmm," she purred. "Are you in?"

"Landed. Miguel is ten minutes out with our SUVs. Once they get here, the guys and I are going to go over the equipment and make sure Miguel got everything we need. Might sneak in a few hours of shut-eye, then we head out."

"I'm going to get Rex and we'll go in right away." She sounded much more awake now. "I can see if there's an updated map from the satellites."

"Babe," my shoulders shook as I laughed internally, "our phones automatically update with the most recent shit. You made sure of that."

"Right," she paused. "I should probably check the coding to make sure that I didn't miss something."

"Dev?"

"Yeah," she whispered.

"Everything will be alright," I tried my best to reassure her. "We'll deal with things as they come. If going into the office will make you feel better, then go ahead. If we run into something, we'll all be connected to you. You'll be able to feed us the real-time info as we need it, and if something seems fishing, you'll let us know then, too."

"Okay, Kip," she said in that sleepy voice of hers. She seemed much more relaxed now.

"In the meantime, if you decide to head into the office early, Bryce's sent you something. With the perks of in-flight Internet, he was dicking around on his computer, and it looks like he might have found an in on Ortiz," I told her.

"What kind of an in?" The excitement in her voice was palpable.

"His email account," I said. "Looks like your phishing scam idea paid off, sweetheart."

"What do you mean?"

"Brycen decided to try a little something after I told him about your gut feeling that we were missing something. Once he hooked Ortiz, he whaled him," I announced.

The woman burst out laughing. "Babe, you should stay away from hacker terminology," she gasped between giggles. "You meant a whaling attack?"

"Yeah," I chuckled. "Anyway, he sent you a bunch of the guy's login credentials. I'm going to need you to go through those, see if you can access his emails, and keep us posted on what you find."

"I'll give you more than that," she said, determination lacing her words. "Let's just hope I have enough time."

"Okay, sweetheart." The crunch of tires over gravel had me turning to find two Range Rovers approaching. "Babe, I've got to go."

"Be safe, Kip," she said.

"You too, babe," I said. Then threw in, "Love you," for the second time in less than twelve hours, before hanging up without waiting to hear her answer, or her goodbye.

The first time I'd said it, I hadn't meant to, but once the words were out, I belatedly realized I'd meant them. Completely. This time, I consciously said the words, testing them on my tongue as they came out. Hanging up the way I did though, was a pussy move. I wasn't quite ready to deal with her refuting my feelings or to feel like I was pressuring her to say the words back to me either. I simply wanted her to know.

thirty-four

DEVOLIN

HE'D SAID IT AGAIN.

And he'd hung up on me again, too.

It had been just after three in the morning when Dalton called. I'd spent the next few hours laying there tossing and turning, thinking of how I'd go about to work with the information that Brycen had dug up on Ortiz.

Since work and Dalton dominated my thoughts, I called it quits on getting any more sleep by five a.m.

Jumping out of bed, I made a beeline for the bathroom. It wasn't until I was rinsing the conditioner out of my hair that I noticed how the air return vent looked off-kilter. I didn't think anything of it, aside from making a mental note to straighten the thing when I had time.

Maybe I'll get Rex to fix it.

Making quick work of dressing, choosing my comfy yoga pants over jeans and a loose-fitting tank, layered with a hooded zip sweater, I made my way to the kitchen.

"Morning, Rex," I said, as I grabbed the carafe from the coffee maker, poured out yesterday morning's dregs into the sink, then gave it a good wash.

All I got from the man was a grunt.

Turning to face him, after pulling the coffee grinds and a new filter down from the upper cabinet, I noticed how tired he looked. "You didn't take the pullout in my office, did you?"

He shook his head to indicate the negative, dry scrubbing his face.

"I know it's early, and I'm not much of a breakfast person, but if you want—"

"Just coffee," he replied. "Black." Then he disappeared into the hall, closing the bathroom door behind him.

An hour later, I was at my desk, studying what Brycen had done to get to Ortiz. It had all started with a shelf-baby. Plainly speaking, a shelf-baby is a digital identity that is created, and then made to look like it's led a full life before using that identity for nefarious purposes. Case in point, to lure Ortiz into providing information he wouldn't think twice of providing a site he was familiar with, like his login information.

It's surprising how much illegal business goes on online, right beneath everyone's noses. Hell, I once read in the paper that a woman had been stabbed and nearly died, had it not been for the 7-Eleven clerk that saw the whole thing, and called 911. She'd tried to sell a purse online and had agreed to meet the buyer in the store's parking lot. He'd asked her to wrap the Coach purse she was selling in red paper. She had no idea that *Coach* was code for cocaine, and that red had something to do with the quantity of said product.

See? Even something so innocent can be dangerous.

I kept sifting through Brycen's work. From that false identity he'd created, all it took was a Backdoor Trojan sent to Ortiz's inbox, made to look like a message notification coming from a site he visited weekly to conduct some of his business.

It was what I would call a Hail Mary Hack. The reason being that the email was coming from a different server, which meant had Ortiz's email security settings been programmed to the highest level, the hack would have never worked, seeing as the email would have made its way to his junk mail and been purged within a matter of twenty-four hours, or however frequently he'd set his purge settings.

But it had worked which made it a massive break for the team and me.

Once Ortiz logged into the mirror image of the site to retrieve his message however, the Trojan got straight to work, populating Brycen with so much information. Information I was now responsible to sift through.

The first thing I noticed was that he had multiple email addresses and profiles. I set forth for a brute force attack, attempting every password combination to get in, starting with the one Ortiz had provided on that spoofed site.

By the time the monitor on my far upper left pinged with a visual popup that the men's comms units were active, I put my earpiece in and turned it on.

"Morning, sunshine!" I chimed. "I need a roll call so I know everyone's devices are working."

"Hey, babe," Dalton went first, chuckling. Someone snickered, then each man announced himself. Even Preacher, who'd opted to join them, and Miguel, Dalton's Mexican law enforcement friend chimed in.

It took some work, but I managed to narrow things down to three buildings that Nadia was most likely being held in—one of which being the main house.

The compound housed thirteen buildings on farm acreage. The Juan Cartel was known for its drug trading quite prolifically. Their drugs of choice: cocaine, heroine, methamphetamines, and marijuana. They were also involved in money laundering, prostitution, and human trafficking along the West Coast waterways, usually through California's various ports. The drugs, however, were being run throughout the U.S. at an alarming rate, and the DEA was having a field day collaborating with the Mexican military and law enforcement.

"This would work so much better if the power went out," I heard Shane state.

"Brycen?" I called out.

"What's up?"

"You think you can get onto your computer and access the grid to shut it down? I can't do it from here," I told him.

"Sure."

"I'll guide you through it now so you can when the time comes," I told him.

The man was tapping away at the keys on his laptop. "Giv'er, Huss," he chuckled.

"Funny," I snorted. "I should call you my script kiddie."

"Now, now," he chided. "I may be at a lower level of talent in the hacking world, but I can still best you in programming if I wanted to." Meaning I'd accused him of only being proficient while using someone else's codes and not creating any of his own.

I barked a laugh. "We'll see, kiddo."

thirty-five

DALTON

DAY 1

DAYLIGHT BROKE SHORTLY after our arrival, which meant we'd spend the day doing reconnaissance.

Satellite imagery was an asset during missions such as this one, but being able to physically circle the grounds, even at a distance, and getting the lay of the land had its perks. We were able to get a feel for how Ortiz ran his operation: how many enforcers per building, shift changes, generally getting a pulse on everyone's habits.

We spent most of our time in the woods outside the compound, exchanging information over our comms units about the goings on surrounding the three buildings we suspected our mark was being held in.

Ortiz and a few of his higher-level enforcers had been sighted. They'd taken off together in some old, rusted out military Jeep right at dusk.

"Everyone ready to go in when I give the signal?" I asked. "Remember, tonight's strictly a recon effort. We're going in, checking things out, then getting the hell out of Dodge. If you get a visual on Ms. Alvarez, let me know. We'll regroup, then decide what to do from there. No one's playing hero tonight, got it?"

I heard a slew of *copys* and *Roger thats*.

"Uh, Kip?"

"Yeah, Huss?" I had reverted to her old nickname for this operation. It was easier to keep things platonic. Most of the guys called her that or a variation of it, instead of using her first name.

"I'm running an infrared imaging software on the live satellite feed over here, and based on what I'm seeing, the two warehouse buildings you're about to check out are empty," she said. "The house, however..."

"Okay, boys, you heard the lady," I said. "T, Shane, Preacher, and Miguel, you guys are up on Building F. Cade, Tate, Babyface, and I will take Building H. Once you've cleared the outside, you may enter, but I want your eyes on everything. Huss, I want to know the second you think someone's onto us. With what we've seen over the last fourteen hours, if anything looks unusual, I want to know about it. Got it?"

"Copy."

Half an hour later, I gave the all-clear to move out.

"All clear outside Building F," Theo, the lead in his group, said ten minutes later. "Going in, now."

My team and I cleared the perimeter of our building a few minutes after Theo's. "All clear outside H," I declared.

There were two points of entry on both buildings we were searching. I pulled up the schematics on my phone, the men huddling around me to study the floorplan. Tate picked the locks on the door facing the woods, then stood back.

I entered first, my Glock drawn. My eyes began to water immediately, and my nose burned. I'd just walked into a lab.

"Masks on," I ordered, taking mine from my cargo's thigh pocket, sliding the half mask on. We'd just have to deal with the stinging eyes for the time being.

It didn't take long to figure out the place was deserted, but it left me surprised that it was. My gut started churning, my brain telling me we needed to get the fuck out of there.

"Theo, we're out. All we have here is a lab. Meet at our rendezvous point."

"Check," the man said. "Wish I could say the same, boss."

Him calling me boss had my hackles rising.

"SITREP, T," I told him.

"There's something wrong with the schematics Huss gave us for this building," he explained. "I know walls can be torn and floorplans can change, but there seems to be missing a good fifty square feet to the back of this place."

"That's impossible," Devolin said. "I compared the satellite images to the floorplans. The measurements match." She sighed. "Hold on." Seconds later, we could hear her furiously tapping away at a keyboard. "Fuck."

"Talk to me, Huss," I growled.

"I just found another set of plans. Looks like Ortiz had some kind of underground bunker designed a few years back. Found them in his email folders—it's never been logged with an inspector, or some sort of authority. I'm sending them to your phones right now," she said.

"T, we're coming in," I said. "We don't know what you're getting into, but a bunker doesn't say anything good."

"I agree," the man said.

It turned out the bunker was one of the cartel's merchandise storage and packaging points. And I had been right in joining in the fun. Two men were standing guard. We wondered why Devolin's infrared didn't catch them, but she explained that infrared was only good for surface heat. Apparently, if you're far enough underground, you can't spot a heat location. Judging by the number of stairs we took down, I'd estimated we were a solid fifteen feet below the floor above us.

The two enforcers we'd encountered were taken down. This wasn't a kill mission, since we were civilians, but when someone whips out a gun, you shoot first and ask questions later.

Not wanting to give ourselves away, we brought the bodies

with us, then dumped them outside of the compound, away from our rendezvous point.

DAY 2

We spent the day much like the one before, scoping out Ortiz and his men. Suffice to say, Ortiz seemed to notice the absence of the two guys we took out last night. The boys and I were forced to move back, which put a wrench in our surveying plans, because he'd had men patrolling the compound perimeter.

By nighttime, we were ready to take our last target—the large house.

Ortiz was present tonight. Then again, so were dozens of others. It looked as if the man was having a party by all the high-end vehicles parked all around.

"Huss, d'you manage to get any details on our guests here?" I asked her.

"You've got some high-rollers in there tonight," she said. "I'm talking police force officials, a U.S. Senator, most of the others are CEOs and business owners. A mix of Mexican and American."

"He's having a sale," Tate stated, disgust heavy in his words.

"Could be a sampling," Cade surmised.

A pain-filled cry by a female rented the air.

"Girls," was Shane's hypothesis.

I concurred.

"What's our infrared look like, Huss?" I asked.

"Looks to be groupings of two to four in various rooms. I have a large grouping with weak signatures. I'd be willing to bet that those are coming from a shallow basement," she said.

I bit my lip, then asked my next question. "Any available entry points?"

"Front door only," she said. "I'm sending you an image of what I'm seeing right now."

Seconds later, my phone chimed with Devolin's text. One look said that it would be possible, but there'd be no way we'd get out of there without being found.

My hand was forced. "Pull back," I gritted through my teeth.

"We could——" Brycen started, but with one look from me, he halted.

"Pull back," I repeated. "We'll try again tomorrow."

DAY 3

A complete clusterfuck. We were forced to sit back and wait again.

DAY 4

It seemed like the inside of the house was always bursting at the seams with people at night, so in the interest of getting the fuck back home with our mark in tow, I sent Shane and Theo to check things out during the day. That large heat signature—the weak one Devolin had found—hadn't moved or cleared from her screen since our arrival.

"We're in," Shane whispered over the line.

"Found the basement," Theo added. "Going in."

A few minutes later, I heard all hell break loose. At first, I heard some guy yell out what sounded like, "What the fuck!" in Spanish, then two other males joined the fray. The distinct sound of a gun going off with a silencer on it could be heard, just moments before a regular gunshot rented the air.

"Leave one of them alive, guys," I said. "We need to ask them about Ms. Alvarez."

Then everything went silent.

"T? Shane?" I asked through the grunting noise.

No answer.

"T? Shane, do you copy?" I repeated.

"We're gonna need backup," Shane said. "I'm counting eighteen women here. The fucker's got them in a large cell."

Caged like animals.

My blood boiled. "Any sign of Alvarez?"

"Nothing," the two men said at the same time.

"Get those women to talk, T," I said. "I'm coming in. We need to get this done before the shift change."

DAY 5

Leaving those women behind had been the hardest thing I ever had to do. Eighteen women sharing a single toilet. No beds, just a pillow and blanket each. A single meal a day—usually bread and water. There wasn't even enough room for them to lay down all at once. They'd been held captive ranging from three months to ten days for the most recent arrival. What made me sick was that they'd all stated a woman had played a part in their capture—Nadia Alvarez to be more precise when we'd shown her picture from one of the guys' cell phone.

As to whether our mark was a partner, or she'd been coerced and threatened to cooperate with Ortiz, remained to be seen. Devolin was now tasked in digging into Nadia's past to see if we'd missed something. Until she came up with concrete proof, we were treating this operation as it originally was: a kidnapping rescue. That also meant that we were sitting back yet again and evaluating which ones of our options was still viable, and which ones to scrap due to this new turn of events. The waiting also allowed us to come up with some new contingencies as well.

DAY 6

It took most of the night before Devolin could find concrete proof that Nadia Alvarez had ties to the Juan Cartel. Turned out, her father had been an arresting officer during a raid of the compound back when she was in the States, living with an aunt and uncle, while in college. The pageant world sure as hell had worked out for her.

The aunt and uncle had passed, a little over two years ago in a carjacking, while visiting family in their native country.

The more Devolin dug up, the more Nadia appeared as a woman scorned in search of revenge. The pieces of the grand puzzle were coming together, and it was becoming clear quite quickly that Minister Wentworth and his son had both been used —at least initially—as peons in Alvarez's quest to get to Ortiz.

Rustling in the trees behind me had me freeze. The distinct

sound of a hammer cocking back on a pistol had my blood turning to ice.

In what felt like a lifetime, but was only seconds, a muffled woman's squeal made me jump into action, only to find our mark held against Tate's chest, his hand over her mouth, his other arm wrapped tight around her torso.

The man wore a shit-eating grin. "Mark secured, boss."

thirty-six

"MIGUEL?" Nadia whispered as the man came into view. "Oh no! No, no, no, no, no! Take me back," she demanded, her Spanish accent quite thick. "If he finds out I'm in with the cops, I'm as good as dead."

She tried to get up off the hotel bed, but I halted her movement. "When he finds out you've been playing him this entire time, you'll be good as dead, too," I told her.

"He's right, you know," Miguel chimed in, her shoulders tensing under my hand. "Your best chance at survival here is to give us what you have on Ortiz and his operation, and let us do our jobs. Dalton," he motioned toward me with a tilt of his head, "is only here to take you back to Wentworth."

Her eyes rounded. "I'm not going back there!"

"We'll talk about that later," I said. "First, you're going to give Miguel all the information he needs, then we'll talk about returning you to your fiancé."

"What about the women?" she shrieked.

"We'll get to that in a bit," Miguel reassured her. "Right now, I need to know about your affiliation with Ortiz. How deep are you in with him, Ms. Alvarez?"

. . .

Nadia had gone quiet after copping to being the lure for the women Ortiz had kidnapped, by acting like the damsel in distress, a perfect act to prey on her fellow womankind. She'd provided Miguel with Ortiz's associates, as well as various ports he'd used to ship the women out to their buyers. Unfortunately, she was unable to provide us with buyer information, but she had mentioned that Ortiz carried his laptop with him everywhere he went. She was sure he had buyer history stored on the device. As much as Ortiz loved having her around, she was never allowed to mix and mingle with the rich men that would come to sample the *product.*

"I love him, you know," she whispered. "Max. I'd seen him with Ortiz a few times, and I knew he'd be an easy in. He came off as a pompous self-serving jerk at first, but he isn't that kind of man." She pressed her lips together before continuing. "I didn't know Scott was in with Ortiz, though. That's why I can't go back. Ortiz will know that I double-crossed him. Scott will tell him. He hates his father, so it won't take much for him to turn. I can't risk Max's life by going back there."

"That won't matter when Enrique Ortiz ends up in jail," Theo supplied as he entered the room with food.

The woman looked at Theo as if he had three heads.

"That man can get to anyone and everyone when he wants to."

"Wentworth will be in his own cell by the end of this too, Nadia," Miguel stated. "And I'm not going to lie, once they're done with you in Canada, since your crimes are here, you'll be brought back. You've been cooperative, and that'll help you out, but I make no promises you won't see the inside of a cell yourself."

The woman nodded. "I knew that might happen. I'm okay with it. I'm just sad it all had to lead to Max's career being finished. I didn't mean to—"

"You didn't do this to him." Theo crouched down in front of her, a sympathetic expression on his face, then reached into the brown paper bag in his hand and pulled out a sandwich, handing it to her. "He did this to himself by being involved with a known cartel head."

Her nod was curt as she fiddled with her lunch's wrapping.

"There's no way Max can hide from this when the authorities

go in. It's not going to be tonight, but I expect that he'll be apprehended within the next few days," Miguel explained to her.

Setting her sandwich down, she got up and walked toward the hotel room's only window. Releasing a sigh filled with defeat, she whispered a watery-sounding, "I know."

Giving the woman time, I turned to Theo, then asked, "The guys get off okay?" as I dug into my lunch.

Preacher had taken Shane, Cade, Brycen, and Tate back stateside so they could fly home before coming back for myself and Nadia, who wasn't done with Miguel's debrief. Theo had stuck around, not only of his own volition but Morgan had served to enforce this decision.

"Yeah."

It was eight the next morning by the time Nadia and I awaited our transfer that would take us from Washington to Ottawa. We'd left at three in the morning, hopping on Preacher's bird, which took us to Houston, barely making it on the next flight out.

Theo was already up in the air, on his way back home.

Home.

I so badly wanted to be there. With Devolin. In bed.

I didn't care if we were naked or clothed, I just wanted her in my arms. I'd missed that woman something fierce, despite having her voice at my constant disposal this entire week. Not having spoken to her in nearly twenty-four hours, I was going crazy trying to get a hold of her at this very moment, and she wasn't answering. Considering it was early in the morning for her to be out and about, I immediately hung up, then dialed Rex's number.

"She's fine," he answered. "We're at that lady, Morgan's, place again. Call me crazy, brother, but playing in the dirt at the ass crack of dawn is not my idea of a good Sunday morning."

It wasn't one of mine either, but I couldn't help imagining what Devolin would look like in Morgan's gardens, smudges of dirt on her cheeks, smelling of earth and the sweetness that came from the flowers.

Trying to keep my musings for when I was traveling alone, I cleared my throat, sticking to the business at hand.

"Anything else since we last talked?" That had been more than a couple of days ago now.

"She had me fix the vent above her shower," he said. "It must have slid a bit after I removed the camera, and she noticed it."

"And?"

"When the guys got back last night, Devolin was still working on her computers. Brycen came in and dropped an envelope on her desk." I had a feeling of where this was heading, and I knew it wasn't going to be good. "She opened it."

"And?"

"I think this is why we're here so early this morning," Rex said. "She told me she was concerned about Morgan being out here alone during her pregnancy. She doesn't know I read the letter after she thought she'd tucked it away in her desk. The other woman and her husband have both been mentioned."

"Theo?"

"Yeah," he confirmed.

"Fuck!" I punched my thigh, garnering attention from a few passengers milling about, along with Nadia's concerned gaze meeting mine. I shook my head, giving her a wave of my hand to let her know I was fine. "I'll be there as soon as I can. Letting you go now. I need to get a message to Theo before he lands so he knows what to expect."

"Got it," he said. "Later."

I disconnected.

thirty-seven

AN EAR-PIERCING SHRIEK rented the air, making me jump from my Dalton-induced-daze.

Next thing I knew, Morgan sent her shears flying and was up and running through the backyard in her too-big-for-her-small-feet rubber boots, gardening gloves and all, the imagery so comical that I forgot about my panic and started laughing.

That's when I noticed the truck coming to a halt in the driveway next to my car.

Theo was home.

My heart beat at a staccato pace at the sheer excitement the moment exuded.

The second the man's feet hit gravel, he sprinted toward his wife, catching her as she leapt with another shriek into his arms, their lips meeting in a fierce welcome home that made me feel like an interloper.

Pausing to grab my and Morgan's baskets, as well as the shears my friend had chucked ten feet away, I proceeded toward the reuniting couple, noticing Rex leaning against the front porch, taking in the scene just like I was.

"Oh God, you reek!" Morgan gagged, but her arms were still firmly wrapped around his neck, her legs around his waist. "Where the hell have you been? Why didn't you call when you landed? I would have—"

Theo slammed his lips back onto Morgan's then pulled away. "Shut up, woman," he growled. "Please tell me that you're done for the day. I haven't seen or spoken to my wife in a week. I've barely slept because I worried about her and our baby. I've been told I smell bad, which means I need to hose myself down before thinking about going into my house to take a shower and spend the rest of the day sinking myself deep inside my wife to remind her of how much I love her."

Thinking it best to announce my presence, least I heard something more they didn't mean for me to hear, I cleared my throat. "I guess we're done here for today?"

Morgan began giggling into her husband's shoulder.

Theo spun around grinning from ear to ear. "Well, if it isn't our little Hussy!"

I could feel the blush spreading over my face. "You can stop calling me that now that you know my name, Theo."

"You'll always be Hussy or Huss to us, Devolin," he told me.

Feeling shy, despite all we'd been through together, I nodded while staring at my feet. "I'm glad you're back safe," I whispered.

The operation was now deemed a closed case, but I hadn't heard from Dalton in nearly twenty-four hours now, and that had me worried.

Oh, I knew that he was on his way to drop Nadia off into Canadian officials' custody, but I'd expected at least one call from the man, or even a few words in a text.

"I—I guess I should get going. Morgan, give me a call if you need me." Meeting Theo's gaze, I forced a smile, then turned to leave.

"Hey, Dev?" I turned to acknowledge Theo. "He's okay."

Relief was potent, but seeing as I wasn't quite sure what was going on, I figured a look of indifference would be more appropriate. Something about the way Theo sized me up though, told me he wasn't fooled one bit.

Shaking it off, I waved to both Morgan and her man, jumped in my car, finding Rex already buckled in the passenger seat, then drove off.

"He called," Rex said in that gruff voice of his.

"Hmm?" I mumble absently. I was busy piling slices of meat and cheese, along with whatever else my fridge had to offer, onto the sandwiches I was making for lunch.

"Dalton called," he said again.

"What are you talking about?" I turned to pick up my phone, intent on showing him that the man in question hadn't when I stopped dead, to see the ten unanswered calls.

All from Dalton.

"You left your phone in the car's console," he reminded me.

I had.

But it still didn't explain why I hadn't heard from him until just this morning.

Call me crazy. Maybe it was that I'd finally gotten myself some for the first time in my life, and when I did, the man left for another country, where I had to sit back and curb the urge to upchuck whenever he was in a dangerous situation. Okay, so it's his job, I knew that. Maybe it was that we had yet to discuss where we stood with one another, despite the man's two proclamations of love. Hell, maybe it was that I was one of those needy bitches I swore I'd never be. When it came down to Dalton, I've never been able to think or act rationally.

Or maybe it's because you know something is up around here, and somehow you think Dalton knows all about it and he hasn't said anything as of yet?

I'd caught the long studying looks Rex had been giving me over the last week. I'd even caught the tail end of a conversation between the man and Dalton once, too. The way Rex had rushed out of my apartment to get rid of the trash the other day. The way he obsessively stared at my hand last night when Brycen had handed me that letter, as if he didn't want me to read it because he knew who it was from.

Choosing to go for nonchalant, I put my phone back onto the counter and said, "He did," before turning to our food once more.

It was early Sunday night, and I was tired of the day, wanting to see the end of it. So, I bedded down early.

After lunch, I had tortured myself by listening to Dalton's three voicemails then promptly erased them, sending him a text that all was okay. Then I'd powered my cell off and unhooked my landline for the remainder of the day.

I even stayed away from Rex, giving him free range to my apartment, while I perused my book collection and settled for a sweet romance, something I didn't normally read. I preferred the hot and dirty. The alpha male that knew what he wanted and brought it out in his woman. Being in a morose mood, one where I didn't see any hearts and flowers coming my way anytime soon, I figured I'd get it from a book.

The only time I left the comfort of my room was to hit the kitchen to grab myself a soda, a large glass of milk, a bag of potato chips, and Oreos.

Somehow, between the massive family-sized bag of chips, the half-empty package of Oreo cookies, and a Bridget Jones marathon, I managed to fall asleep.

Something was tickling the side of my face.

Swiping at nothing, I settled down only for the same sensation to happen again, this time, a distinct fragrance hitting my nose.

Stargazer lilies.

Around the same time the smell hit me, so did the solid heat pressed against my back.

My body stiffened.

"I know you're awake, Devolin," Dalton cajoled.

"No," I groaned petulantly, "I'm having an amazing dream where you're being sweet and not an ass at all. Let me sleep."

The bed began to shake with Dalton's silent laughter. "I said I could be sweet, didn't I?" He tickled my shoulder with the bloom, running it down my arm, where goosebumps followed its trajectory.

Then his lips brushed my temple, trailing down to my cheek, my shoulder, up into the side of my neck, where he buried his nose. Inhaling deep, he then chucked the lily he was wielding onto the bed beside us, before wrapping his arms tightly around me.

"Jesus fucking Christ I've missed you," he whispered. "I'm sorry I didn't call until this morning. I know you're pissed."

"No, I'm not," I argued even though I had been. Now, not so much. Not with him finally being here, with his arms surrounding me, his heat warming me from the inside out. Not with him being sweet like he was, when I knew he probably was exhausted from the last week. If my alarm clock was anything to go by, he'd come to me the moment he'd landed. Hesitating, I confessed. "Well, I was. But I'm not now."

The mattress shook again as he pressed his lips against my neck again. "Okay, sweetheart." After a lengthy pause where neither of us said anything, he sighed, "I'm staying."

"I kind of figured as much," I said, smiling into my pillow. "Now sleep, Kip."

"Mmm." He squeezed me against him then mumbled, "Love you."

thirty-eight

DALTON

I COULD HAVE SWORN I heard her whisper, "Love you too, Kip," but I was too far gone to know what was real and might have been a dream. Instead, a smile spread on my face as my body melted toward hers, the darkness of the early morning hours taking me within its grasp.

I woke up on a groan the following morning, Devolin's ass fidgeting against my hard cock.

"Stop," I whispered.

"I would if you'd let me go, you oaf!" she snapped in a low tone. "I need the bathroom."

My arms released her immediately as I mumbled, "Sorry, babe," then rolled over to my back, watching her as she left the bed with her barely covered ass and that see-through tank, before covering my eyes with a forearm. I didn't move from this position, even when I felt the mattress dip with Devolin's return a few minutes later.

She burrowed into my side, playing an indiscernible pattern over my chest with her fingertips as I savored the calmness of the morning.

"Did you send Rex home?" she murmured against my pec.

"Yeah."

"So..."

That suggestive tone of hers had me rolling her onto her back, pushing her hands up by the headboard, and fitting my torso between her thighs.

"I can't believe I left this for an entire week after finding it," I whispered against her jaw, giving her left hand a squeeze before releasing it, then trailing my right hand down her arm, to her side, where her shirt lifted to bare heated flesh.

"What would you have done had you stayed?" She nuzzled at my nose.

"I would have drowned myself in you," I told her, pulling back to gauge her reaction. "I wouldn't have let us come up for air. I would have fucked you on my desk. I would have taken you on yours. Up against the wall." That netted me with a whimper. "Whenever. Wherever. If the mood struck me, I'd take you. And you'd give in to me." I nipped at her lips. "Because you'd want it just as much."

Her vehement nod was joined with a purred, "Yes."

Her response had me smirking as I released her other hand, then proceeded to push her tank top up and over her head, leaving it in a tightened tangled mess at her wrists.

My palms skimmed the smooth skin of her chest, downward until I reached those tiny, short shorts. Devolin's eyes flared with an even more intense heat as she lifted her hips, granting me with an easier chore of removing them.

"Fuck," I muttered. She'd gone commando. "I thought this skimpy little bedtime outfit was enough to make me sweat." I lowered myself until my face hovered above her sex. "Knowing you were wearing nothing but this, while Rex was here and I wasn't, makes me see red."

"He didn't see me—"

I reached up, pinching a pert nipple, making her squirm. "It also makes me hungry," I growled against her pubic bone, inhaling her scent.

Her breath quickened. "Please."

"You mean this?" I teased her opening with the back of my index finger.

She shook her head from side to side. "Your mouth," she pleaded. "I want your—"

Lowering my mouth to her pussy, I gave her one long lick from bottom to top before diving right in.

Devolin's entire body went taut, her back bowing, mouth open in a soundless scream. Her orgasm had me damn well near coming in my briefs.

I fused my mouth to hers, dizzy from watching what I did to her, and mindless with the need to be inside her.

Rolling us over, so her body lay over mine, I gave Devolin the opportunity to pull away. Instead, she managed to disentangle her wrists from her tank top, chucking it to the floor, then proceeded to use her hands along with her mouth to explore.

Her delicate tongue circled one of my nipples, sending an electric jolt of lust straight down to my groin. To stay grounded, and not take matters into my own hands, I busied them by sifting them into her hair. When she shimmied down my body, I fisted the sheets.

I lost purchase on my sanity when her mouth covered the middle of my shaft and blew warm air through my underwear before pulling them down to my thighs.

Knifing up to a sitting position, I grabbed onto Devolin's hips and pulled her against my front. Settling onto my lap, I could feel her slickness coating my cock which was nestled against her folds.

Her breath fanned against my face in short pants. Our eyes connected, hers filled with urgency.

"Lift up, sweetheart," I whispered.

Her thighs flexed as she did, and I guided myself to her entrance as she held on to my shoulders. Without prompting, she let herself slide down onto my length, sheathing me from root to tip on a keening moan. Her chest pressed against mine. Her neck on display. I couldn't help myself. I bit down on the tendon gently, adding a little suction. Her muscles twitched around my length. Once she started to move, I knew I was absolutely lost.

I held on for the ride.

Bodies slicked with sweat, chests sliding against one another, eyes fused. We were as close as two people could get, and I still didn't feel like it was enough.

It wouldn't be until her pussy pulsed around me, clutching, sucking at my length, greedy as it pulled me further into her depths. And when it did, the way Devolin let go with abandon at the peak moment of her climax had my orgasm railroading me.

Flipping us, so she was under me, I slammed myself into her twice more before I roared my own release, realizing—albeit a little too late—that I'd fucked up.

thirty-nine

I KNEW what Dalton was getting at around the same time he uttered, "Fuck me!" into the curve of my neck, his fist clenching the pillow beside my head.

We hadn't reached for a condom.

Feathering my fingers through his hair, I kissed his temple. "It's okay." It sounded hesitant, but I hoped that it was reassuring enough. "I uh...I—"

"You're on something?" Dalton said, lifting his head expectantly.

I shook my head in response, biting my bottom lip. "Not exactly."

His brows furrowed in confusion. "Then what, *exactly?*"

"I can't get pregnant," I confessed, turning away from his gaze.

I hadn't planned on telling him like this. I didn't want to tell anyone about the fact that getting pregnant would be like winning the lottery for me—it was damn well near impossible.

I could feel Dalton's gaze boring into the side of my face. Being the man I knew he was, he was assessing how to approach the conversation at hand. His doing so had tears filling my eyes. Tears for me. Tears for any relationship I would end up having, because surely Dalton wouldn't want to stay, and every other man after him would pale in comparison and leave me alone with my inadequacy. The tears were also for Dalton. If he so chose to stay with me, he'd most likely be denied a proper legacy.

That's if he even wants kids.

Regardless, I was defective.

Less of a woman.

What man would want that?

Stuck in my own head, the touch of Dalton's hand on the side of my face, tilting it to force our eyes to connect, had me back in the here and now.

"Sweetheart?" His eyes were filled with sadness, but not the pity I expected to see.

"I can't have kids," I repeated, my voice hoarse. "After two bouts of leukemia and the chemo, they said that there might be a possibility that everything would be okay," I explained. "But when my period became more and more irregular...They'd warned my mother and I that if that happened, that the likelihood of getting pregnant would be slim to none. Then there's the anemia and the lupus. Did you know that you can get that from too much chemo?"

Dalton simply shook his head, no.

I didn't realize that I was full out crying until his hands were cupping my face, thumbs brushing at the tears.

"I want kids," he whispered against my lips, his eyes never wavering from mine. "But I want you more."

"But—"

His fingers covered my lips. "Sweetheart, I want you more," he reiterated. "I'll always want you. Your being able to give us babies isn't a deal breaker for us, Devolin."

"Don't you want a kid with your blue eyes? That dark hair? A boy you could teach...I don't know...how to skip rocks on a pond, how to fish, hunt, how to be a good man like you?"

Dalton's soft smile made me feel a little smidgen of hope. "All of that can be taught to any kid, baby." He smiled. "As for the dark hair and the blue eyes? If I were to picture a kid, a biological one, I'd picture a little girl with your auburn hair, in pigtails and black ribbons because pink isn't her thing." This made my lips hitch up slightly at the edges. "Our little girl would be as hilarious as her mother, and tough as nails like her old man."

"Kip," I whispered.

"No." He was adamant. "This is heavy shit we're talking about first thing in the morning, but we're done with this subject for the time being." He kissed my forehead. "Right now, I want you out of your head." He trailed his lips gingerly down to my cheek. I could feel him rising to attention inside me. "I want to make love to you," he whispered over my lips. "I want to tell my woman I love her and watch her face change like it is right now."

I melted into the mattress at his words. My eyes filled with tears once more. Ones of joy this time. I'd heard him say those words before, but this time...this time, I knew he meant them with all his worth. I could see his emotions swirling in his dark baby blues, the conviction in his face. I heard the sincerity in his voice. He hadn't thrown those words at me before, and he certainly wasn't now.

"How..." I struggled with getting the words out. "I..." I tried again. Sucking in a deep breath, I gave it all I had. "I love you too, Kip." My voice came out shaky, but it held the depth of my feelings for him. "I'm terrified that this is all happening so fast, but I can't help the way I feel."

"Say it again," he pleaded, voice gone gruff.

Grabbing on to the sides of his face, I anchored my eyes to his. "I love you." His dick flexed inside me, making me grin.

"I fucking love that you gave me those words while I was buried deep inside you." This caused me to giggle. Humor shone in his eyes, even as his expression softened. "Sweetheart, I don't give a shit if anyone thinks it's fast. For all intents and purposes, and from where I'm standing, what's going on between us has been a year in the making. It felt right a year ago, and that feeling's only gotten stronger since you fell into my life again."

I agreed with him. There'd been something that set Dalton apart from the rest of the team that night when we worked together to find Morgan. The pull I felt toward him had never faded. If anything, it had intensified. Giving into him, into this version of us, had been my only option. As it turned out, it had been the smartest decision I'd ever made for myself, too.

forty

DALTON

THE IDEA of spending an entire day in bed with Devolin had proven to be too good to be true. At least we'd made it through lunch before reality came knocking.

From the kitchen fridge, I heard Devolin's panicked, "Mom, what's wrong?"

Bottles of water forgotten, I slammed the door shut and rushed into the room, only to find Joleen's eyes red-rimmed and her face pale.

Devolin led her to one of the chairs, easing her down in it.

"I was on my way over when I got a call from your uncle's lawyer," she announced. Joleen's eyes found me and rounded with surprise. "Dalton?"

"Hey, Jo." I gave her a small smile in greeting and made to leave, sensing that perhaps Devolin's mother would be more comfortable without my being there. It didn't take a genius to know that whatever was plaguing the older woman would weigh heavy on both women before this visit was up.

"You can stay, Dalton," she said. "Devolin shouldn't be alone when I leave."

That's a little cryptic.

"Mom?" Devolin prompted, while I found a seat on the sofa.

The older woman's sweet demeanor turned to one of anger as her face suffused with red. "Where the fuck have you been, and when were you going to tell me that you were working for your uncle?"

"Mom—"

"Don't *Mom* me, young lady!" she shrieked, getting up to her feet, setting a pacing rhythm. "We talked about this. You promised! Promised, Devolin!" She skewered her daughter with a venomous look.

"Mom—" Devolin tried again, coming to sit next to me.

"No! Max called you up and asked you to help him" she growled, pointing her finger in our direction. "You and I talked things over, and I told you that this was dangerous business that you were getting into. You assured me you wouldn't."

"I know." Devolin's shame was evident in her words.

"Then why? Why would you do this?"

"Because he's family," she answered. "You taught me that no matter what, family is always there for one another." Joleen's mouth opened, then snapped shut. "I told him to contact Dalton and his team." She grabbed my hand and squeezed it.

Devolin's mother didn't miss the act.

"That's why you were here that day, wasn't it?" Her look of accusation was directed at me. "You dragged my daughter into this after she'd given me her word."

"No, Mom!" Devolin cried. "Dalton and I worked a case on a missing woman a year ago. That's how I knew he would be able to help Uncle Max. I just didn't expect to find what I did, which is why—"

"Which is why she got in touch with me," I supplied. "I brought her onto my team because she's amazing at what she does. Her talents were wasted with Hewitt."

"You put my baby in danger!" she raged on.

"I kept her safe." My tone was firm. Unwavering.

The older woman met my gaze and locked there. Her posture relaxed some within seconds. "You're not just her boss, are you?" Running out of steam, her ass met the chair she earlier vacated.

"No, ma'am," I admitted.

Joleen's eyes shifted from me back to her daughter, then filled with tears. "I got a call from your uncle's lawyer this morning." Taking a calming breath, she pushed forward. "Scott was found dead in his cell last night. He was shanked." Devolin gasped beside me, her nails digging into our joined hands. "They found out Nadia had played them, but I expect you already knew that." Devolin and I both nodded. Shaking her head, Joleen leaned forward, massaging her temples. "I suspect you haven't gotten word of this latest news just yet, though."

"What is it?" Devolin prompted her mother.

"This morning, the RCMP was sent to arrest your uncle. They got there too late. Nadia's body was found badly beaten. Max was hospitalized with similar injuries. They don't think he'll make it either."

My breath caught in my throat.

"What?" Devolin whispered her disbelief, then looked at me. "Y-you told me that she would be safe. You told me that they were all going to be safe. Kip—"

"Baby." I released her hand, grabbing onto her shoulders while I shifted to face my woman. "I told you that they'd do everything they could, but you know there aren't any guarantees."

Devolin gave me a feeble nod as her mother continued her explanation.

Turning to Devolin's mother, I sighed. "I need details, Jo."

"They said it was a break and enter gone bad. The house was ransacked, but nothing seemed to be missing except for Max's computers, and the safe was found empty."

On Devolin's soft sob, I pulled her into me. She followed my guidance easily before mumbling, "Ortiz is going to get away, isn't he?" in my chest.

"He might," I gave her the truth. "But Miguel will do everything he can to make sure that doesn't happen. Nadia made sure he had all the information he would need to put him away. It's out of our hands now, sweetheart. I know it's not fair, but we did what we had to do to make things right."

"And we failed." She balled up a fist and slammed it against my chest, beside her face.

"We succeeded, Devolin," I told her. "Eighteen women got their lives back. All because of you, me, Nadia, and our team."

Another feeble nod.

I sifted my hand through her hair until Devolin regained her bearings enough to pull back. Pecking me on the mouth, she said, "You're right. But it doesn't make it easier."

"It doesn't," I agreed, then grabbed at both sides of her face, dipping mine into hers, "but it doesn't make what we do any less important." Her eyes cleared a little as she contemplated my words. "Come here." Kissing her forehead first, I pulled her in for a hug.

Despite the tears streaking down her face, Joleen's smile was hard to miss.

I think I just won the woman's stamp of approval.

forty-one

DALTON

DEVOLIN WAS A MESS.

Even with my years of training and experience in the army, losing a charge or a client was always a tough pill to swallow. It was hard for me to remain detached from the entire situation this time, however. Where every case was a job to me, the Wentworth case hadn't ended that way. Normally, I would close a file and move on, usually never hearing from my clients again until they needed something else. This time, I was privy to the aftermath, and I didn't like it.

Not for me.

Not for Devolin.

Losing a family member wasn't an easy thing to get past. When you lost a relative because of something you were involved in however, it left a mark. A dark one. A stain that may fade, but never truly disappeared, even after a lifetime.

Believe me, I know.

Call me crazy, but that commonality with her made me want to share.

"I was seven when my mother died," I whispered against Devolin's hair.

We were cocooned under the fleece throw on her couch. She'd

been quiet. Dejected even, and I wanted to bring her back to the here and now. Get her out of her head.

My words apparently worked.

Shifting so she could push herself up, I was met with a sympathetic gaze studying my face.

"She was sick," I proceeded. "She suffered from seizures."

"She was epileptic?"

I nodded. "They started after I was born. Dad stayed with us, working from home most of the time, back then," I explained. "She was diagnosed with postpartum preeclampsia a day after giving birth to me. The seizures started a few weeks after that. By the time I was three, the doctor had diagnosed her with epilepsy. The preeclampsia caused too much damage to her nervous system."

Devolin's hand cupped my cheek. "Why are you telling me this?"

"Because I need you to know that you're not alone in your guilt," I told her. "I know how you feel, believing that you could have done something to stop what happened, but not doing it. Even when the truth of the matter is, that there wasn't anything to be done."

Devolin forced me to my back, crawling over my body, her hands grabbing each side of my head. She stared me down.

"Kip, you were seven!"

"Young enough to be selfish, but old enough to know better," I muttered. When Devolin's brows furrowed, I kept talking. "Mom's seizures were almost nonexistent by then. She was on medication and it worked for her. She'd only had one seizure that year, and it was July.

"I was outside, playing with a friend when we decided to climb the old willow in my yard. I'd done it dozens of times that summer." Licking my lips, I geared up for what came next. "Dad warned me to stay out of the thing after a bad storm. I didn't listen. I never listened. I guess boys will be boys, right?" She nodded, one corner of her mouth tilting up. "I should have listened, sweetheart," I whispered. "I climbed that thing like I always did, but something went wrong. The branch I was standing on snapped while I shuffled back to make room for the other kid. I fell about ten feet, but it was enough to snap my upper arm."

"Kip—"

"Steve, that's the kid's name, ran to find my mom. I remember the panic in her eyes as she cleared the broken branches away from me. She wasn't thinking clearly and ushered me to the car. She wasn't supposed to drive, but I didn't know this. Everywhere I went, my parents were always with me. But Dad was out of town on business that day." I closed my eyes so I could tell her the rest. "I don't know how much you know about how seizures are triggered with epilepsy, but an emotionally charged state...stress...can bring one on." And it had.

Devolin's grip on my face tightened as she braced. "We were a block away from the hospital when the seizure hit. She ran a light, the car coming from our left smashing into us."

"Oh, Kip," she whispered, her voice shaking.

"It was my fault, Dev." I finally opened my eyes. "She died because of something I did. Fuck, she died because of something I didn't do."

"No! No, Kip." She shook her head vehemently. "You were just a kid. You can't—"

"Old enough to know better, remember?" I held her gaze. "But you're right, I was just a kid. I didn't know everything like I do now, and even though I do, it doesn't change the fact that I carry that guilt with me every day."

A silent tear escaped Devolin's eye and I reached up, catching it with my thumb.

"So what are you saying?" she asked. "That I'm entitled to feel guilt?"

My eyes searched hers and I nodded. "That, and the fact no matter what we did or didn't do, it most likely wouldn't have changed the outcome. It took me years and the army to come to terms with that, Dev." Another tear trickled down her cheek. "We can only do our best, and ask for help when we need it. Then we need to deal with the outcome."

Her lips quirked up. "We can only control our actions, not everyone's reactions."

I nodded, my lips tugging upward. "Yeah. Basically, it doesn't matter what we ended up doing for Nadia, Max, and Scott. You couldn't control what they ended up doing. When someone wants something bad enough, especially a bad someone, they'll take every measure to get it. Had Ortiz missed his opportunity to get to them, he'd have found it some other way, some other time. Criminals like Enrique Ortiz are resourceful and patient."

"Yeah." She swallowed hard, one hand moving to my chest, above my heart, and the other, to skim her fingertips over my lips. "I'm so sorry about your mom, baby," she whispered.

"I'm sorry about Max, Scott, and Nadia." Wrapping a hand around the back of her head, I leaned up to kiss her forehead before pulling her into my chest where she started sobbing again.

forty-two

Devolin

I WAS SO FUCKING sick of crying.

So when Dalton announced that his sister was on her way over, I welcomed the family drama I knew was about to ensue.

Skylar greeted me with a tub of rocky road and one of her tight hugs. "I'm so sorry, Dev," she whispered. I nodded against her shoulder. "Any news on your uncle?"

"No. Mom's on her way to him right now," I explained. "She'll call when she gets in."

Dalton's arm wrapped itself around my middle and pulled me back into his front.

This caused Skylar to smirk, but her demeanor quickly changed to one of annoyance. "By the way, I talked to Dad."

"And?"

"*And?*" she snorted.

"Yeah, *and,*" he said. "In case you haven't noticed, I've been out of country."

"I know," she growled. "I got that little tidbit of information on Sunday, when I called Devolin to find out where the hell you were because you weren't answering my calls or messages. He was waiting on you."

Dalton didn't say anything to this.

As for the tension between father and son, I knew it had something to do with Skylar's mother, Dalton's stepmother. I'd never met the woman, but the things my best friend had shared with me sent chills of revulsion down my spine. I couldn't blame Skylar for keeping her distance from the woman. I also had a feeling that what she'd shared with me wasn't the whole of it.

"Was she there?" he asked.

Skylar sucked her lips in between her teeth.

Guilty.

"That's what I thought," he growled, let me go, then started pacing my living room.

"She just showed," Skylar whispered. "Dad hasn't invited her to these things in months, D. Not since—"

"Say it," he growled.

Skylar's gaze met mine, then flickered to her brother, then back again. "Not since..." She shook her head. "D, she doesn't know."

Feeling uneasy about the direction this conversation was headed, I started to back away from them, moving toward the kitchen. "I should—"

"No!" Dalton exploded, making both of us jump. "If you're not going to say it, I will, Skylar. She nearly ended your career before it fucking started! Because of her shit, I nearly landed my ass in jail after she encouraged that bastard to keep trying for you. You almost got raped!" His hands feathered through his hair, yanking at it angrily. "It took her nearly killing Dad for him to see the light," he bellowed.

My head was spinning with all that I'd just learned. Skylar had confided in me about her near rape, but I had no idea her mother had a hand in that. Vile as a description of the woman no longer sufficed. I'm pretty sure they still haven't invented the word to describe her yet.

"D—" Skylar started.

"I'm done with this conversation," he said with finality and locked his gaze on his sister.

"And what should I tell Dad?" Skylar asked, arms crossed over her chest.

"Tell him he's got dinner at Kip's on Friday night," I blurted out.

Matching silvery-blue eyes stared at me like I'd lost my mind.

"Kip?" Skylar inquired with an amused expression, while Dalton demanded, "What?" simultaneously.

"And I'll cook," I added, taking the few steps I needed to come to my man's side. Wrapping my arms around his waist, I looked up at him. "I didn't know much of the story, but I have heard your sister complaining about how you never show up at family dinners. I think it's time you changed that. Starting with a new date and location."

Dalton's expression gentled as a humored glimmer entered his eyes. "Okay, sweetheart."

A snort made us turn to our visitor. "It's been what...*a day* since you two have gotten together, and here she is laying down the law." Skylar giggled. "I'm liking this role reversal, brother."

A grin made its way onto my face, while Dalton groaned at his half-sister's words, his gaze flaring with lust.

"I think we can both agree there's one place I'll always be the lawmaker," he said, smirking down at me.

My heart kick-started, my blood warmed. Biting my lower lip, I gave him a subtle nod. This earned me those dimples of his and I found myself leaning up toward them.

"My eyes are burning!" Skylar dramatically exclaimed.

I couldn't help the eye roll that made Dalton laugh as he leaned into me, whispering, "I'm going to want to know what just went through your mind right now. Later." His all-knowing grin had me squirming against him, blushing ten shades of red.

forty-three

DALTON

FRIDAY ROLLED AROUND.

I hadn't seen Devolin since late Tuesday morning, when I dropped her off at the airport for her flight.

In the early hours of Tuesday morning, she'd received a call from her mother. Max hadn't made it through the night, having suffered a massive heart attack.

The funerals and interment were yesterday. Joleen had stayed behind to take care of her brother's estate. Devolin, on the other hand, was all about rushing back, letting me know, that in no uncertain terms, was she going to miss our dinner with my father.

With that said, I left work early to run some last-minute errands for my woman. To be honest, I had no idea what to expect when I walked through that door. All I knew is that I couldn't wait to hold Devolin in my arms again. We hadn't had time to breathe and just be us since we began. I wanted normalcy. I needed it. So did she.

What I witnessed when I walked into my house had me smiling.

First, I was hit with the smell of spices and garlic.

Second was the sound of Melissa Etheridge's, "Come to My Window" mixed with their giggles.

Creeping up on them, I was greeted by a lip-syncing half-sister and a dancing Devolin, both too busy to notice they had an audience, even when the song ended and segued into Etheridge's, "I Want to Come Over."

In the midst of belting out the chorus, Devolin turned and finally noticed me. Skylar was too busy giving it her all with her back to me, chopping away at vegetables. The girl could never carry a tune. Hell, she sounded like a screeching cat on the best of days.

"I'll be right back," Devolin called out, not waiting for the other woman's response.

Slapping her hands onto my chest, she led me backward around the corner from the kitchen's entryway, into my living room.

That's when I took over.

Picking her up by her ass, I slammed my mouth onto hers. She didn't hesitate to wrap her legs around my hips as I pressed her back into the wall, taking what I was denied for days.

Her taste exploded on my tongue, and I couldn't help grinding my hips into hers, eliciting a tortured moan from Devolin. One I swallowed, feeding off it before I slowed things down.

Keeping her pinned to the wall, our lips parted enough for me to nuzzle her nose with mine.

"Let's make a deal," I whispered, sneaking a quick kiss. "If either of us needs to leave town, the other follows." The woman's body began to shake against mine. "I mean it, Dev."

"But we haven't had phone sex yet." She gave me the cutest playful pout, the mischievousness shining in her eyes.

"Trust me." I grinned. "You're not missing much, seeing as you're about to get the real thing before the night is up." Then an idea hit me. "But if you're adamant in living that fantasy of yours, we could always combine it with that other one of yours."

Sure, my overtness had her blushing, but the glazing over of those green eyes of hers told me that her curiosity was piqued.

"Tell me, baby," I rasped. "How wet are you for me right now?"

"Kip…"

"I fucking love the breathless way you say that." I nipped her lower lip. "Now tell me. If I were to strip you bare right now, would I have to go slow, or would I be able to pound into—"

Devolin snapped.

Fingernails dug into my scalp as she pulled me by the hair, covering my mouth with hers in the most aggressive kiss she'd given me yet. I swear, I was ten seconds from combusting.

"For the love of Christ!"

Devolin ripped her mouth from mine as soon as Skylar announced her presence.

Fuck!

Dropping my head to my woman's shoulder, my body started shaking with laughter. "Hey, sis," rumbled out of me. "You mind giving us another minute?"

On a huff, I heard her feet shuffle. "Fine. Dad just texted. He's five minutes out, and I'm pretty sure Dev doesn't want to meet him looking like a puffer fish."

Devolin released a horrified gasp. "Put me down, Dalton," she whispered her panic.

I pulled back enough to take a good look at her, but I didn't let her go.

She'd put some work into her appearance. Her hair was down, a slight wave in it, making the reds in her auburn locks more pronounced. She was wearing a sexy little sundress. Her makeup was heavier, yet still subtle, only because she rarely wore anything more than mascara, or so I'd discovered since meeting her. Those pink lips of hers were closer to a dark rose color now, and swollen.

"You look beautiful," I told her.

"I need to fix myself up," she rebutted.

"Babe?"

"Put me down, Kip," she stated exasperatedly, fussing against me.

"Babe," I groaned, then pressed my still swollen cock against her. "You're not helping me with that wiggling of yours."

"Then put me down, Dalton," she growled. "I don't need to

meet your dad for the first time with you flying at full mast, looking like you are about to fuck my brains out."

Recognizing how important this first meeting was to her, I loosened my grip on her ass and slid her body down mine until her feet met the floor.

Sighing, she leaned her forehead against my chest. "Thank you."

"I love you," I said against her hair.

Tilting her head back to look up at me, I was gifted with that beautiful smile of hers. "I love you, too," she said just as the doorbell rang. "Shit! Fuck! Damn!" she blurted, pushing me back and making a beeline for the bathroom.

As for me, I headed for the front door, laughing as I opened it, coming face-to-face with someone who shouldn't be standing there.

"What the fuck are you doing here?"

forty-four

DEVOLIN

"AREN'T you going to invite me in?"

That wasn't Dalton's father.

"I'll ask again, Suzie, what the fuck are you doing here?" Dalton ordered.

Suzie?

"Fuck, what is she doing here?" Skylar whispered from behind me, making me jump.

"Shit, Sky! Don't creep up on me like that!" I scolded her. "Who's Suzie?"

"You remember Suzanna from the other night?" She was referring to the night we'd gone out to McAskill's with Tamara.

"Uh...how can I forget?" Now that I thought of it, the woman's voice sounded familiar.

Suzanna had been what had driven me to drink so much that night.

Bumping into her, on our way to pick up our takeout, the woman had gone off about Dalton, right before she zeroed in on me. I'd never met her before, yet she claimed she knew all about me, and then proceeded to tell me she was shocked Dalton would choose to be with someone like me: the poor sickly recluse. It stung, and I tried to let the insult slide, but Skylar jumped to my defence.

I had no idea what I'd done to deserve that stranger's wrath.

Regardless, she'd been a stranger who Dalton had wanted to marry according to Skylar—his ex-fiancée to be more precise.

After that run-in with the wacko, I'd asked Skylar for details. She'd cheated on him repeatedly, getting herself knocked up in the process. For a man I knew wanted a family, I felt for him. Thing is, no matter which angle I chose to look at things, I couldn't picture the high-maintenance nut job with the man I'd come to know. As much as Dalton was structured in his work life, he was pretty down to earth on a personal level. Sure, he was intense no matter what, but he knew what he wanted and went for it balls to the wall. No one could fault him for that. If anything, it was one of the traits I admired most about him. That and his integrity. The man didn't do anything if it would mess with his belief system. He was very black and white to my grey in views, which seemed to balance us out perfectly.

"What's going on here?" A man bellowed from the front door. "You shouldn't be here, Suzanna."

"Dad," Skylar whispered at my back.

"I was only here to warn you, but I can see it's pointless." Her eyes were trained past Dalton's shoulders on me. I hadn't realized I'd moved away from my hiding spot. "If you think I hurt you, you have no idea what you're in for with her."

After a brief stare down with me, a maleficent glint in her eyes, the woman turned on her heel and left.

As soon as the front door latched shut, Dalton's father turned his attention to me, sporting that familiar grin, a singular dimple appearing on the left of his face. "Who do we have here?"

"Daddy!" Skylar started for our visitor.

Dalton backed away from father and daughter, coming to snag me around the waist and pulling me into his side.

"You okay?" he whispered.

Nodding, I mumbled, "We need to talk," below my breath.

He didn't say anything. Only nodded.

When Skylar parted from her father, the man immediately zeroed in on Dalton's arm around my waist.

Shaking his father's hand, Dalton took care of introductions. "Dad, I'd like you to meet Devolin. My girlfriend."

The older man's brows rose as he gave a questioning glance at his daughter. "Your friend Devolin?" Skylar nodded. "Well, hell!"

He sauntered the rest of the way, grabbed my hand, and pulled me toward him as Dalton and Skylar uttered, "Dad!" in warning.

He froze before he could get his arms around me, sympathy spreading across his face the moment he read my stiffened posture, and what most likely could have been taken as panic in my eyes.

Knowing that the man standing before me was who'd raised the one at my side, it was easy enough to get past my standoffish behavior. To be honest, I'd been making strides in that department since meeting Dalton and the crew at NSI, and the first person I'd approached for a hug after my man, had been Brycen. To say the man had been shocked was an understatement. So now, after taking a centering breath, I moved toward Dalton and Skylar's father, hesitantly offering him an awkward hug.

"Sweetheart," he said gruffly, his arms coming around, holding me loosely. "You don't—"

"You're a hugging family," I said by way of explaining, the side of my face pressed against his chest, my eyes trained on Dalton, who was smiling sweetly at me with what looked like approval in his gaze. "It's not your fault I have...issues I need to work on." The man released me, his hands grabbing my hands to hold them between us. "I suppose it's the curse of being used as a pincushion for most of my life." I shrugged.

The man harrumphed. "How are you feeling? Skylar's told me a lot about you." He grinned.

"I'm much better." I returned his smile. "Can I get you a drink?"

forty-five

DALTON

THE WOMEN HAD PUT SO much work into dinner, that I'd sent them out onto the back patio, promising coffee, tea, and dessert as soon as Dad and I had tidied up the dishes and kitchen.

"I like her," my father said, as he stacked the last of the dishes into the dishwasher, and I finished with the last of the pots, draining the sink.

We'd succeeded in ignoring the elephant in the room the entire evening for long enough. I felt like a heel having to put an end to something we hadn't had in several years. Ever since Cora, Skylar's mom, had sent all three of our lives into a tailspin, things hadn't been the same. Thanks to Devolin, the evening had felt like the good old days.

"We need to talk," I told him.

"Yes, we do." He sighed. "I'm sorry, Dalton."

Drying my hands on the dish towel, setting it on the counter by the sink, I turned to meet his gaze head on. Skylar was right. Upon my own quick inspection, something weighed heavily on him. It was in the way his shoulders slouched in defeat. It was in the glimmer of failure in his eyes.

"Dad..."

He lifted a hand to halt my words, shaking his head to enforce that I remain silent.

"You haven't had it easy, son. When we lost your mother—"

"Dad, I know it wasn't easy on you either," I said.

"You needed a mother," he said. "I couldn't believe my luck when I met Cora. When she told me she was pregnant, I'll admit, I didn't love her, but she gifted me with another child to love, so I did the honorable thing."

"You don't need to explain," I told him. I would have done the same.

"I do, son. I do." Taking a deep breath, he continued. "I didn't love Cora the way a man should love a woman, but I did grow to love her in some way. It simply wasn't enough. After years of trying, I couldn't do it anymore." I remember those days as if they were just yesterday. "She was sucking the life out of me, D. I didn't handle it well when you told me you saw her with another man." He hadn't. "I was pissed at her. Pissed at myself, and I was pissed at you for having to be the one to point her bullshit out to me, even though I could feel that something was going on."

"The day she signed the divorce papers that bled me dry, I couldn't have been happier," he confessed. "I didn't give a shit about my inheritance. So long as she didn't touch yours and your sister's, I would have given her every fucking cent."

The apple doesn't far from the tree. It's why my father and I butted heads so often.

"I know you would have." I sighed, running a hand through my hair. "It's the fact that she's still around after it all. I get Skylar needed her mom. Don't get me wrong, I agree with that. And she was a good one for a while afterward. Until—"

"It's done, son."

"Dad—"

"It's done," he said with finality.

I pinned him with my gaze. "Then why was she there last weekend? Even though I wasn't, she should have stayed away. Did you think Skylar and I wouldn't talk about Cora showing? I see my sister at least once a week, Dad, of course she'd tell me *that* woman had been around."

"She was trying to warn me. I haven't seen her since I was in the hospital, son." It had been two months since his heart attack.

"Warn you?" My laugh came out with all the sarcasm I intended for it to hold. "What could she have to warn you about?"

"She ran into Suzanna, who told her she was back in town. Permanently. In fact, she's been back for quite some time."

Oh.

"I knew about it, since I had to learn from Shane, when I visited the precinct, that you were thinking about taking another restraining order out on her," he explained.

I nodded. "She's been calling nonstop, so I knew it was the next logical thing to do, even though it hadn't worked the way I thought it would the first time around. Before you ask, I have no idea what she wants from me."

"Have you looked into her?"

"No." It was stupid, and I knew it, but things have been so neurotically chaotic for me lately. "I'll get one of the guys on it."

Dad gave me his nod of approval. "Good. I'm done with this bullshit. I want my fucking family back, because if what I see brewing between you and that pretty little thing out there is as strong as it looks, I want to be able to enjoy it." He grinned. "I'm too fucking old for my own drama, but I'm never too old to watch that woman," he pointed toward the patio door, "make you run in circles around her."

It fucking felt great to laugh with the man in front of me. "Who says she won't be the one doing the dancing?"

His laugh came out loud and boisterous, then calmed, but the humor still dominated his features. "Because...if she wasn't, you wouldn't look at her the way you do. I was like that with your mother." His smile was forced, the sadness taking over. "I would have done anything for that woman, and she knew it."

"I told her about Mom," I confessed. "I haven't told her everything else, but I want to."

He seemed as surprised as I had been when I'd made the decision to give Devolin some of my darkness, starting with my mother. "You did?"

"I love her," escaped me in a whispered reason.

Wrapping a hand behind my neck, he squeezed and said, "Then dance, boy." He pulled me in for a hug and a slap on the back. "Love you, son."

"Love you too, old man." I smacked him back.

Skylar and Dad had left less than an hour ago, and Devolin had retired to my bedroom to get into something more comfortable.

"Babe?" I called out toward the bathroom where I heard water stop running.

"Yeah?"

Stripping my shirt and chucking it into the hamper next to the closet, I sat down on the edge of the bed. "Can I talk to you for a sec?"

"Uh-huh."

She walked out of the bathroom wearing one of my t-shirts. I struggled to keep my mind on track. I wanted this conversation to be done and over with. Hell, I'd been happy if I didn't have to have it at all, but Suzanna needed to be dealt with, and Devolin needed to be in the know on how I planned to do that, as well as what to expect.

"Talked to Skylar earlier, when she came in looking for dessert," I told her.

"Yeah?"

"Why didn't you tell me you met Suzanna?" I stuck out my hand for her to take. Now I knew why she'd called me a heart-breaker.

She grabbed hold, and I pulled her until she stood between my legs, settling my hands on her hips.

She snorted. "Meeting would imply an introduction. One I never got directly. And it wasn't exactly a conversation I wanted to rehash until I was ready."

"You weren't just pissed at my demanding you explain about Hewitt that night you went out with the girls, were you?"

"No." She made to touch my cheek, her thumb rubbing against my day worth stubble. "That basically put me over the edge though. The shit she knew about me. I don't know how she did, but I don't get why she'd even rub it in my face." Biting her bottom lip, I could see she was fighting something in her head.

"What is it, sweetheart?" I asked. "Just ask and I'll tell you."

"Skylar told me that she cheated on you and got pregnant with the other man's kid, but what exactly happened with her?"

By the time I finished explaining my history with Suzanna, Devolin was pacing my bedroom, anger pouring off her in droves.

"Do you think she'll stir trouble?" she asked me.

"I hope not, but now that she's back in town, who knows."

"I...I." She was so flustered, she couldn't even speak. "I want to rip her throat out, right now, for what she did to you. Cheating was bad enough, but no...she had to do it with a friend? And she aborted the baby without him knowing?" She huffed, "This is a real-life soap opera, you can't make this shit up, Dalton!"

Her defense of my character had me going to her.

Too busy with her rant, she never saw me coming. Putting a shoulder into her stomach, I picked her up, then flipped her onto her back on my bed, making sure not to crush her as I landed over her, smiling.

"I don't see anything worth smiling about," she snapped.

She braced her hands on my chest as I played with a strand of her hair by her temple. "You're hot when you're spitting mad."

Her brows furrowed. "I am?"

"Downright sexy." I nuzzled her nose, my eyes studying hers. "But as much as I appreciate you defending my honor, I rather move on to a more enjoyable part of our evening."

Not waiting for a response, my mouth crashed to hers.

forty-six

DEVOLIN

THE INSTANT DALTON'S mouth hit mine, I lost myself in him.

That's what he did to me.

He transformed me into a glutton for all things him. The more he gave me, the more I wanted. My obsession was my salvation when it came to him.

His lips moved to my neck, his hands migrating to my hips, sneaking underneath the soft cotton of the shirt I was wearing.

"Have I told you how much I love you in my shirts?" he rumbled against my carotid, his tongue licking up the column of my neck to my jaw, where he nipped its edge.

My breath caught momentarily before kicking in at a pant. "I love having something of yours wrapped around me," I confessed. "I think I might highjack a tee or two to take home with me."

This netted me a growly laugh, even though his mouth continued to play with the skin of my neck, his hands questing, finding my already pert nipples. "Or you could just stay here and have unlimited access to all the tees you want," he mumbled against my ear, scraping his teeth on the tender skin just below it.

I arched up into him. "I...I—"

"Lift your arms, sweetheart."

Doing as he asked, my shirt was shimmied up and was over my head, onto the floor, somewhere behind Dalton in the next second.

"Kip," I said breathlessly.

His eyes snapped from their hungry perusal of my body, up to my eyes. "I know." He leaned back onto his knees, undoing his jeans, pushing them off his hips, over his thighs, and came right back to me.

"Please," I begged. "I want...I need...I need you inside me."

"Are you ready for me, Dev?" he growled, the vibration warming me to a fever pitch.

My nod was vehement. "So wet." I licked my lips. "For you, Kip."

He groaned, rubbing his length into my folds. "Christ, woman. You're a walking contradiction."

I reached between us, grabbing his cock in hand, a hiss escaping his lips, and positioned him at my entrance. His hand joined mine as his hips pressed forward, our eyes fused to one another's, and stayed there, unmoving.

Rubbing the abundance of my moistness over my clit with his fingers, Dalton then proceeded to paint the wetness over one of my nipples. His tongue darted to flick that same nipple, circled, then his mouth engulfed the entire tip with a long pull.

"Fuck!" I cried out. "This is better than what my mind can conjure." My hands circled his shoulders as he continued to feast on my breast.

Releasing my nipple with a loud pop, he smirked down at me, those dimples peeked out.

Lifting my head, I tongued the right one, giving him a sheepish smile. "I've been wanting to do that for a while now."

He shook his head at my antics. "You can do whatever you want, baby." Withdrawing from my depths, he plunged in hard. Taking my breath with it. "Just not right now. Right now, I want to be the one wrapped around you. Not my shirt. All fours, Devolin."

My entire body quivered, my pussy squeezing his girth. Dalton's eyes deepened to a near navy blue.

Before I could get settled, Dalton lifted my ass up, and

slammed himself inside my heat. My head snapped up toward the ceiling on a loud cry.

Truth is, it hurt a little. Hurt so good.

He was so deep, and when he ground against me, he felt as if he was deeper than I'd ever taken him.

The heat of his body leaning over my back, his warm breath fanning over my shoulder and into my neck, had me feeling safe, despite the dominant fashion he was taking me.

Dalton's hands skimmed the skin of my arms, up to my shoulders. I shivered. "Are you scared?" He licked my earlobe.

"Never," I breathed. "Show me."

His lips pressed against my left shoulder before the warmth coating my back left me. "Tell me if it's too much." Fingers digging into my hips, he pulled nearly the entire way out, then plunged in just as hard with a grunt.

"Fuck me, baby," I wailed.

His palm met the cheek of my ass with a slap that had my insides clenching on him.

"You like that?" He repeated the treatment.

"Yes," I hissed.

"Fuck me, my baby's got more kink in her than I could dream." He ground himself against me again. His thumb now feathering lightly over the rosebud of my tush.

There was no time to ponder my words. They were out before I knew it. "You have no idea." My body pressed tighter to Dalton's, his thumb pushing harder against that forbidden zone, black spots clouding my vision.

I was so close.

"Give it to me, baby," he ground out.

His thrusts came harder. Faster. I loved every fucking second of it.

When his thumb breached my ass, he destroyed me. I exploded.

My body locked as a wailing scream broke through the sound of slapping sweat-slicked skin. I was flying high, and I never wanted to land.

"Fuck! Again!" Dalton roared, his hips hammering into me now.

Pulling his thumb out of my ass, his arm came around to my front.

"I—I can't!" My body shook against his. The touch of his fingers on my clit proving to be nearly painful from that first cataclysmic release.

"You can." He pinched the bundle of nerves. "And you will. Your pussy is going to suck me dry, baby."

That did it.

On the hardest thrust yet, all my air left me. No sound escaped as the orgasm to rival all orgasms broke me. My body went completely limp, leaving Dalton bearing my weight. His body bowed tight as he shouted his release and a slew of curses.

Seconds later, he collapsed on top of my back, flattening me into the mattress.

"I think you might have broken me," he whispered into my neck before kissing it.

My laugh came out in a huffed breath. "There's no question, you succeeded with me."

forty-seven

DALTON

NOSE IN HER PHONE, Devolin froze midstep as she entered my office on Monday afternoon. The action was so abrupt that my head snapped up. It didn't take much more than her paled complexion to get me moving toward her.

"What is it?" I asked.

Fingers flicking on the screen, she dismissed whatever it was that clearly had her spooked, then shoved her phone in her back jeans pocket.

"Dev?"

It took her a while to meet my eyes. "It's nothing, Kip," she whispered.

My eyes narrowed on her. "Then why do you look like you're deciding between bolting out of here or upchucking your lunch?"

She huffed. "I've been getting these weird emails," she explained, as she whipped out her phone again, punching in the code to unlock the screen. "They started the day I left for Ottawa for my uncle's funeral. The one that bothers me the most is this one." She brought up the message. "I don't understand what this person means by cameras and pictures."

Oh, I knew. What I should have remembered though, was that

keeping all this Hewitt stalker bullshit from Devolin would back-fire and bite me on the ass.

"Babyface!" I bellowed out to Brycen. "Get your ass in here!"

The wheels were turning in her head, and Brycen and I seemed to brace for the inevitable fallout.

"So what you're saying," she sifted through the file of photos I'd gotten from Rex last week, when she'd been away. "Gordon did this?" I nodded. She dropped everything onto my desk, hugging herself. "I think I'm going to be sick."

Setting a hand on her shoulder in comfort—I knew that she wasn't quite ready to be close to me—she shrugged my touch off.

"Sweetheart—"

Her eyes came to me, hurt evident in them. "You kept this from me!" she yelled. "I thought I was getting someone else's emails. My name wasn't even in them. Sure, it fucking made me nervous that some of my favorite chapters from books I've read were included in them, but they're from bestsellers, so I told myself not to read too much into it."

"Dev—"

"You should have told me. When did you know?" she demanded.

I could taste blood I was biting my lip so damn hard.

When I didn't answer, she looked to Brycen, who avoided her spearing gaze by whistling.

Turning to me, she skewered me with her fiery gaze once more. "When, Dalton?" she growled.

"Mexico," I said.

Her eyes widened at my truth. "Rex," she surmised.

I nodded in confirmation. "It wasn't just about the flowers he sent you, or how forceful he was about that date he wanted, or the fact that he was following you. It wasn't just for my peace of mind. I know how he operates, Devolin. You're forgetting that I've had eyes on him for a while. He's been having you followed when he can't do it himself. He gained access to your apartment and installed cameras."

"*What?*"

"Rex found and removed them right away, after seeing these photos." I pointed toward my desk.

"Oh my God!" she whispered, letting her ass drop back to the couch, covering her face with her hands. "Rex has seen me naked?"

Seriously?

"There's more to worry about here than who's seen your sexy as fuck ass, sweetheart," I said.

Her head snapped up. "Don't be so fucking crass, Dalton!"

"It's the fucking truth, Devolin, and you know it!" I exploded.

Shooting to her feet again, she rushed the desk, grabbed the file, snapped up her phone from Brycen's fingers, and turned for the door. "I'm out of here."

"I'll call—"

"No!" She whirled around, venom filling her eyes. "No Rex. No Brycen. No one from this place. And no *you*. I need to look at these closer. I need to think. I need to be alone."

The fact she'd emphasized that she didn't want me around, stung. Then again, I'd walked into that situation two weeks ago.

"Dev, I don't—" I started.

"I need to think, Dalton." Sad eyes met mine. "About a lot of things." Then she walked out.

"Fuck!" I yelled after my office door was slammed. Bracing my hands on my desk, leaning forward to look down, I shook my head. "Call Rex and put him on her," I told Brycen.

"But she—"

"I know what she fucking said. It's either him or me," I eyed him. "She's comfortable with him. She's pissed at me a whole lot more than him. Tell him to follow her around for now."

The man nodded and left me to my thoughts.

forty-eight

DEVOLIN

KIP

> Make sure you activate the alarm. I love you.
> ~your Kip

"DAMN THE FUCKING MAN!" I threw my phone onto the couch. Dalton's text had come in just as I was walking into my apartment.

Flipping the deadbolt, I headed to the alarm panel and entered the code to deactivate it, then entered the one to activate it with an *at home* status.

My satchel hit the carpet with a gentle thud as I went straight to my bedroom, peeling one layer of clothes off at a time and dropping them wherever, leaving a trail behind me.

I was numb. Too many thoughts rolled about in my head. One thing I knew though—and I concentrated on it with all my being —Gordon Hewitt was about to be eviscerated in all things. Electronically, of course!

Slipping into a pair of yoga pants and a loose-fitting hoodie, I headed for my sanctuary.

. . .

My head ached and my eyes were starting to blur, but I had to keep going. I ignored everything around me. It didn't matter that Dalton, Skylar, and Morgan were trying to get a hold of me. This shit show was going to end and quickly.

At quarter after midnight, I gave into my rumbling stomach.

I was on my way back to my computers when I heard the knock at my door.

I debated leaving whoever was on the other side hanging, but my mother's voice in my head nagged at me about my manners, and I gave in.

Dropping the bag of Oreos and large glass of milk, I hit the *disarm* button on the alarm panel, flicked the deadbolt and opened.

What I didn't do is check the peephole.

DALTON

12:30AM

I was still at the office when the call came.

"What you got?" I barked.

"She's gone," Rex groaned, sounding more like a pained one over an annoyed one. "Got clocked out before I could even get to her."

"Fuck! Are you okay?"

"Nothing a few stitches won't fix."

"Get your ass looked at, then I want you back at NSI." I hung up. Scrolling through my contacts, I brought up Theo's number and hovered over the *call* button. Deciding against it, I hit on Brycen.

"She's gone," I said by way of greeting.

"Already on my way, bro." I heard the bleeping of a car alarm being activated. "Figured that out when I saw Rex's tracker still at Devolin's, while hers was heading out of town."

"You have her low-jacked?" I asked with incredulity. How had I not thought of that?

"Her phone. Her car. Her favorite pair of running shoes. Her satchel, and one of her jackets," the man answered. "It's the satchel I've picked up."

The lock in the main door to NSI turned and Brycen loomed in the entranceway, staring straight at me, the panic in his face unmistakable.

"Don't say it." I shook my head.

"I'm not, but you know that it's possible," he said.

I did.

"We've got to call the guys in."

"Already done," the man said. "Called them up as soon as I realized that something was going on."

I hissed, running my hands into my hair, pulling at it. "Fuck."

Brycen's hand squeezed my shoulder. "Calm down, we'll get her back. This was the only way. According to your sister, Devolin can hold a mean grudge. When she says she wants time alone, she means it too. She wouldn't even allow Morgan in."

"That's what I'm afraid of."

As my words came out, the front door crashed open to show Theo, his brother, Paxton, Tate, Shane, and Cade walk in.

HANK

My stomach roiled as I took the scene unfolding before me.

Tucked away in the driver's seat of my car, I watched as an unconscious Devolin was carried toward a black sedan.

Some large man approached them, unbeknownst to him, the man depositing my son's woman in the car had an accomplice.

The man my son had set on his woman went down like a ton of bricks after suffering a hit to the back of the head with what looked like a tire iron.

Both men got into the car, driving off with the squawk of tires on asphalt.

I followed, the man crumpled onto the ground starting to rouse, but I couldn't go to him. Knowing my son, he'd want me to put Devolin first.

.   .   .

When Dalton told me about what was going on yesterday, when my kids had come over for Sunday dinner, old feelings got into the mix with those for my son's present situation.

I had still been working for the Jacksonville PD when a file with Gordon Hewitt Jr.'s name had hit my desk what felt like a lifetime ago.

Knowing the slippery fucker that I hadn't been able to put away was now after my own child and the love of his life didn't sit well with me.

Dalton had told me why Devolin hadn't come over with him.

He'd fucked up by not telling her the truth, and that's why I was there.

But I'd fucked up, too.

forty-nine

Dalton

3:05AM

"I'VE GOT THE SATCHEL, but her—" Brycen says over the line. "Shit!"

"What?" I demanded over the speakerphone so the group could hear.

"Her fucking computers!" I didn't see why this warranted excitement. "They took her laptops. Dude...okay, hold on." I heard a car door slam, then some tapping of keys. "Devolin has an instant Internet connection on those beasts," he explained. "I can't believe I didn't think about tracking her location through that this entire time."

I nodded to myself. "Makes sense. Ditch the bag and only take what's needed," I hypothesized. "He'd want those computers. Hell, he wants the information that's on them, some shit she got on two guys for him that she never gave to him. I'm betting that's what he's after."

"Me, too," Brycen agreed.

My phone beeped with an incoming message.

"Got a message. Stay where you are until you get a bead on her, then call me back," I ordered Brycen.

"Roger that."

Disconnecting, I found I'd missed a call from my dad.

The man answered after the first ring.

"Dad?"

"Newport. That shipping yard you and your boys found Theo's woman in last year. Fifteen."

Before I could say anything, my father hung up.

I looked down at my phone. "What the fuck?"

"What?" Theo took a step toward me, Morgan standing at his side.

With Devolin kidnapped, and because Rex had found that letter that contained the threat toward Morgan and Theo, I'd told Theo to go get Morgan and bring her to the office.

"The old man's on the case, apparently," I grumbled to the group. "She's in Newport."

Theo's eyes rounded. "Not..."

"Yeah."

Four tries and I still hadn't reached Dad. That heavy feeling in my gut was only getting heavier. Something bad was coming, I knew it with every fiber of my being.

By the time we pulled up outside of the shipping yard, Brycen was there waiting for us.

"Did you see Dad?" I asked him.

"Nothing."

"Dammit!" I took a large breath, hoping for patience. "Everyone knows what they're doing?" I received a collective nod.

Time to roll.

We found Dad first, tucked away behind Warehouse Fifteen, a bloodied heap on the ground. His breathing was shallow, but he was conscious. Barely.

"Where's the car?" he mumbled.

"Car?"

"Black Olds. Sedan. Last year's model," he rattled off.

There hadn't been one of those in sight. "Dad, all we saw was an old RAM drive off at the other end of the lot." That's when it hit me. "Get in that warehouse now!"

Somehow, I knew we wouldn't find what we'd come for.

That was proven as fact when we came into the large structure, a table at its center, a chair, some tangled rope on the ground, and a body.

Shot up multiple times, but still quite fresh since the oaf was still warm.

"T, turn him over, will you?" Theo walked up to the body and flipped him from his side onto his back. Taking my phone, I snapped a shot and walked right back out to where my father lay. "Is this him?"

"One of them," he groaned. "There were two."

Where the fuck had they gone?

DEVOLIN

I'd shot someone. Dead. Or at least I think he was.

Holy shit, I shot someone!

Let me explain that...

Gordon had taken off with his car, leaving me alone with his muscle, to put to rights what I'd been messing with the entire night.

You see, I'd finally found an access point to Gordon's bank accounts, as well as proof that he was siphoning money from his investors in less than legal operations.

Looks like I succeeded a little too well at drawing the man out.

When Marcello-the-Brute, as I had vowed to call him, went to inspect a loud clanging noise coming from the back of the building, I'd followed him, even though he'd instructed me to stay put.

That's when I saw him beating some man to a pulp. A man I didn't recognize right away until he rolled over. Shrieking my shock at seeing Hank, Dalton's father, plastered with blood and beaten; Marcello had turned to find me noticing the gun he'd been holding, but had somehow ended up on the ground. I made a dash for it, having to shove my elbow into the bruiser's nose to get away and into the warehouse. He was hot on my tail, but I had enough time to get the safety off the weapon and take aim.

I pressed the trigger, surprised that three shots rang out due to the trigger's sensitivity. Considering I'd never shot a gun off before, I was shocked to find that Marcello was on the ground.

That's when I made my escape, carrying my laptops with me.

Checking that Hank still had a strong pulse, while he lay there unconscious, I dialed 911 to report the incident.

I then wandered the shipping yard, looking to find some way to catch a ride, when I spotted a Dodge Ram, the driver inside, eyeing me as I approached.

"Not exactly where you should be this time of night, is it, sweets?" the man said.

I decided to go for honesty. He seemed harmless enough, and I still had the gun tucked in the back of my pants, my hoodie doing a great job at concealing the weapon. "I need your help." I looked behind me to make sure I wasn't being followed. "Earlier tonight, two men took me and brought me here. I need to get back home."

"You need to talk to the cops," was his rebuttal.

"M-my boyfriend is the cops." So I told a little white lie, sue me!

Despite the warmth in the air, I was shivering. The man noticed.

"Get in." Putting the truck in reverse, he asked, "Where to?"

fifty

I COULD ONLY IMAGINE what went through Dalton's head when he read the text I sent after I'd found my safe haven, this also necessitating the removal of the tracker I found magnetized to the framework of my car. I couldn't be too careful.

Earlier, Doug, the owner to the RAM, dropped me off in front of my apartment building. The night guard at the security desk recognized me, and helped me in. I could tell he was wondering what the hell I was doing out that late at night.

Walking into my place, I didn't waste time. I'd gone to my room, packed a few changes of clothes, and some bathroom necessities. Checking my office, I saw how it had been ransacked. Someone had been in my place after I'd been taken, but I didn't have time to search everything to know if anything was missing. Opening my duffle, I shoved my laptops in it, buried the gun under some clothes, grabbed my untouched bag of Oreos—because a night like tonight definitely deserved a cookie binge—sought out the spare set of my car keys, then hit the road.

Half an hour later, I was sitting on the bed of a dingy hotel, procured under an assumed name, thanks to my trusty hacking skills, and I'd just pressed *send* on my text to Dalton.

Now it was time for me to work my magic. As for Dalton and the gang, I'd deal with him, my anger, and feelings of betrayal later.

Your man's dead.

It took all but three seconds for my phone to start ringing. After discovering that Brycen had rerouted my calls from Hewitt's number, I'd reversed his efforts.

"Listen, you cunt!" Gordon yelled over the line.

I tsked. "You kiss your mother with that mouth?"

"Put my money back where it was," he demanded. "You have no idea who you're messing with here."

"Au contraire mon cher," I singsonged. "I know exactly who I'm dealing with."

"Bitch, I'm going to—"

"End up in jail or in a pine box...or maybe both," I finished. "I have enough proof to take you down, Gordon, and it's all on its way to Jacksonville PD, via an anonymous source." I hung up before he could say anything more, then I silenced all incoming calls. Reaching for one more cookie, I shoved it whole in my mouth, smiling like a loon, and set to work on sending everything I'd finally managed to put together to Shane's JPD email.

It felt fucking good to cut down the bad guy at the knees and give back to the good people.

"Fuck, I love my job!" I sighed, laying back and watching the progress of the file transfer until it hit one hundred.

It had been two days since I'd sent Shane all the information I had on Gordon. Between what Dalton had compiled over the years, and what I had record of, I'd managed to sift through both and figure out where to go from there.

This morning, local newspapers were spreading the news that real estate mogul, Gordon Hewitt was indicted on multiple charges. Funny how embezzlement was the lesser of all the charges, but he'd been found out for so many cases that those charges alone—provided they stuck—would be enough to put him away for two lifetimes.

Still, I'd paid myself full up for the next week. Feeling weak from my latest bout of excitement, I needed to rest. Lupus caused me to force rest on myself when I encountered great moments of stress. Also, I wanted to make sure I wasn't found by Dalton and the NSI gang, not to mention Hewitt's men, before I made my next move. God knows how many people were out there looking for me.

I missed Dalton like crazy.

Was I still furious with him? No, not really. I was disappointed he hadn't trusted me enough to know I could handle the information.

We'd had zero communication since that text I sent him on my arrival at Twin Oaks Motel, warning him about his father, and it was getting increasingly hard to keep ignoring his messages.

Multiple times a day, I'd sit there, activating my message app, debating if I should read them. I'd dial into my voicemail, only to hang up instead of punching in my password.

To make sure I wasn't found, I'd removed the tracking software that Brycen had installed on my computers. I'd gone as far as reinforcing them with extra coding. I'd also deactivated any tracking options on my cell, only powering it up when needed for added precaution.

It was an email two days later that had me breaking down on my self-imposed exile.

The email had come from Skylar.

Hank had another heart attack.

fifty-one

DALTON

"DO you think she'll fall for it?" Skylar asked from her chair in my office.

She'd just sent our baiting email a few minutes ago.

"I hope so," I mumbled, one of the donuts she'd brought, shoved in my mouth.

We'd been canvassing her favorite haunts—those that Skylar knew about anyway. I'd set a man on her apartment building. I'd even gone as far as to call Joleen to see if she'd heard from her daughter. All of it wasn't netting any results, except for me successfully freaking Devolin's mother out.

Two hours after the email was sent, we hit pay dirt, when Brycen confirmed that my woman had opened Skylar's email.

I hightailed it to the hospital to hopefully catch my ghost.

Lack of sleep had me fighting to stay awake. My appetite had taken a hike too, but I ate whenever someone shoved something in my face, just so they'd shut the fuck up. I must admit, I was a bear of a man to those around me. After five days without a sign of life from Devolin, could you really blame me?

With Hewitt on the loose, I understood why she'd sequestered

216

herself somewhere safe. I even got why she'd stayed away for a few days, until things stuck, and she'd known for a fact that the man wouldn't be let out on bail. Hewitt had a long reach. I'd have done the same.

It had been three days after the man's arrest, and she could have at least initiated contact. She hadn't. Something told me there was more than just Hewitt to do with her little ghost routine, and it all boiled down to me.

That's why we flushed her out with that email. She may not have come out had the email been from me, but Dad had been there that night. She knew he'd been hurt. Hell, she'd called 911 for help before leaving him. She also knew of his heart history. Because of that, it was the perfect setup.

Cloistered in a dark corner, continuing my good fight against exhaustion, and failing, I missed her slipping into Dad's room.

I shot up to a proper sitting position the moment I felt the kick at my boot followed by, "Yo, D."

Morgan and Theo were standing over me, the woman holding an extra cup of coffee, extending it my way.

"Thanks," I mumbled, rubbing at my eyes with one hand and taking the cup with the other.

"Anything?" the man asked.

I shook my head, taking a hefty sip of the hot liquid. "No." I went to pull my phone out of my jeans and noticed the blanket laid across my lap.

"Looks like someone took pity on your miserable ass," Theo said.

"Hmm," I mumbled as I unlocked my screen, noticing I had a text.

From Devolin no less.

DEVOLIN

My heart told me I needed to see Hank for myself.

My gut was churning with the fact that this whole heart attack business was a ruse to get me to come out of hiding.

Before acting on my emotions alone, I decided to be cautious. It's a good thing I had too. Breaking into the hospital mainframe and accessing their patient records wasn't all that easy. It took me about an hour to get in there, but when I did, I breathed a sigh of relief to discover Dalton's father was just fine.

Thank God.

Despite this, however, I still felt a burning need to see the man. After all, he had tried to save me. I know, in my heart of hearts, had I not interrupted my captor, Hank most likely wouldn't have been here with us any longer.

I'm going.

With my decision made, I started planning.

Even in sleep, I could sense Dalton's presence. I took a moment to study him. His face was pale except for his jaw. He looked as if he hadn't shaved in days. His eyes were puffy, the bags under them prominent.

Not for the first time, but this was the worst, I felt guilty for staying away. I knew that Dalton could have helped me stay safe. I also knew that I could achieve the same result on my own too. It was hard to let old habits die. It was even harder to admit that, even though he'd hidden important things from me, he'd done it out of love.

Looking around the hall, I spotted the rolling cart of blankets. Nabbing one, I slowly made my approach, unfolding the material as I got closer. Careful not to wake him, I draped the blanket over him. The strand of hair that I absolutely loved chose that moment to fall over his face. My hand stopped centimetres away before I softly brushed it aside, vowing that I'd have another opportunity to do more than just that, soon. When I was ready.

Walking away from him was the hardest thing I had to do. I'd come to do one thing, and that was to check up on Hank.

Sneaking into his room, I saw the large mass of a man, laying there.

"You came," he mumbled once I stopped at his bedside.

"I did," I whispered.

"No flowers?" He smirked.

Heat suffused my face. "I'm sorry."

"Don't be."

I took the time to take in his appearance. Hank had some bruising on his face, a nasty mix of green and blue, but he looked none the worse for the wear.

"How're you feeling?" I asked.

"I'm fine, girl." He patted the hand I hadn't realized had made its way to his, covering it. "They want to make sure everything's okay with my ticker. So long as the tests come back good, I'll be home in my own bed by tomorrow."

"Is there anything I can do?"

"You did enough." His eyes held mine for longer than I felt comfortable, but I matched his intensity because it's what the man deserved. "I should have known better than to go in there without my gun," he whispered, closing his eyes.

I'd seen this same reaction from Dalton before. It was his way of controlling his emotions when they threatened to get the better of him.

"Thank you for coming for me," I told him. "I should go. I promise I'll check in on you soon." Turning, I made it to the door, pausing when Hank spoke.

"Girl, if you really want to do something for me, keep making my son happy," he said. "He needs that in his life. He needs you, Devolin."

On a nod, I took my leave, hurrying out of the hospital. It wasn't until I'd gotten back to my room at Twin Oaks that I gave into the tears. I also gave into my urge to get in touch with Dalton, sending him a text.

> I'll be home soon. Sleep well, Kip.

And I didn't turn off my phone for once.

fifty-two

DEVOLIN

SOMETHING FELT off the moment I set foot in my apartment, but I just chalked it up to the fact that I'd been taken a week ago, and it was just me trying to get familiarized with my own space again.

I should have known to trust my intuition.

"It's about fucking time, bitch." I startled as it came from behind me once I'd entered my bedroom.

Trying to get my heartbeat back down to normal, I turned to be faced with a face I'd never formally been introduced to.

Suzanna.

Suzanna pointing a pistol at my face from five feet away, to be more precise.

What the fuck? "Suzie?"

"That's right!"

"W—what are you—"

"I tried to warn him," she said, maniacally shaking her head. "But no! You just had to get in there deeper with him, didn't you?"

"Suz—" Fear had me frozen in place.

"It wasn't enough that you had Gordon, you just had to have Dalton, too."

Bile filled my throat. "Gordon?"

"Yes, Gordon!" she yelled. "He's mine, just like Dalt was. He didn't tell you he was taken, did he?"

I wanted to say something along the lines of, *You can have him,* about Gordon, but I figured that lashing out at the woman was probably not in my best interest if I planned to evade what could be coming out of that barrel at any moment.

"H—how'd you find me?" I asked instead.

Her laugh was borderline psychotic sounding. "Does Anna Sue Kendrick ring a bell?"

Holy fuck!

"That's right, Devolin Payton Taylor. I know all about you, right down to your Social Security number," the crazed woman said. "Imagine my surprise when I couldn't find you anymore, only for Gordon to hand me that change of address form. It couldn't have worked out more perfectly that I'd find you on your own." That and what she told me next went a long way to explain how she knew all she did on the night Skylar and I had bumped into her.

Anna Sue Kendrick was the head of human resources at Hewitt Realty. We'd never met, because I'd gone in for my interview with Gordon, then was granted permission to work from home, mostly because of the type of work I did for him, but also because of my health issues. The last was why I'd taken the job to begin with.

I'd never really had a reason to meet with the HR department since my forms had been filled, signed, and personally handed to Gordon himself over a lunch. I'd rarely gone to Gordon's office; our meetings were usually over lunch or dinner since the man claimed it was the only time he was free.

I never questioned it, but hindsight is twenty-twenty, right? Skylar and my mother had met him briefly, and they'd both had felt the man was shady. I'd worked for him for two years, and despite the odd vibe I got from him, his creepiness never truly registered.

Seeing as this past week I'd been in hiding, scared that Gordon would send someone else after me, I asked the obvious, "D—did he send you for me?"

The glimmer of satisfaction entered her gaze. "He did." She

licked her lips like a she-wolf cornering her prey before pouncing on it. "But I'm here for my own reasons."

Keep them talking. That's what they said was the key to living through something like this, right? Until help came?

Well, help wasn't coming because I'd been stupid. I knew going it alone was going to bite me on the ass at some point. Today looked like it was going to be that day.

Damn you and your stubbornness, Devolin!

"It's time to go." Suzanna brought me back to the present. "They'll be here soon."

"Who?" I asked.

A loud crack rented the air, followed by a searing pain in my side.

She'd shot me!

Dropping to my knees, my hands went to my right side, lifting my shirt and inspecting the wound. It looked to be a graze, but I couldn't be certain. There was so much blood.

Looking up at my intruder, I could make out the shock as clear as day on her face. The bitch didn't know how to shoot a gun, and thankfully, her aim really sucked, since the fucking weapon had been aimed at my chest.

For the first time since I'd been faced with Suzanna, my fight or flight response was starting to kick in. Realizing that I could use this latest happenstance to my advantage, I decided to give that a try.

She wasn't going to be taking me anywhere.

fifty-three

DALTON

A SIMPLE SENTENCE that scared the shit out of me, but also had me smiling for the first time in nearly a week. How soon was soon though?

Not fucking soon enough.

I wanted Devolin home now. I wanted to come home to her, or for us to leave work and go home together. I wanted to be able to curl up on the couch with a beer, and just be. I wanted my dad to pop by, and see my woman and Skylar cooking up a storm with their singing and dancing shenanigans. I wanted to wake her up in the middle of the night, just for the sake of reminding her what she means to me. In one night, she broke me, and I haven't been the same since. Like a thief, she snuck in and stole my heart, never giving it back—and I didn't want it back. It was hers. I was hers. All of me. All I had to give.

My dreaming about my future with Devolin came to an abrupt halt when I heard my phone chime.

"Yo," I greeted the caller.

"Mr. Kippers?"

223

"Speaking."

"It's Hugh at Riverside Estates. I was informed that if I saw Ms. Taylor on the premises to contact you."

My heart beat at a wild gallop. "Where is she, Hugh?"

"She went up in the elevator, so I assume she must have gone to her apartment," he said, a phone ringing in the background. "I haven't left my desk all night, and she hasn't come down."

"Thanks, Hugh." Instead of hanging up right away, my gut told me to hold on.

"Mr. Kippers, that's the tenants' line, do you mind holding for a sec?"

"Not at all."

Soon enough, I'd know why I'd waited.

Ring after ring, the man named Hugh fielded calls until he came back to the line.

"I think you better get here," he said. "I've just received three calls reporting something sounding like gunshots coming from Ms. Taylor's unit."

"Hang up and call 911," I told him. "I'm on my way."

Pocketing my phone, I rushed to my safe, pulled my weapon and some extra bullets, shoving those in my pocket, and the weapon in the back waistband of my pants. Grabbing my keys, I locked the door to the house that would no longer be just mine, if I had anything to do about it, and jumped in my truck while hitting Shane's contact.

"Just got the call," the man answered. "I'm on my way to the scene now."

"Good." I hung up, started my truck, put it in reverse, then hit Brycen's contact.

"What's up?"

"Bryce, get your ass to Devolin's and call the guys," I told him.

"She back?"

"Yeah, but we've got a problem. Shots fired. No one's come out yet."

"Be there in ten. I'll round up the crew."

Hanging up, I threw my phone into the middle console and floored it.

. . .

Five minutes is all it took me to get to Devolin's. It had been enough time for emergency personnel to start crowding the place.

Parking in the only free spot I could find in front of the building, I took my keys out, grabbed my phone, locked my vehicle, and ran across the road to Shane, who was talking to his partner.

"D," he greeted me.

"Give it to me straight," I demanded.

"No one's come in or out. We've got a few witnesses stating that they'd only heard the one shot. Some are stating up to three. The lady next door was the one who confirmed three," he explained, pointing to Devolin's neighbor.

"I'm going in," I told him and made to head for the door.

The man stopped me with a hand to the chest. "Not without backup, you're not." His face brokered no argument, and doing so would only waste precious time.

"Fine."

"I'll lead." He did just that. I followed on his heels, Will, his partner hot at our backs.

"Do we know who's in there with her?" I asked as we entered the elevator.

"No idea, but the neighbor thought she'd heard two women," Shane said.

The fact that Devolin wasn't up against a man filled me with relief, but when it came to guns, it didn't matter if you were a man or a woman. What mattered was if the person manning the weapon knew how to shoot. The worst kind of shooter, however, was the inexperienced one.

With that thought, I vowed that I would be bringing Devolin to a shooting range and teaching her all there was to know about defending herself with a weapon. Adding on to that, I'd teach her hand-to-hand combat maneuvers, too, while I was at it.

There was no way my woman would ever be caught in a situation like this, or like the one she'd ended up in a week ago, ever again.

As the elevator arrived at the twelfth floor, my focus returned on the task at hand.

A few doors opened as we walked down the hall toward Devolin's unit. Residents watched us, relief palpable that the authorities were in the building.

Will ordered each neighbor to shut and lock their doors, telling them they'd be notified when it was safe for them to leave their homes.

When 1203 loomed in front of us, half an apartment length away, Shane turned to his partner and me. "I'll go in, Will's got my back. Not that I don't trust you, man, but you're emotionally vested in this, and you're not wearing Kevlar." He pulled his weapon, as did the rest of us.

I nodded.

We were almost right up on the door when we heard a loud shriek, some grunting, followed by the crash of broken glass.

My body went solid at, "You fucking bitch! I'm going to kill you!"

I knew that voice.

"Guys, I know that voice," I told them over the ensuing scuffle going on. "It's my ex." I was seriously regretting not getting Brycen to look her up now.

"For real?" Will said at the same time Shane said, "Psycho Suzie?"

"The one and only," I replied.

Before we even breached the door to Devolin's apartment, a gun went off. Repeatedly. Five times to be exact before Shane made his move.

"Freeze!" he yelled, Will next to him.

As for me, I was thinking the worst. Especially as the gun kept firing until I could hear the sound of the trigger clicking.

"Devolin, put the gun down," Shane ordered.

That's when I rushed to action, freezing as soon as I took in the sight of her.

It was apparent that the woman was in shock. Letting her arms fall limply at her sides, the hand holding the gun shook before it released the weapon, allowing it to thump against the carpeted floor.

"You need to teach me how to shoot," she whispered before she hit the floor hard.

Rushing to her side, I fell to my knees beside her, feeling for a pulse, and finding a strong one. Looking up, Shane met my gaze and shook his head as he removed his hand from Suzanna's carotid.

fifty-four

DEVOLIN

PAIN. So much fiery pain. That's what I woke up to.

"You know," I heard whispered in my ear, "we really have to stop meeting like this."

"Please tell me it's over," I whispered.

Dalton's hand was clasped around mine. "It's over, sweetheart."

My entire body sighed with my relief, and everything went black in the back of that ambulance.

"Ms. Taylor?" A nurse walked into my room.

"Yes?"

"We've got a gentleman here who says he's your fiancé."

"My *fiancé*?"

The woman nodded. "He's putting up quite a fuss out there and scaring the patients."

There was only one person I knew who'd be like that. "Let him in."

Dalton appeared in my hospital room's doorway, looking beaten with worry, his clothes soiled by what I knew was blood—I'd been covered in it by the time they'd shown up—and defeated.

"Kip." I extended my hand to him.

It seemed to be all he needed to move closer. He didn't say anything. He simply took his seat next to me, holding my hand in both of his. Lifting it to his mouth, he began to kiss my bruised and scraped up knuckles. Opening my palm, he then pressed it to his cheek and held it there.

"You fucking scared the life out of me, sweetheart." My thumb rubbed over his unkempt scruff. "I thought I'd lost you for good when I heard those shots."

My breath burned in my throat at the tortured look on his face. "I should have come back after I shot that bruiser, and stayed," I whispered. "I'm sorry."

"You should have." He turned his head to the side, kissing my wrist. "But I understand why you didn't. Still...it doesn't mean I liked it."

I couldn't help the small smirk that played at my lips. "I kind of got the sense of that from your messages."

"I've been miserable without you," he confessed.

"Kip?"

"Yeah?"

"I missed you too, baby," I told him. "Now, kiss me."

He didn't hesitate. Leaning over me, his hand found that strand of hair of mine he loved to play with so much. "With pleasure."

The moment our lips met, I knew we'd be okay.

Pulling away, Dalton's eyes traveled my face studying me. "I wasn't sure I'd get to do that again."

"Mmm." Arching my head up, I pressed my lips against his for another quick taste, before letting it drop to my pillow. Then I asked about what the nurse had told me. "So...fiancé?"

He shrugged. "They're only letting family in to see you; I very well couldn't tell them I was your brother."

My eyes burned. "No, you couldn't do that." Swallowing the growing lump in my throat, I whispered the next thing to pop into my head. "I killed two people."

"Shh." Dalton covered my mouth with his fingers, his other

hand tightening around the hand he had yet to let go of. "Shane's on it. You'll be in the clear before you leave here."

I shook my head, tears sliding down my face. "There's no coming back from that, Dalton."

Staying true to the kind of man he was, he didn't sugarcoat things. "You'll never forget, sweetheart." His eyes were flaming with fury, but they were gentle too. "It was you or them. They didn't give you a choice to be who you are."

My brows knitted together. "A killer?"

"No." This came out sure and final. "A survivor." I melted. "Some people give up. Some play along, thinking they'll be set free if they conform to others' demands. Others...they fight. You're a fighter, Devolin. A survivor. You had an entire lifetime of practice, so it's engrained in you."

"I so fucking love you, you know," I mumbled through my now steady-flowing tears.

"I so fucking love you too, sweetheart."

"Has anyone called Mom?" I asked.

Hank sat on the chair next to my bed, while Morgan sat on the other, Theo standing behind his wife.

Shane had come looking for Dalton. Even though they'd been on task together, formalities with JPD needed to be observed. That meant my man had a statement to deliver.

"She flew back this morning." A man I wouldn't have recognized, if it weren't for his eyes and hair, walked through the door. I shared the same hints of reds as him, his definitely greyer now, however. "I'm sure she'll be here shortly. I was on an earlier flight."

I gulped. "Dad?"

"Hi, sweetheart."

The term of endearment grated on me, and I'm sure everyone knew it, what with the room growing thick with tension. After all this time, I only had two more words for the man who used to be my favorite person in the world. "Get out!"

"Dev—"

"The woman said to leave." This came from Hank, who got to his feet, Theo coming to his side. A show of loyalty and protection.

I fucking loved these people. For the thousandth time today, I kicked myself for running when I had, even if at the time, I knew it was what I needed. My rest. Time to think things over, to simmer down from my snit.

"I want to talk to my little girl," my father demanded.

"You don't have a little girl," I spat. "You had a daughter. One who you let rot in a hospital bed because you couldn't deal with her illness. Now, I only have a mother. That's all. Now get out!"

The room buzzed with awareness the moment my father reached into his back pocket. I guess anyone—law enforcement or military—would brace with such a move, especially when one of their own had just been shot. He pulled out his wallet, fished out a business card, and handed it to Hank.

"My number, if you need anything." With one last glance my way, the man turned and left my room.

"So that's your father, huh?" Hank pondered aloud.

I snickered. "That's dear ol' Daddy all right."

"Seems nice enough a man," he smirked.

I looked at him, then to Theo and Morgan, and snort. "Oh sure," I rant, "I get cancer twice, and the man bails. I graduate high school and college, the man never bothers. I end up in the hospital again with lupus because of the fucking cancer treatments, he still doesn't care. But I get kidnapped, beaten, and shot at, and the man comes running? Yeah, a real winner. What the fuck!"

"Language, Devolin Payton Taylor!" my mother scolded, as she entered the room.

Theo lost his hold on his laughter, the sound making the walls shake as it exploded out of him. Hank was looking at me, a large grin on his face. Morgan was holding onto her stomach, giggling quietly.

"Oh, come on, Mom," I snapped. "I think I'm entitled to a few choice words, don't you?"

"Baby girl, I swear, when you leave this hospital, I'm locking you up." She crossed her arms over her chest. "Now why are you talking about your father, and what in the hell is going on?"

fifty-five

DALTON

"THAT'S what I want to know." I stood by Devolin's room's entryway, arms crossed over my chest. "Who the fuck was that I saw walk out of here five minutes before your mom showed?"

"That would be my father," Devolin growled.

"What?" Joleen shrieked. "He's here?"

My woman skewered her with her eyes. "You didn't know?"

"I was with him when I got the call from Dalton that you'd been shot."

"Mom!"

"It's not like I get to pick where the man gets his coffee," she said.

I smelled bullshit but I wasn't about to give my two cents. The woman was still pissed at me for failing to find and protect her daughter like I'd promised I would.

"I think we should go," Morgan said, trying to usher Dad and Theo toward the door, but my father wasn't moving.

His eyes were fused to Joleen, much like hers were now on him.

"Officer Kippers?"

"Just Hank, Jo-Jo," his voice came out deep.

What the fuck?

"You two know each other?" Devolin shrieked.

The two simply nodded.

It was Dad who answered everyone's lingering question. Somewhat. "How's business at the bookstore?"

"Good." The older woman smiled. "We haven't seen you visit in a while."

He nodded. "Been busy." Turning to me, he added, "I'll get going."

Without waiting for an acknowledgement, he was out, Theo saluting me as he followed, Morgan offering a sweet smile, stopping in front of me so I could bend over and kiss her cheek.

"See you later, mama."

Before we could get into it with Joleen, for a more in-depth explanation as to how she and my father knew each other, Shane and Will walked through what could have been Devolin's revolving hospital room door.

"Hey." Devolin forced a smile at the two officers.

"Ma'am," Will greeted Devolin's mother. "We'll have to ask you to leave the room for the moment."

When he and Joleen left the room, Shane stared at me.

"Am I in trouble?" Devolin asked. "Can he stay?"

Shane turned to her, a soft smile at his lips. "He can stay," he confirmed. "And no, you're not in trouble from what I'm able to tell, but your statement will help us close things down."

She nodded. "How'd you want to do this? I can tell you what went down since that night Gordon tried to take me, or is this a Q and A kind of deal?"

I laughed internally. Here she was, looking at accommodating an investigating officer over him accommodating her.

"How about you tell me everything from the time you left NSI headquarters, to when we found you? Then we'll fill the gaps if you leave any."

"Okay," she said softly.

"I hope you don't mind me taking notes?" She shook her head to indicate that she wasn't bothered with it. Opening the file he'd brought with him, he clicked his pen, then said, "Whenever you're ready."

That had possibly been the longest two hours of my entire life.

Hearing practically a minute-by-minute account of what Devolin had been through in the last five days had been torture for me. She hadn't left anything out; talking about our fight, how she walked out with vengeance on her mind. My blood boiled as she recounted how she'd snuck up on Marcello Mancini as he'd beaten my dad down, then proceeded to give chase to her, but she'd shot him with his own weapon. A weapon she'd kept, telling us it was at the bottom of the bag she'd left on her bedroom floor.

I felt guilty that my secretiveness had contributed to her running. She explained she was so used to working on her own, that at first, it never occurred to her she could reach out for addi-tional help.

Devolin explained how she'd managed to get the information JPD needed to put Gordon Hewitt away.

"And what made you come home?" Shane asked.

Her eyes met mine, then just as quickly, fell to her clasped hands on her lap.

"I almost fell for Skylar's email," she explained.

"You tapped into the hospital's database, didn't you?" I asked her.

"If you were me, what would you have done?" She speared me with a look. "I had to make sure." Turning to Shane, she continued. "I came. It was late, last night...or more like early this morning."

My eyes widened. "You did?" Then I thought about it. "The blanket."

"Yeah." She smiled. "Your dad didn't tell you?"

"No," I grumbled. "Old man's got some explaining to do."

"Let's get back on point," Shane reminded us. "What happened after you left the hospital?"

She'd gone back to the hotel, stating that seeing me so beaten and exhausted, then having spoken with Dad, she knew she'd made a mistake by running and trying to handle things on her own.

Once she'd finished her long crying jag, she'd packed up and gone back home. Where she was met with Suzanna.

When Devolin recounted how my ex and Hewitt were linked, I almost lost my damned mind. Turned out that Psycho Suzie—as Shane and some of the others on the team had dubbed her—was a lot crazier than I'd ever imagined. She'd been involved with Hewitt for a number of years. It had been about the money. Forget love, that woman had not one idea on how love worked. When Hewitt voiced his infatuation with Devolin, Suzanna had set a plan in motion that would ultimately lead to her demise.

"She shot at me, catching me in the side when I told her I wasn't going with her. We were in my bedroom." Devolin winced as she tried to readjust. "I remember watching or reading something on the Internet about not letting your captor take you to a second location."

"That's right," Shane said. "What happened next?"

"I jumped her. I managed to knock the gun out of her hand, but we both ended up on the floor, me on top of her legs. The gun landed just outside my bedroom door. I managed to straddle her. I sent my elbow into her face, then I rushed out into the hall, to get to the gun." She struggled to take a breath, her eyes cloudy as she relived the entire thing for a second time. "I made it to my knees to get up, but she hit me in the back with one of my bedside table lamps. I went down and flipped onto my back just in time to kick her in the stomach. I got to the living room and pointed the gun at her. She was screaming that I'd hurt Dalton like I'd ruined Hewitt. I don't even know what that means! Gordon and I were never involved in more than an employer-employee type relationship." Her eyes were wild. "Then she yelled that she was going to kill me." Closing her eyes, a singular tear trailed down her cheek. "There wasn't any time for me to get my phone to call anyone. I'd left it on the couch when I first got home. So I lifted the gun and started shooting. I knew she wouldn't stop until I was dead." By now, Devolin's eyes were clenched shut and her body shook as she sobbed. "I shot her. I don't know how many bullets came out of that gun, but she kept coming at me, and I kept shooting until I ran out of bullets. That's when you all came in."

Knowing how the rest unfolded, I got up from my chair and took a seat on the edge of Devolin's bed, cradling her head in my chest as I let her cry things out.

Shane met my gaze with his own sympathetic one. "Devolin, I'm going to step out for a bit and let you get some rest." Devolin nodded. "I'll be back in a bit so we can go over everything before you sign off. Would that be okay?" Another nod. "Okay, Huss." That got him a humored hiccup. Setting a hand on her shoulder, he gave it a slight squeeze, then leaned down to kiss the back of her head. "You're a true fighter, Huss. You'll get past this, you'll see. We're all here for you." Her sobs only got louder.

His eyes coming up to meet mine, we gave each other a nod, then he turned and took his leave.

<h1 style="text-align:center">fifty-six</h1>

DEVOLIN

EARLY THE NEXT MORNING, I was released to go home.

Mom had argued that I should be with her, but all I wanted to do was curl up in Dalton's arms and sleep for a century. In his bed.

Truth be told, I doubt I'd be able to walk into my apartment any time soon—too much had transpired there in such a short amount of time.

To appease my mother's hurt feelings about not staying with her, my man offered up his spare bedroom. That way we'd all be close to one another. She refused, but I could tell she appreciated the offer, citing that if it was okay, she'd go home, get some sleep, then pop by for a visit around lunchtime.

I was glad of that.

Not that I didn't want my mother around, but Dalton and I had some things we needed to discuss. Even if we didn't talk about everything today, we needed time to ourselves. Time to just be us. Something I'd realized we never really had since that day at Theo and Morgan's.

Dalton handed me one of his t-shirts.

"I could use help with changing the bandage," I said.

His eyes bored into mine as he gave me a gruff, "Okay."

He escorted me to the bathroom, taking the bag of medical supplies and prescriptions we'd filled and purchased on our way home. Setting everything on the vanity, he turned to me, his potent gaze asking for permission as his hands reached for the hem of my shirt.

I nodded.

Slowly lifting, he peeled my shirt over my head, chucking it onto the floor.

"Fuck me." The torture in his voice had me watching him take in the bandage on my side, as he sat on the toilet seat, and pulled me to stand between his legs before his forehead met my stomach. "I'm so fucking sorry this happened," he whispered.

My hands sifted through his hair, his hands gripping my hips. "Kip…"

"Let's get you cleaned up." He peered up at me. "You still have some blood on you. And then you're going straight to bed."

Giving him room, he went to the linen closet and pulled out a facecloth and ran the water to soak it.

As physically and emotionally exhausted as I felt, I could feel the familiar tingling my body made whenever Dalton touched me. It was an intimate moment. One so far from sexy, and nowhere near geared to anything sexual in intent, but it was candid. It was a moment just for us, filled with the *what-ifs* of life, regret, gratitude, and hope.

Chucking the cloth into the garbage can when he was done, he proceeded to spread some ointment on my stitches and redressed my bullet wound. By then, I could barely stand on my feet.

Leading me to his bed, Dalton sat me down on its edge.

"Bra on or off?" he asked.

"Off."

Not once did he look away from my eyes as he unhooked, then slid the garment from my body. Grabbing the shirt he'd taken out for me earlier, he set to put it on me.

"Let's get you to bed." Kissing me on the forehead, he pulled back the sheets. Settling in, he pressed his lips to mine and lingered. "Let me go lock up, and I'll be back."

. . .

Dalton didn't come back.

And after an hour of trying to fall asleep, I got up.

I found him nursing a glass of whiskey if the bottle on the coffee table was anything to go by.

The floor creaked beneath my feet, giving my presence away.

"Hey," I whispered, stopping at the edge of the couch.

"Hey."

I studied him. "You okay?"

He snorted into his glass as he took another sip. "Better than you," he rasped.

"You're not okay," I surmised out loud and let my feet take me directly to him.

Taking his glass, I gave it a quick sniff before taking a sip for myself, then setting it down next to the half-empty bottle. I didn't care that it hurt like a bitch when I lowered myself to sit astride his lap.

Wrapping my hands on either side of his face, I tried to meet his eyes, but he didn't seem to be able to hold my gaze. "Baby, talk to me."

"I should have told you about Hewitt."

Okay, so we were going to have this conversation now.

"Kip..."

"If I'd told you everything from the get-go, then we'd have been able to catch him and turn his ass in together," he explained.

"True, but what about Suzanna? It's not like we would have known what she'd planned."

"You're right," he sighed. "But it doesn't make me feel better knowing that my ex nearly took you away from me. Dad asked me if I'd looked her up to see what she'd been up to since we broke up five years ago, but I didn't. I could have stopped any of that from happening. It's on me."

"No! I think she was more about taking me away from Gordon, even though you were mentioned," I told him. "It doesn't matter anymore, Dalton. It's over."

"Yeah."

"Come to bed with me, Kip," I whispered over his lips. "Hold me. Make me feel safe. I'm home when I'm in your arms."

The haunted look in his eyes evaporated. "Okay."

Minutes later, Dalton was wrapped around me, my back to his front, under the cloak of sheets and darkness.

"You're my home too, sweetheart," he whispered against my ear, before depositing a kiss to the back of my shoulder. "You'll always be my home."

For the first time in nearly a week, I felt at peace.

fifty-seven

DALTON

OPENING THE FRONT DOOR, I cringed as I let our guests in, closing the door behind them and ushering them further into the living room.

"Who is it?" Devolin asked from the hallway, her footsteps coming closer.

I looked at the two people standing there. "It's—"

"Mom! Dad?" I turned to find her eyes flitting from one parent to the other. "What the hell?"

"Let me explain," Joleen started.

"I don't want him here," Devolin stated.

"He's your father."

"He is?" she snapped, crossing her arms over her chest, grimacing when she nudged her side. "I no longer have a father. I haven't since I was eight."

I could see my woman was becoming agitated, and I went to her side, wrapping my arm around her as a show of support.

"Is this why you wanted me to stay with you? So you could ambush me with *him*?" Devolin speculated aloud.

"Baby girl, please listen to what he has to say, then you can make up your mind," Joleen said.

"No!" She stared daggers at her father. "You don't get to walk back into my life again. Not right now. Not like this. Twenty-one years, Dad!"

"Sweet—" he started.

"Don't you dare!" she growled.

"Honey..." Joleen tried to run interference. "Please."

"Mom, I can't believe you'd do this to me," she said. "This is the last thing I need right now. I love you, but I need you to go. Take him with you. Give me a couple of days."

"But—"

Having heard enough, and hating that my woman was suffering, I took things in my own hands.

"Listen to her. She's had enough. She's telling you she's not ready to deal with it. Please leave. Devolin will be in touch when she's ready, and not a second sooner." Letting go of Devolin, I proceeded toward the front door and opened it, staring them down until they did as requested.

DEVOLIN

I'm not sure if I'll ever be ready to talk to my father.

I can't imagine the list of excuses he'd present.

Honestly, I knew I'd hurt him by denying him a word with me, but he'd hurt me for twenty-one goddamn years!

"Are you okay?" Dalton knocked me from my thoughts, the front door now shut.

I huffed. "No!"

"Baby..." He approached me, his hands grabbing onto my hips, lining up his front to mine.

My forehead met his chest. "I'm so sick of this. Can't I have a bit of normalcy for once? Dalton, it's been four fucking weeks and we haven't even had a day to ourselves. I just..." I sighed. "I just want to be."

"Then we will." He kissed the crown of my head, then reached down to tilt my chin up so our eyes could meet. "I'll keep them away," he vowed, pecking my lips. "All of them." He punctuated that by brushing his lips from side to side against mine. "For as long as you need me to," he whispered.

My hands met the planes of his chest as my breath quickened. "It might take forever."

Dalton's body shook with silent laughter. "Then I'll be in great fucking company." Still laughing, he snared my mouth with his, dipping his tongue into my mouth for a thorough taste.

Following his lead, my arms reached around his shoulders to pull him closer, and I opened further.

Yeah, forever wouldn't be all that bad if it was with Dalton Kippers.

fifty-eight

DALTON

2 MONTHS LATER...

MY FIST RAPPED on the door. "Sweetheart?" She'd been in there for well over an hour. What could possibly be taking her so long?

"Gimme a sec!" she shouted through the wooden barrier.

"Babe, we've got to go, or we'll be late."

Seconds later, the door opened, and my breath caught.

Holy fucking shit!

"Do I look okay?"

"Are you kidding me right now?" There's no way I'd survive tonight. "I'm about two seconds away from calling in to cancel our reservation and stripping that fine ass of yours bare. You look amazing, baby."

She strutted—yes, *strutted*—the five steps toward me, lifting on the tips of her toes to press her lips lightly to mine. "Such a charmer," she murmured. "Let's go. I've got some showing off to do." She winked, walked around me, and left me salivating—I mean following—after her and the imagery she evoked had me peeling off that little strapless black number she was currently wearing. Don't get me started on those strappy black fuck-me-heels.

DEVOLIN

Torturing that man of mine has become one of my favorite pastimes these last few months.

Things have never been greater between Dalton and me. If I thought I loved the man months ago, it was nothing compared to how I felt for him today.

I'd have been happy to stay home, but my man had pulled out all the stops for today. After this morning, I was excited.

Waking up to my dream man was great. Waking up to him, playing with something wrapped around a very important finger of mine, was another.

It was perfect.

The moment, I mean.

Dalton brought me back from memories of this morning with a kiss over the large rock sitting on my left hand as he drove us to dinner. "Have you decided yet?"

"Mm-hmm." I smirked, not telling him anything more.

"And?"

"Is tomorrow too soon?" I grinned.

This netted me a boisterous laugh. "Funny, I was wondering if today was possible."

"I wish," I sighed dramatically. Truth was, if it were at all possible, I'd be running down the aisle, straight to him.

Moments later, we'd reached the Hilton's gardens, where Dalton had planned some ornate catered meal for us to eat under the stars.

Guiding me by the hand, he led us under a beautifully sculpted archway, toward a white linen table surrounded by people I wasn't expecting.

"Surprise!"

Dalton braced me from behind so I wouldn't fall over from shock.

"I have one more thing to ask of you," he whispered into my ear before turning me to face him. "Will you marry me today?"

"B—but..." I bit my bottom lip as I pondered what this meant. Looking into his eyes, I felt myself calming. Hadn't I just told him that I'd marry him right away if we were able to? Instead of giving him the answer we both wanted, I blurted, "I don't have a dress."

"Right here," Skylar came from behind everyone, a garment bag slung over her arms.

That's when I realized that everyone in attendance was decked to the nines. I took in the faces surrounding us, then looked at the one I wanted to see every day for the rest of my life. "Yes, Dalton. Let's do it!" Jumping up into his arms, I fused my lips to his, clapping and catcalls surrounding us.

Mom, Skylar, and Morgan helped me get dressed in the beautiful white lace strapless, that Skylar insisted was made for me. I don't know how she'd managed to get it so it fit me like a glove, but I'd forever remain grateful.

Mom was a ball of emotions, and every time she started to tear up, it was a double battle for me to keep my cool because Morgan would join in on the waterworks, thanks to her pregnancy hormones.

It had been fifteen minutes since I'd said yes to Dalton's second proposal of the day, and I found myself alone, tucked away in the Hilton's lobby when Hank came around the corner.

"Mom mentioned she knew the right man for the job." I smiled at my soon-to-be-father-in-law. "I was wondering which one of the guys I'd get, and I was hoping it'd be you." I knew it wouldn't have been my father. After that afternoon at Dalton's, the man never once tried to get in touch again. Part of me wanted to know why he'd given up so easily. I mean, if he was so desperate at mending fences, then why couldn't he make all the effort? But he didn't, and so I let the proverbial sleeping dog lie.

"You're radiant, honey," he muttered, bending in closer to kiss my cheek before reaching into his suit jacket. "I have something for you. It was Dalton's mother's and I know she'd want you to have it." He pulled out a tattered velvet box and opened it to reveal the most beautiful bracelet I'd ever seen.

I gasped, tears springing to my eyes, and all I could do to stop them was wave my hands frantically in front of them and breathing deep.

"They're emeralds," he said as he undid the clasp. I presented him with my wrist. "I bought it for Amara for our first anniversary. They matched her eyes, just like they do yours." Securing the clasp, he took a moment to admire the piece of jewelry. "Just where it was meant to be."

I lost my battle with the tears, throwing myself at the man in a blubbering mess. "Thank you," I whispered. "I'll cherish it forever."

"You're welcome, sweet girl." Setting me back, he pulled out a hanky from his back pocket and dabbed at the wet under my eyes. "There. Now, what say you we take you to your groom?" Presenting me with his arm, I hooked mine through it, and we were off. "If I know my son well enough, he's probably pacing like a caged lion right now."

"You sure he's not dancing in circles?" I grinned.

His laugh boomed out, making everyone's eyes turn toward us. "He told you about that, did he?"

Oh, he had.

epilogue

DALTON

I KNEW something was going on for a little while now, and I've been expecting Devolin to say something, but she hadn't.

It's been two weeks since the wedding, and I can honestly say that I haven't been happier. What would make me ecstatic would be if she quit living in denial and finally admit it.

Turning so she could snuggle into me, I heard her, "Good morning, babe," as she pressed her lips to my chest, kissing it.

That's when I would normally flip her onto her back and proceed to *greet* her for the day. This morning was no exception, except that when I leaned down to kiss her lips, her eyes rounded in horrified surprise, she pushed me off her, and made a beeline for the bathroom.

Well, maybe that'll clue her in.

Seconds later, I heard her wretch into the toilet, followed by, "Oh, God!"

That was my cue to get up and take care of my woman.

Padding into the bathroom, I grabbed a washcloth and wet it with cold water. I went to crouch down behind her, but she yanked the thing out of my hand and pushed me away. "Go. I don't want you to see me like this." Then she began to heave again.

"Sweetheart, I take the *in sickness and in health* portion of my vows seriously," I joked, garnering a groan from my wife. "Plus, I'll have to get used to it, because it might be happening more often from here on out."

Once she'd regained her breath from her non-productive heaves, she held the cloth to the back of her neck, then turned her head to look at me. "What in the hell are you talking about?" she asked.

"Sweetheart." I knelt onto the floor, far enough away so that I couldn't see last night's dinner in the toilet bowl, and gently pulled Devolin to me. She came easily, straddling my lap. "I think you're pregnant."

She shook her head. "That's not possible, Kip. You know I can't—"

"You said you never had the fertility tests done, baby." I played with the strand of hair that had fallen into her face. "It is possible. And judging by the fact your tits feel and look larger, you've been eating—"

A hand covered my mouth, and my wife gave me a death glare. "Don't fucking say it. I can't help it. I'm just hungry."

Pulling her hand down from my mouth, I grinned down at her. "Bullshit."

DEVOLIN

I'd been putting off that test Dalton had gone to get me for most of the day now, choosing to ignore the proverbial elephant in the room. On one hand, I didn't believe I could get pregnant. After all, my life had never allowed me to be that lucky. Why would my luck change suddenly, right? On the other, I knew that being pregnant was a possibility, no matter how minuscule, but I refused to hope.

We were now working on movie number two of the evening when I ended up having to rush to the bathroom for my third bout of puking for the day. All because of that stupid fucking bag of Doritos I'd just popped open.

Feeling Dalton crouch down behind me, holding my hair and

dabbing at my neck with the cloth I'd set aside from earlier, he said, "Sweetheart, take the test."

"What if I'm not?" I voiced my worries. "What if it's something else; something bad? It could be my lupus...or what if that anemia is back? Stem cell treatments don't always work, Kip."

"I promise it isn't." He kissed the back of my head before straightening himself and heading to the sink to fill me a glass of water and handing it over. "Drink slowly. I'll go get you some saltines." He left the room.

"No! Cookies! I can't eat any more saltines. Get me the Oreos, please," I told him as I got up to brush my teeth. You'd have to kill me before you could hope to get those slices of sawdust in my mouth again today. Cure nausea? Oh no they didn't!

"Yes, dear!" he hollered from what sounded like the kitchen.

Four cookies and a full glass of water later, the urge to relieve myself hit.

Grabbing the test that had mocked me since its arrival in our home this morning, I headed for the bathroom.

DALTON

She finally caved.

The more the day wore on, the more I felt my hopes climb. The symptoms were all there, and some of the physical signs, too.

My guess was that she never entertained the possibility, simply because of what the doctors told her years ago, but had never actually medically confirmed it.

"Son of a bitch!" I heard yelled behind the bathroom door, which slammed opened moments later. Devolin's shocked eyes snapped up to look at me as she mumbled, still holding the stick, "You knocked me up!"

The moment was too comical not to laugh. "You're damn right I fucking did, baby."

She smiled at me. "Baby." I nodded, moving toward her. "Our baby."

"Yeah," I whispered. "Our baby."

"I'm pregnant," she said as if still in shock.

"You're pregnant," I parroted her.

"Know what else I am?" she asked coyly, that mischievous glimmer making its way into her eyes.

"No, what?"

"Horny."

Then she jumped me.

DEVOLIN

The exhilaration I felt at that positive test result had me flying high. Seeing Dalton's face light up with excitement like it had, was a dream come true.

I was giving him something I never thought I'd be able to.

It was a miracle.

The minute I'd wrapped myself around Dalton, he had taken control.

Now here I was, my hand between my legs, sitting spread-eagled against the headboard while Dalton sat on the lounging chair in the corner, watching me as he jerked himself off.

"I was right," I licked my lips. "This is so hot."

"Oh yeah?"

I nodded. "Yeah, but now I have another fantasy."

His eyes smoldered. "Tell me," he growled.

Pulling my fingers from my pussy, I crooked them. "I want to sit on your face while I suck you dry," I said, licking my own juices off my fingers.

The man pounced.

DALTON

Hours after our lovemaking, in the break of the night, I smiled to myself as I watched Devolin sleep, our hands entwined over the belly that would soon grow larger with our child.

I'm not sure what woke me up, but glad for the solitary

moment of introspection, I finally could agree with my mother's words.

Dream big.

I didn't know when I quit living by those words, but somehow, I'd started doing it again, and it all hinged on one dark night when a band of brothers set off to save a damsel in distress.

In my arms lay the woman I loved, my legacy, my world. My home.

There's no better dream than the ultimate one of happiness—and I got mine. Finally.

about the author

Born and raised in small town Northern Ontario, Canada, award-winning author, Carey Decevito has had a penchant for reading and writing for as long as she can remember.

A writer of erotic romance, paranormal romance, and romantic suspense, this lover of food will throw in a bit of heat, a dash of sass, a pinch of comedy, and a dollop of real-life experience in order to provide her readers with a story that will mess with their emotions from start to finish.

Family and friends are her lifeblood, but Carey also enjoys conquering the outdoors, sports, traveling, and playing tourist in Canada's National Capital region. When life gets crazy, she seeks respite through her writing and submersing herself in the latest addition to her library. If all else fails, she knows there's never a dull moment with her two daughters, her goofy husband, and their dog who she swears is out to get her.

She is the author of *The Broken Men Chronicles* series, the *Essence Extracted* trilogy, and the *Nightshade* series.

For more book updates, visit
www.careydecevitobooks.com!

facebook.com/carey.writes

instagram.com/For

x.com/ItalRT4u

bookbub.com/authors/carey-decevito

amazon.com/author/careydecevito

also by carey decevito

Nightshade Series

Night Break

Night Shift

Night Hunt

Night Hack

The Broken Men Chronicles Series

Once Written, Twice Shy

Almost Forgotten

Play Me to Infinity

To Forgive & Hold Safe

A Heart's War

Essence Extracted Trilogy

Essence Derived

Essence Redeemed

Essence Surfaced

Collections & Anthologies

Love at First Sight: a first-in-series collection